Above all, the ape was marvelously adaptable. Omnivorous as a rodent, thriving on any food available. Three and a half feet tall: the most acquisitive, curious, inventively vicious hominid Barion had ever found, and quite the hardiest on this violent world next to the cockroach and the rat.

Long after this day's work the ape would produce Christ, Beethoven, Auschwitz, thumbscrews and philosophy, Magna Carta and white supremacy, poetry, poison gas, nuclear fission, and romantic love. For the moment it crouched by the water hole, munching a succulent grub discovered under a stone, warning off the large creatures that somehow would not be frightened away. They were unclassifiable, therefore a threat. The ape made the brave noises of its kind.

"Good morning," Barion said softly. "Welcome to evolution."

"Something like *Cat's Cradle* meets *Network* meets *Stranger in a Strange Land* . . . fleshed out with some razor-sharp detail and peopled with believable characters. Godwin's best so far."
—*Kirkus Reviews*

"Godwin's never been in finer form. His dialogue crackles; his humor isn't the slapstick from TV sitcoms, but a true humor based in part upon the human condition and all the stronger and more poignant for that; and most important, he doesn't take any easy ways out."

—*Other Realms*

Waiting for
the Galactic Bus

PARKE GODWIN

BANTAM BOOKS
NEW YORK · TORONTO · LONDON · SYDNEY · AUCKLAND

WAITING FOR THE GALACTIC BUS

A Bantam Spectra Book / June 1989

PRINTING HISTORY
*Doubleday edition published 1988
All rights reserved.
Copyright © 1988 by Parke Godwin.
Cover art copyright © 1989 by Chris Hopkins.
Library of Congress Catalog Card Number: 87-33069*
No part of this book may be reproduced or transmitted in
any form or by any means, electronic or mechanical,
including photocopying, recording, or by any information
storage and retrieval system, without permission in writing
from the publisher.
For information address: Bantam Books.

ISBN 0-553-28066-X

Published simultaneously in the United States and Canada

*Bantam Books are published by Bantam Books, a division of
Bantam Doubleday Dell Publishing Group, Inc. Its trademark,
consisting of the words "Bantam Books" and the portrayal of
a rooster, is Registered in U.S. Patent and Trademark Office
and in other countries. Marca Registrada, Bantam Books,
666 Fifth Avenue, New York, New York 10103*

PRINTED IN THE UNITED STATES OF AMERICA

O   0 9 8 7 6 5 4 3 2 1

*To Marvin Kaye,
for more Incredible Umbrellas*

Charity, by way of prologue

Charity Mae Stovall spent her childhood in a county orphanage. Yearning for a mother or any kind of palpable parent, she sublimated in adolescence to a rigid Christianity. Charity was—and still is—a highly intelligent young woman, although for her first twenty years she never thought herself acute in this regard, nor was the quality noted by the school system that passed her through its portals and curricula without a second glance. Since she didn't read much and no one ever required her to think, Charity's potential remained a string unsounded in the decaying factory town of Plattsville.

She was very active in the house of her chosen faith, the Tabernacle of the Born Again Savior, where she accompanied congregational hymns on the hammer-worn piano, was wooed by an aggressive young man named Roy Stride and, to a more retiring extent, by Roy's self-effacing friend, Woody Barnes. Woody furnished trumpet obbligato for these musical effusions. He played well, Charity with more precision than talent. She was a Fundamentalist and earnest about it, distributing leaflets for the removal from libraries of harmful books like *The Wizard of Oz* and *The Diary of Anne Frank.* On a personal basis, Oz didn't do much for Charity one way or the other, though she did wonder why the Tabernacle was against *Anne Frank*. Outside of her being a Jew, the day-to-day life and thoughts of Anne were pretty much like her own at thirteen. Nevertheless, Reverend Simco thundered against it as an alien blot on a Christian land already imperiled. Dutifully, Charity demonstrated against an abortion clinic, opposed the teaching of evolution as a dastardly onslaught of secular intellect upon defenseless children and believed herself a direct descendant of Adam.

Not entirely without justification.

Barion found her earliest direct ancestor by a Pliocene water hole, a creature with no likeness to Adam other than health, appetite and uncertainty. Unlike Adam, the ape was quite savage. Anything outside its immediate family group was a dangerous enemy. The crucial difference in this primate, for Barion's purposes, was a brain verging on but not quite ready to be called a mind. In this regard, the creature had much in common with its descendant, Charity Mae Stovall.

1

SORT OF GENESIS

■ 1 ■

This was a real nice clambake . . .

Without question the grandest party of a brilliant season. Racketing across the universe through the myriad clusters of stars, across the dark void between galaxies, like a gleaming silver tear glistening on black velvet, the end-of-term celebration became an unbridled riot of the senses for the self-conscious students. On young worlds they bathed in the scarlet splendor of volcanoes, rhymed solemnly to each other and made love in the cold light of moons drawn close to dying mother worlds, dove headlong through the chromospheres of small suns to prolong their high on rarefied gases. They basked and swam in plasma-soupy primordial seas gravid with life to come; roared drunk in a perverse course counter to a slow-wheeling galaxy to reach the outer whorl simply because it was there and looked lovely; came to rest finally on a green savanna in an atmosphere so oxygen-rich that it shot their high even higher and they changed form again to complement it. No one expected a school's-out party to make much sense, not in this generation at least.

A magnificent time—yet Sorlij was bored.

They were the purest and most sublime of sentient life forms: energy to matter to energy at will. Where their kind passed, less advanced creatures called them gods. This generated wise laws among the mature and in jokes among snotty adolescents like Barion and Coyul.

They were neither gods nor the only advanced mutable form, as the recent war had proven. Certain developments might have been predicted by far less advanced cultures, particularly the war's effect on the young. After the inconclusive hostilities, the anthropoid form became a dissident movement among students. Thinking themselves the first to be disillusioned and sold down the cosmos by craven elders, they brazenly adopted any lifestyle and form disapproved by the retiring generation. They transported blithely in their glittering, half-ethereal ships to any planet that pleased them and cavorted on two legs or three as the fancy took them.

Why not? Bodies were fun. They opened a whole new spectrum of sensory highs. Sexual possibilities were narrow and local but with interesting side effects. They found it a real kick to chew certain green leaves with actual teeth and feel the profound effect on a finite being, and if you overdosed, you could always dissolve to energy state to detoxify. Some substances were very dangerous; you had to identify the onset of physical death before coma set in. You could actually die, and some loved to see how close they could come before winking safely back to energy. Fun, danger, uncertainty, courage. Works of art perpetrated in this perilous state were considered ultimate truth. A few extremists formed death pacts, left bad verse in farewell and went all the way.

Older academics considered the anthropoid form an unprofitable dead end for study. The new generation loved being decadent and lost, reveled in irony and romantic self-pity, created sad or savage music like that of Coyul, Barion's bratty little brother. In the bizarre four-limbed form they leaned together, murmured solemn verities, felt doomed and dramatic or glittered defiantly in radical chic.

Though all this could pale. Sorlij, the class leader, was terribly bored. The party was coming down from its high, scattered about the moist grass, too exhausted now even for the queer, comic form of lovemaking peculiar to the bipedal body. They should start home. A long way, Sorlij remembered fuzzily, five galaxies away . . . or was it six?

"Which way did we come?" he asked about. No one remembered.

Meanwhile the party languished. Sorlij's pet hates, Barion and Coyul, were not fun drunks. The brothers were not even of the graduating class, sophomores in every sense of the word, but well connected and precocious. A few of the seniors had thrilled for a moment to Barion's poetry—

"It sings! It soars!"

—and someone else twittered over Coyul's music and flip cynicism. The brothers were invited along over Sorlij's objections. He could always pass on Barion's poetry and interests which centered unhealthily on the possibilities of the anthropoid form. The main thrust of all their studies was life-seeding on new worlds, but Barion seemed obsessed with the one creature far beyond the limits of fashion or fad. Anyone else would be laughed at or disciplined. Barion, the spoiled darling of prominent family, would probably win the coveted first prize in genetic science that should go to Sorlij for his work in marine life forms. To most observers, Barion's faults were drowned in his alleged charm, and Sorlij politely detested him.

As for Coyul, Sorlij considered him a mere added irritant. His ennui and affected decadence could wear on you, especially if those poses had only recently been

7

renounced in one's self. Nothing galled so much as yesterday's follies worn today by someone else.

"The green shoot plays the autumn leaf," Sorlij quipped, not above an epigram himself.

He gazed about at his friends lounging about the grassy slope and found his favorite, Maj, whose radical concepts in the anthropoid form had prompted her to assume something dramatic for the occasion: a scarlet mer-seductress with a broad tail that changed colors with Maj's every whim.

"Stroke my fin?" she invited Sorlij.

"Maj, I think it's time to go home."

"Oh, not yet. The party's a huge success."

"Before it becomes tedious."

Maj covered a delicate yawn with cerise fingers. "There's that, yes. Time to go, everyone. Don't have to be sober, just mobile." Her mer-tail flirted suggestively at Sorlij and became a remarkable pair of female legs. "Shall we?"

One by one the party let go of physical shape and became daubs of silver light against the green and amber of late afternoon, flowing toward their ship. All but Barion and Coyul, prostrate on the grass. Sorlij lingered in substance to prod them with a custodial toe.

"Up, you two. We're going home."

Coyul hiccupped, rumbled somewhere in an unaccustomed digestive tract and passed out again.

"Barion! Gather up your unspeakable brother and bring him to the ship. Time to leave."

The young man turned over, labored up on one elbow. "Leave?" he said thickly. "Ridiculous."

Sorlij booted him again. "Party's over. Come on."

Barion pronounced with drunken care, "It has just begun." He gouged double handfuls of grass from the moist earth and flung them high. "Rich with promise and oxygen, new-made creatures pattering, thundering toward destiny. Primates . . . what's the literal meaning of 'primate' in our tongue? 'Those who look up.' Utter par-*hic*-adise."

Sorlij hauled him to his feet, on which Barion swayed like a tree about to fall. His chosen physical form was advanced primate. Millions of years later on this same world the image would be described as Byronic.

"I would take this birthing world into my hands"— Barion tried to focus on them—"and through my fingers run the saltwaters of oceans, the grains of earth, a cosmos of thought . . ."

"Meanwhile, let's go home."

". . . teach my creations to see the atom and through it to the larger worlds, galaxies within: one vast, concerted, soaring purpose . . ." Barion trailed off, wilting down onto the grass like a garment fallen from a hanger. "Soon's I get a nap."

"Serve you both right to be left here," Sorlij muttered. He nudged Coyul again. One bleary eye opened and found him. "We're going. Come on. You'll have to carry Barion to the ship."

"Abs'lutely. Common sense to the rescue." Coyul rolled over beside his unmoving brother, studied him and then Sorlij. "The lovely thing about being drunk: I don't have t'listen to him or look at you. My dear brother," Coyul mumbled on the verge of maudlin tears. "He believes all that cosmic-poetical nonsense, y'know."

Coyul squinted up at Sorlij with drunken malice and apparently came to a decision. Lurching erect somehow, he balled the novelty of his right hand into a clumsy fist. "I know you don't like him, but he's never been hurt. Which, as of this moment, is more than I can say for you."

Coyul launched a roundhouse right at Sorlij. Unused to real muscles, he aimed the blow where Sorlij's mouth was supposed to be. His target merely dissolved.

Coyul passed through thin air, went down on his face and stayed there.

"All *right,*" Sorlij huffed, a little shaken by the sudden violence that recalled too sharply everything he disliked about the irresponsible siblings. "So be it. For once you two can get your precious selves out of trouble. Just stay here a while and cool off. I'm sick of you both."

"Where are the boys?" he was asked at the ship.

"They don't feel like coming." Sorlij bit off the words. "Frankly, I don't care. I don't want to be bothered with them now."

Maj tittered at the prospect. "That's amusing. Imagine them waking up with nothing to do until we come for them."

The notion caught on immediately. "Doomed!"

"Alone."

"No one to impress but monkeys."

The whole thing was a lark. After all, someone would return sooner or later. They were all still too partied out to care. Anyway, what harm could come to the brothers on a world where the highest form of life was an undersized primate? Crossing the orbit of the system's frozen outermost planet, more immediate problems beset them.

"I've been in some unfashionable neighborhoods," their navigator observed, "but this is really obscure, not even on our charts. Anyone remember where we came out of jump?"

No one did. They hadn't cared much about directions coming out, though in a curved, finite universe, they couldn't stay lost forever. On the other hand, the volunteer navigator was less than expert.

They landed many times on the way home, mostly for a change of scene, knowing certain systems to be in varying stages of civilization. After some bad experiences, they became discreet about asking directions.

On worlds where they were not understood, the higher life forms proclaimed them deities, wrote sacred works, promulgated dogma on what they were supposed to have said, and flattered them with the sacrifice of surplus population. Where they were understood, the natives tried to sell them trinkets, real estate and surplus daughters.

"Thank you, no," they declined, "we're just passing through . . ."

"Unless perhaps you have a son with four arms," suggested Maj, who was quite jaded.

As their near-immortal kind went, they were not appreciably older when they found a familiar sun for reference, but the universe was. By then, no one even faintly remembered or cared much where they'd left Barion and Coyul.

Shortly after their return, a conservative administration came to power. Trends altered, youth no longer flamed. The few post-adolescent gatherings in the now unfashionable human form looked merely anachronistic. Primate studies languished. The family and friends of Barion and Coyul found themselves less well connected than before, though it was understood that Sorlij would have to return for the boys since he knew the way. More or less. Sooner or later.

Meanwhile Sorlij's discipline became high-priority for a newly discovered batch of sea worlds, his academic star in the ascent.

"Of course you'll go back for them one of these days, no question. But now, dear boy—how do you like advanced studies?"

■ 2 ■

Killing time: genius ad lib

Barion stood on the brow of a low hill, seven feet tall, idealized in every fine-chiseled feature, a time bomb of idealism. Eons later in the Age of Romance, this likeness would inspire a plethora of sonnets by repressed ladies who played the spinet and reproduced parthenogenically by thinking of England. A little later, Whitman would write much the way Barion presently conceived existence. By then Barion would be more restrained in taste and method, but the errors of early enthusiasm would be irreversible.

He felt buoyant this primal morning, breathing deeply of the oxygen-rich air and the heady impurities exhaled by this fecund planet. On the flatland below, a mild breeze stirred the tall savanna grass—no, not breeze but movement. A small group of the fascinating primates noted yesterday: two males, three females, shambling through the high grass in search of food, physical differences barely discernible under the silky black hair that covered most of their body.

Their stereoscopic vision and acute color perception would register Barion as alien. Yes; they saw him and halted. Barion faded to energy phase, moving closer. With nothing to see or smell, the primates went

12

on foraging. Barion concentrated on one of the males turning over a stone in search of grubs. It had no forehead at all, merely a thick supraorbital ridge of bone. The brain was almost entirely instinct.

Almost, Barion knew, excitement rising. There were possibilities.

The ape's blunt head swiveled toward a flicker of light, screeching at the others. On the hilltop something like sunlight began to take definite shape. Barion flowed away toward his brother.

Physical but motionless, the brothers watched the wary primates move away from them. "As anthros go," Barion judged, "these are interesting."

"Try this for laughs," Coyul glowered in frustration. "They've left us here. Sorlij, Maj, the whole considerate pack of them. We're stuck."

Absorbed, Barion said, "Nothing to worry about. Probably a side trip. They'll be back."

"I lack your faith in Sorlij."

There were large differences of temperament between Barion and Coyul, quite obvious in human form. As stated, Barion's fancy ran to the Byronic. Smaller Coyul looked like an overdressed Dylan Thomas. Where Barion's costume was thrift shop casual, the fretful Coyul stumped up and down in a gold lamé dressing gown that startled his brother as much as it had the retreating apes.

"Left!" Coyul berated the heavens. "Lost, abandoned, ma*rooned!*"

"Relax; they'll be back. You know Sorlij."

"I do," said Coyul, not at all reassured. "I have work at home: a whole new cycle of études. Notes for a major orchestral piece."

Which demonstrated another basic difference in the brothers. Both were trained to the primary work of their kind, genetic seeding. Barion considered himself a scientist with artistic leanings. Coyul was at heart an

13

artist and something of a dilettante, happy only at his music, competent but halfhearted at the discipline into which fate arbitrarily dumped him.

"I've got a bad feeling about this," he brooded. "Remember the way we came?"

"Not really. Toward the outer edge of the galaxy . . . sort of."

"Ah—which galaxy?"

"Oh, I don't know," Barion confessed without much concern. "How many are there?"

"Your complacency boggles the mind. I hope someone knows. Without a ship we are in trouble."

Relative trouble: in energy form they could streak across short distances, perhaps half the diameter of the present galaxy. Beyond that presented serious dangers of energy dissipation, radiation effects, pollution from star scintillation, all possibly mortal to their electron-cycle life.

"Barion, what can we do?"

"Come on, little brother." Barion grinned. "Where's your creativity, your initiative?"

"I've got plenty of initiative," Coyul blazed. "Just wait'll I use it on you sometime."

"How about now?"

"This is your kind of place," Coyul retreated. "What can we do?"

"Oh, well." Barion looked off after the primates receding across the grassland. "All sorts of things."

Lost on this mud-ball world while more time passed. Whenever Barion disappeared for long periods, Coyul could always find him indulging his obsession with primates, observing the nearest family group in physical form, allowing them to get used to him. On this unknown, uncharted planet, Coyul feared that Barion would find the lure of experiment irresistible, and therein lay the problem. Penalties for premature seeding were stiff enough; for unauthorized experiment they were virtual death: exile for eons on the Rock, some utterly or near-lifeless planet, until the solitary prisoner gave up and bled his energy out into space and oblivion.

Coyul found it ironic that he should be considered the irresponsible one, but a large part of this general opinion was his own doing. Competent enough at carbon-cycle life studies, he had no interest in science at all. Part of his youthful dilettante pose was an affectation of boredom toward any discipline save art, deriving a perverse pleasure from letting elders and peers alike think him an utter waste of time. He reasoned that by the time he was independent they'd just leave him alone to dabble and compose.

On this unpromising day, he found Barion observing a single primate under a tree. Coyul's sudden appearance made it start and gibber.

"Soften your colors," Barion suggested. "The bright confuses it."

Coyul's toga-like creation faded from scarlet and silver to buff-green. "What's it doing that's worth watching?"

"Found some nuts. Tried to gnaw through one and broke a tooth. Doesn't feel at all good about that. Now it'll try that stone."

The ape raised the stone and hurled it at the nuts, missing them altogether. Coyul stirred restlessly. "I hope this improves—*ow!*"

He sprang up, rump stinging, as the offending snake coiled to strike again. "You little—"

The Ur-cobra was evolving a neurotoxin to paralyze its dinner, but the concept was still on the drawing board. Coyul glared murderously, then flowed as energy into the reptile brain, raging, bloating it to grotesque activity. For tortured seconds the snake suffered from conscience, questioned existence, then thrashed away through the undergrowth. Shortly afterward,

15

with suicidal relief, the snake allowed itself to be eaten by a wild dog with fewer scruples.

"Charming place: one huge digestive tract," Coyul muttered, corporating again. He glanced at the bewildered ape pawing at his gritty nutshells. "Any news from the cutting edge of science?"

Suffering with the broken tooth, the ape scooped up the stone with a scream of frustration and smashed it on a larger one. The missile split evenly along a seam.

"Cutting edge," Barion mused. "I wonder . . ."

"Leave the animals alone," Coyul warned. "Don't tinker."

"Obviously on its way to becoming human."

"With all the implied instabilities. Even if he creates beauty at breakfast—and he's not exactly expert at simple feeding yet—you can never be sure he won't murder before sundown."

But Barion heard the siren song of possibility. "At least I can help him with the nuts. Before that other specimen grabs them away."

A smaller male, foraging himself, had wandered close. The first male chattered a warning. When the newcomer made a snatch at the nuts, he scooped up the broken stone—

—the difference was subtle but apparent to Coyul: a little more control in the grip, better aim as the cutting edge slammed down on the marauder's skull. With a shrill scream the smaller male rolled in the grass, clutching its furry head. Reclaiming the prize, the victor laid the nuts on the rock that had shattered and shaped his own missile and pounded at them with the cutting stone.

"Barion, quit messing *around!*"

"I didn't," Barion whispered, jubilant. "Well, not much."

Just a nudge here, a hint there in the small proto-brain, turning it precocious just a little ahead of evolutionary schedule. "Show-off. At least give the loser the same break."

"What, him?" Barion started away toward the hilltop. "Controlled experiment; always a loser. Smart eats, stupid starves. I have some thinking to do."

Coyul sat alone, brooding on the grave and very possible consequences of Barion's impulse, staring morosely at the relative genius picking edible morsels from the mashed shells.

"Congratulations. Try not to get eaten yourself before the day's out. Now get out of here. Move!"

The sudden thunder of Coyul's voice sent the ape fleeing away across the savanna. Safe for the moment, the smaller male brandished a stick after him, achieving moral victory at low cost and healthy distance, then rummaged among the nutshells for bits of meat.

Coyul watched him, thinking on balances of power, his brother's arrogance, the wounded monkey. Blood from its lacerated scalp spattered over the stone missile. The creature hefted the stone in one hand, picked up its stick in the other, looking off after the departed enemy.

"Just this once," Coyul decided. "Only fair."

He made no major intrusion in the small brain, just enough to push one fact toward another to make a working combination. Still intent on his distant assailant, the ape's bright eyes gleamed with new tactical purpose. It remembered dimly making a few tentative swipes at soft wood with harder stone . . . something stone could do to wood.

The nimble fingers with their unique opposable thumbs began to work—clumsily at first, then more surely through a hundred tries until the ape learned how to strike most effectively with the tool. Until there was a formidable point.

With a scream of triumph, the little creature plunged its weapon again and again into yielding earth, brandished vengeance high overhead, then darted away on a direct course after the enemy who hurt it.

17

Coyul lingered a moment to wonder which would survive, then put his figurative money on the spear maker. The other ape might be bigger, but this one was vindictive and *mean*.

■ 3 ■

The serpent's gift

The spear maker became head of his family group by the logical expedient of skewering his larger rival. Barion was peeved at his brother's interference—

"Keep your hands *off,* Coyul."

—but on reflection found aspects of the victor too tempting to pass up. Perfect serendipity: this backwater world would never matter to anyone. Sorlij or someone would pick them up soon enough; meanwhile he could experiment toward results that would surely win him a science prize for seeding in one of the more important galaxies. Barion was young. The urgent rightness of his theories spurred him like a pebble in his shoe.

Suppose . . .

Ninety-five percent of hominid species never went anywhere. Another three percent did somewhat better but coasted eventually down evolutionary dead ends. The viable two percent were no end of trouble, but only —Barion theorized—because no one was allowed to work them to Cultural Threshold until they'd attained 1050 cc of cranial capacity. At that tardy point, the primal tendencies were too deep-rooted a part of them, the memory of the dark in which their nocturnal ancestors foraged while the great reptiles slept.

"No one has ever tried CT at the level of these subjects."

"An unencouraging and totally illegal 900 cc," Coyul reminded him.

But the prospect caught fire in Barion's imagination. "An expendable world not even on the charts at home. An expendable species that won't . . . Look, you know this kind of planet always tends to radical polar tilt sooner or later. They won't make it through the ice. We'll be gone by then, but at least I'll know I'm right."

Coyul shook his head, resigned to sad truth. "You won't breed the darkness out of them no matter when you start. It's part of them."

"Isn't."

"It is when you're a mind capable of conceiving eternity trapped inside a body that dies. I didn't sleep through *all* the lectures, you know."

"Yes, yes." Barion waved the objections aside with his usual know-it-all gesture. "Religion, dualism. Predictable stages."

"Not stages, you idiot! Propensities!"

"Hush, be still. My subject's coming."

The ape moved cautiously to the water hole to drink, wary of the two still figures a little distance away, hissing a challenge out of a mouth and throat still limited in the sounds they could produce. Were she of an empirical bent, Charity Stovall might have been edified to know her direct ancestor was the smartest ape on its metaphorical block. Relative to body mass, the brain was already huge. Other survival traits would have sent Charity gibbering back to Genesis for reassurance.

Above all, the ape was marvelously adaptable. Omnivorous as a rodent, thriving on any food available. Three and a half feet tall: the most acquisitive, curious, aggressive, inventively vicious hominid Barion had ever found, and quite the hardiest on this violent world next to the cockroach and the rat. Long after this day's work the ape would produce Christ, Beethoven, Auschwitz, thumbscrews and philosophy, Magna Carta and White Supremacy, poetry, poison gas, nuclear fission and romantic love. For the moment it crouched by the water hole, munching a succulent grub discovered under a stone, warning off the large creatures that somehow would not be frightened away. They were unclassifiable, therefore a threat. The ape made the brave noises of its kind.

"Good morning," Barion said softly: "Welcome to evolution."

The ape jumped at the sound, afraid but curious.

"I may be wrong about you. You and I have a great deal to learn."

The ape made a clicking sound of puzzlement.

"You won't understand any of this. Even when your mind is clear enough to send your little cutting stone to the moon and beyond, you'll still wonder about this moment but never quite forget the truth of it. Wrap it in religion, a hundred flattering myths, in music, painting and exaltation of pure spirit—"

"Why all the lyrics?" Coyul wondered sourly. "You're only giving it a boot in the evolutionary butt."

"Can't you see it? The implications, the greatest of all dramas, when life stands erect to contemplate itself—"

"My brother, the scientific lemming, headlong over the edge of folly. Don't do it."

"Shut up. This is *his* triumph: this one moment of knowing, when the atom contemplates an electron navel and finds worlds within worlds, will stay in that small brain forever. Your nature will always be to believe," he prophesied to his quivering subject, "but your destiny always to question. I can't make that any easier for you."

Barion began to dissolve, flowing toward the creature. Coyul pleaded one last time. "Barion, don't! It's—"

Too late. His brother became a brief sparkle in sunlight before pouring into the little ape's brain.

"—madness."

Under the beetling brow, it—*he*—blinked. A great light had flashed somewhere behind his eyes. Blood pounded in his ears. He was alone by the muddy water hole and still thirsty, but now, as he bent to drink, there was a difference. Always before, he'd seen the other creature come up to meet him out of the water, then vanish somehow in the small ripples caused by his drinking. The image had always frightened him; now he knew it was his own. He snarled at it, knowing he existed and would end, rejecting that horrible truth for all time with a howl of terror and rage and a primal loss he would labor through countless eons and creeds to rationalize and define. With all the terrible weight of consciousness, *knowing* he was. The beginnings of expression in the eyes, a dawn-sense of the tragedy Barion had taxed him with. As for the lost thing never to be found again, even his far-distant daughter Charity would call it the Fall.

Stunned by sentience, the miserable human did what came naturally—growled as Barion reappeared beside Coyul.

"Now you've done it," Coyul reproached him with a full measure of disgust. "I don't care if you are my brother. You're a rotten kid."

"We'll see." Barion inspected his handiwork like a critical painter gauging perspective on a canvas. Abruptly he swung away, covering the ground in great strides.

"Where are you off to now? Haven't you done enough damage?"

"Got to do the same for his group," Barion flung back. "Can't have him maundering around thinking all alone."

"Fine . . . just fine." Coyul dissolved to energy out of compassion for the miserable creature that Barion had just kicked upstairs. Whimpering with a new fear all the sharper for having no clear shape, the creature bowed his besieged head in hairy paws and felt vastly sorry for himself.

"All right," Coyul sighed. "You're a self. Suddenly apart where you used to be part of. I'd have left well enough alone."

The same sympathy kept him from leaving the human, who was weeping now, already trying to make sounds for unguessed meanings.

"It's not all bad. There'll be insights now and then. I suppose there's a chance."

The pathetic human went on sniffling. He didn't seem to know where he was anymore.

"Look, it's not my fault, not up to me to help you at all. He shouldn't have done it. So many other life forms more suited to sentience than you'll ever be. Oh, stop whining, will you?"

The weeping human raised his blunt head at the sound of a distinct reluctant sigh.

"All right—here: it's the least I can do."

Weeping made him feel thirsty again. As he bent to drink once more, knowing the reflected image for himself, fear transmuted to something lighter, the ugly sound of his sadness to an even more alien emotion. He couldn't help it. The effort strained his throat that barely had the muscles for laughter.

So much for motivations. Barion wanted to win a science prize, Coyul only to go home and write music, but the thing was done. A great deal of bloodshed, art and religion would be perpetrated in both their names, and neither would be understood at all. As they had done to him, the human modified them to a lesser but more flattering truth he could live with.

23

Dazed, intermittently sobbing and laughing like a squeaky hinge, the creature deserted the water hole and scampered away toward history and other mixed blessings.

------------------- ◼ **4** ◼ -------------------

Topside/Below Stairs

The relief ship didn't come. And *didn't* come.

A great deal of time went by. The Pole tilted, the ice came and went. Barion's creature moved across the land and oceans, the skies, touched the moon and groped beyond. Barion began with a passionate belief, encouraged to vindication with every advance. Coyul took his own conclusions from the dismal weight of evidence.

Humans *were* dualistic. Consciously forgotten, the primitive eons still lurked in the subsconscious, a huge dark forest against the small bright leaf of civilization. With new language they put new names to the gods of light and dark, put them at a distance but could not escape. Called the dark evil but found it always there inside them, a kind of spiritual schizophrenia. Persisted in seeing existence in terms of this struggle between "good" and "evil," producing a great deal of belief, violence and, now and then, actual thought.

"The darkness will wear away," Barion was certain.

"Sure," said the dubious Coyul. "Any millennium now."

And then a new problem cropped up in which dualism was only an aggravating part. Matter could be neither created nor destroyed. The human brain was matter that generated energy. At a certain point in its evolution, a residue of personally defined energy began to stockpile, wanting somewhere to continue after physical death and, above all, something to do. Even Coyul had no flippant answer for the quandary. The small body of work their kind had done with the ill-regarded species never included sufficient follow-up on side effects. A few inspection reports on this post-existent energy pool (couched in *very* cautiously conservative terms) filtered in, were misinterpreted, buried and forgotten in the academic catacombs for irrelevant information and the pressure of more immediate problems at home. Barion never realized—

"They don't die, Coyul. They just go *on*. And they keep asking about one god or another."

"Me, too. I tell them I'm just waiting to go home. Then I tell them where home is and nobody believes me. For all their violence, they have a remarkable capacity for supine adoration. Throw 'em a grand party; that always works."

Worked for some and for a while. Egypt and Sumer passed. Most of them forgot about gods and creeds after a time and got on out of habit with the kind of life they'd known on Earth. Babylonians came, greased and gauded, brought wine and cheese and loved the party. Britons sang, Irish drank and mourned, Chinese discussed aesthetics, Indians chased phantom buffalo, Jews argued. Their combined energy was incredible, but Barion managed after a fashion, directing by indirection.

Then the Christians started to arrive, simple folk for the most part who didn't want much. Nevertheless, the Apostles had definite and aggressive views, the martyrs felt they were owed the Presence of God and grew sharp with Barion, who was, to them, merely a ubiquitous handyman and certainly dressed like one. Unlike Coyul, Barion dressed for function, inventing denim ages before America popularized it.

26

Very few had the perception to discern Barion's real power. One who did was a young Nazarene named Yeshua who had problems of his own in what people thought he was and expected of him.

"Sometimes," he admitted to Barion, "I wish I'd minded my own business."

"*You* wish? Have you met Augustine yet?"

"I've avoided him," said the candid Yeshua. "He doesn't like Jews."

"Well, he's after me all the time about seeing God. And you: where and when does he come into the Presence?"

Yeshua gazed out over the grassy riverbank he and Barion had imagined for a few moments of relaxation. There was a directness to his glance and a stillness that the unsure found disturbing, the pompous insolent. "Just tell him you're . . . You, I guess. Something."

"You were an extraordinarily wise man in your time," Barion said, "and even you had to use parables. You think Augustine, that doggedly passionate saint, would accept what I really am: a student from a galaxy on the other side of the universe and likely to be in a lot of trouble when I'm found? He's growing insistent on seeing you, too. What he thinks you are."

"He'd just be disappointed. They all are. A pity, too. I like being with people." Yeshua rested his chin on drawn-up knees. "There's one friend I'd give anything to see . . . talk to. He hasn't come here."

"Judas?" Barion guessed. "He's with Coyul."

"Judas could have understood the truth, but he ran from it."

"You two!" The stentorian voice startled them.

Barion winced. "Speak of saints . . ."

"I would speak with you." The short, bull-shouldered man in late Roman dress strode along the bank and halted before them, peremptory as a drill sergeant. His wide-set eyes gleamed with strength and the steely light of the Believer reborn from self-defined sin.

Nothing for it; Barion greeted him pleasantly. "Hello, Augustine."

The Bishop of Hippo brushed the courtesy aside. "Give me no more excuses or subterfuge. Tell me where I may find what I have in life suffered, fought, endured enmity and slander for. Where—is—He?"

"Haven't seen him."

"Oh, not again!"

"I've never seen him." Barion shrugged, choosing his words carefully. Augustine was skilled in debate and played dirty. "But in time you'll understand more than you did."

Augustine bridled: a strong, courageous but narrow man. "I need no nondescript porter in outlandish garb to give me understanding. Where, then, is my Lord, Jesus Christ?"

"Visiting a troubled friend," Yeshua volunteered truthfully.

Augustine, that most embattled of the early saints, subjected Yeshua to disdainful scrutiny from the sensitive face to the provincial garb of Galilee. "And here another riddle. I do not understand, among other mysteries sufficient to drive the Faithful to drink or women, why *you* people are suffered to remain here. You destroy, you question everything and accept nothing. When Christ offered you salvation, you spit on it and nailed Him to a cross."

"That was a bad day," Yeshua agreed with authority. "I was against it myself."

So it went. Time continued to pass. More people arrived, prejudiced as Augustine. Barion was forced to subdivide his nebulous domain into different realities. Pagans were no problem so long as they had sunlight and greenery, nor the Jews so long as they could suffer and argue and Hasidim didn't have to deal with the new Zionists. If you needed to feel Chosen or Elect, there were miles of exclusive high rises set aside for the purpose, and never a wait for vacancies. Only the most radical few made permanent residence there. A lifetime of extremity was one thing, eternity quite another.

With the Protestant Reformation and its spread to America, Barion's problems became truly complex. In their passion for exclusivism and damning others, they gave his establishment so many names that Barion simply affixed a nonsectarian title that stuck.

Newcomers were greeted: "Welcome to Topside."

Coyul could look to no more respite than his brother. Post-existent energy began collecting in his vicinity as early as in Topside. Like Barion, he was forced to maintain an office for some kind of organization. Barion's taste in decor never got beyond functional government surplus, but Coyul's office was more of a salon, reflecting the march of style through the ages —grand during the Egyptian Middle Kingdom, a fine Athenian period. He went a little gaudy with Imperial Rome, overtapestried during the Renaissance. The seventeenth century grew a bit lacy, the nineteenth very busy and Pre-Raphaelite, the twentieth by turns Art Deco, Scandinavian, chrome-and-Lucite. The grand piano obligingly modified its finish to match changing styles.

Those lusty ancients who came to Coyul just wanted to relax and enjoy themselves. Romans were marvelous in this respect, especially Petronius and Martial, but eventually Coyul had to subdivide to accommodate the variety of human experience, prejudice and folly. Seeding Cultural Threshold so early had lasting repercussions; by the time of the late-medieval Christians, human notions of an afterlife were as violent as the one they'd suffered Earthside. Since Coyul's neighborhood was clearly not heaven, they considered themselves damned and expected to suffer. Coyul found that they ultimately defined themselves by pain and were used to it. After a time he gave up trying to dissuade them and provided a space large enough but of no specific character—until he read Dante and comprehended their geometric and grisly expectations.

"These people are sick. Well . . . all right."

Drama they wanted, drama they got with full staging, lights and stereophonic sound. Their subdivision hell was very German Expressionist—dark, windswept and romantically bleak. Coyul provided only scenery and props, leaving pain to humans with more talent for it. As with Topside's high rise for unreformed ecstatics and the insufferably blessed, the reality of eternal penance quickly palled. The sector had well-lighted exits, and their use was encouraged.

Occupied with their own problems, the brothers saw less and less of each other as the ages passed. When Barion did visit he was appalled.

"What do you call this—whatever it is going on here? Looks like a cross between a procession of flagellants and a Polish wedding."

"Hadn't thought to name it," Coyul said, stroking idle chords from the piano. "Topside is catchy; what should I be? Downstairs? The Cellar? No, it doesn't ring."

"I heard you visited Luther Earthside."

"For all the good it did. I presume you got him."

"Didn't I just. Don't meddle, Coyul."

"Oh—the original pot blackening the kettle. Did you straighten him out?"

"I don't try anymore," Barion said unhappily. He no longer looked Byronic, just hassled. "Left off that with the Druids. They all think I'm sort of a janitor."

Coyul surveyed his brother's worn denim jeans and work shirt. "Can't think why. Now, drama works very well here—below stairs, as it were."

"But do they believe you?"

"No." Coyul played a few minor chords. "Most don't believe me, the rest don't give a damn. I hope they find us soon—fun as this place can be sometimes."

"Just keep your hands off Earthside. We're in

30

enough trouble—" Barion broke off abruptly, listening intensely. "There—you hear it?"

"Hear what?"

"That sound. Voices. Been hearing them on and off for several years. Americans," Barion concluded vaguely. "Don't like it at all."

"Wait. Where are you going?" Coyul asked hastily as Barion began to dissolve.

"Out . . ."

His curiosity tweaked, Coyul turned his ear Earthside, sifting the voices and spirits that echoed as energy from that violent little ball in space. He heard them soon enough: American voices that somehow didn't *sound* American, like a sudden change of pitch in a smooth-running engine. Coyul sought out Barion's energy, found him sweeping over American mountains and flatlands, a solitary hound on a scent. Blending with that energy, Coyul knew what his brother did, read the names though they meant nothing to him.

Charity Stovall. Roy Stride.

To Barion came the masses of simple folk, lost, neglected and ground down through history, bearing nothing but their bewilderment, injustice and the brutalized monotony of their lives. The passionate but inarticulate needers of a flaming God to redeem their humble faith or at least help them get even.

Coyul fared better for personalities. There were problems, to be sure: malcontents, injury collectors, bureaucrats (dull but useful for keeping records), fascists, reformers, assorted chauvinists and bigots. Coyul grew adept at fitting the right ambience to the individual spirit. As time went on, this rather than any schism became the difference between Topside and Below Stairs. Both were more or less efficient without much organization, but Coyul maintained the more colorful establishment. Along with the thorns of the professional sufferers came the occasional blossoms: the musicians, the stimulating thinkers from the Vienna coffeehouses. The artists, the newsmen with cynical eyes and large thirsts, rowdy poets and agnostic scholars. The actors like Edmund Kean, whose visceral *Othello* could thrill new generations of deceased . . . and the dashing, incendiary, utterly mad John Wilkes Booth, who came bathed in his own perpetual spotlight, ready as ever to be a star.

Early on, there came one man who wanted absolutely nothing except to be left alone. He lived in solitude on an isolated moor on the fringe of suffering, received no guests, troubled Coyul not at all. Now and then he drove a cab or did other odd jobs for the mislabeled Prince of Darkness, who knew him immediately but, out of courtesy, did not trouble him for a name.

"Jacob will do," the newcomer said—a brooding, sardonic man with troubled eyes and a manner designed to keep folk at a distance. In later times, tooling his cab through the byways of Below Stairs, he simply offered, "Call me Jake."

■ 5 ■

Management problems
among the mad

"No! I will not! Never, ever again!"

Wilmer P. Grubb was not an aggressive man, but driven by last-ditch frustration, he barged into Coyul's salon, slamming a pale hand on the piano top to punctuate his passion. A slight, sallow academic who never looked quite kempt, his happiest expression that of a child forced to drink something good for him.

"I will not!" he bleated. "Excuse me for not knocking, Prince."

"No one ever does," said the inured Coyul, "but you might start a trend. What is it, Mr. Grubb?"

"Booth."

"Again?"

"As ever, the bane of my existence."

In life Wilmer Grubb had been a professor who wanted nothing more than to teach Shakespeare as a poet, not a playwright. The immortal lines, he felt, were fragile and unsafe in the braying mouths of players. Not choice but biology sent Grubb to a galley oar in theater. He had an ardent love for his comely wife, Elvira, and stated it redundantly with eight children, forcing him to earn extra money as a drama critic during Lincoln's administration. In his jaundiced scholarly view, actors were déclassé, plays the opiate of a benighted public— but the mad John Wilkes Booth, younger brother to Edwin, was Grubb's bête noire. When Booth opened, Grubb quite often wrote his review before trudging to the theater as to execution, sometimes without bothering to go at all. He died of acute gastritis brought on by questionable oysters and Booth's *Hamlet*, never once blaming the seafood. Wafting Topside to the requested strains of Handel, Grubb was told that his wife had preferred Coyul's establishment. Before departing south, the scholar indulged the dream of a lifetime and asked to meet his icon, Shakespeare.

The meeting was unfortunate. The balding, bibulous son of a Stratford glove maker possessed a lyrical vulgarity that might tickle his tavern cronies but revolted the prim Grubb, especially when well-oiled Will did his uncensored Mercutio. Grubb fled the Mermaid and the neighborhood, arriving Below Stairs in profound cultural shock. He was greeted by an affable Coyul in a lilac chesterfield.

"Do come *in,* Mr. Grubb. Your charming wife is already with us, presently doing—uh—social work in the downtown area. We have lacked you, sir. Our actors, particularly Booth, need your critical rein."

Grubb blanched and shuddered.

"House rules are quite lenient, though we discourage children and pets."

After eight children, so did the Grubbs. They renewed their connubial passion unfettered by issue. Paris being worth a Mass, Grubb continued to review and flay the impossible Wilksey Booth—but enough was enough.

"Prince, I am, in most respects, a happy man. If I must review, I am allowed infinite space—"

"Infinitely employed."

"But far too often"—Grubb's tone went pallid—"I have to review that . . ."

"Booth. Yes." Coyul struck an idle chord on the piano. "And you are driven now to Draconian measures? Miltonian depths? Want to review books?"

"Anything!" Grubb seized on the notion as on a life preserver in a maelstrom. "Even the new works of Hitler."

"He's Topside with Eva." Coyul rippled an arpeggio. "Never sees anyone but Wagner, reviews his own books."

"Possibly romance novels," Grubb offered with waning hope—then, in broken tones, the final indignity: "Even epic fantasy."

"Grubb, remember your pride. All those unicorns . . . I'm in a bind where Wilksey's concerned," Coyul confessed. "Groundlings dote on him, uncritical virgins swoon, older women pursue him with Merovingian intent. No one reviews that painful ham with any detachment except you, Mr. Grubb. My last, best critical hope. You can endure actors."

"I don't like actors," Grubb complained in a voice like a damp sock. "I don't like writers. They're never as nice as their books. All they do is get drunk and arrogant and sick all over the furniture."

Well, Coyul suggested, he might relocate Topside. "There's Woolf and T. S. Eliot: they're frightfully sane."

"HA! *There,* villain!" They were transfixed. "There you are!"

"Booth!" Grubb paled at the sight of the vengeful figure in the entrance. "Protect me, Prince. He's violent."

"Nay, stand! Your next move is your last." The hissed command became the *whish* of a rapier unsheathed, the lethal point on a line with Grubb's pigeon chest in the grip of a black-clad, lithe young man. Still in his Hamlet costume, John Wilkes Booth crouched before them, malevolent and handsome, bathed in his ubiquitous spotlight. He advanced like a demented but purposeful cat. "Grubb, you ratcatcher, I have found thee."

"Provincial raver!" Grubb retreated behind the piano. "Confederate assassin!"

"Prince, I entreat you." Booth suited word to action, down on one knee. "Have you heard what this baneful scribbler wrote about my current Hamlet? List then: 'a hyperthyroid mannequin,' says he, 'overstuffed with conceit as his codpiece with batting.'"

Coyul frowned at the cringing critic. "Now, that was mean."

"Puissant Prince, hear the most loyal among thy liege men. Is't not enough I had to live in Edwin's shadow? Nor that I died for the Confederacy? Now in death must I suffer and create only to endure the calumnies of this unfeeling fungus on the fundament of art? The sword's too noble for such as he." Booth dropped the rapier, drawing a wicked dagger. "A bodkin's work, by heaven!"

He launched himself at the miserable Grubb, spotlight following the fine body as it hurtled to vengeance. A scant inch from Grubb's breast, the dagger became a limp daisy. Not that Booth could have done any damage, but Coyul hated even the idea of violence.

"Wilksey, you silly ass, knock it OFF! Mr. Grubb, if you please." Coyul ushered the trembling teacher to the door. "The matter is in my hands. Meanwhile, you need no longer review."

"Thank you, Prince. Thank you," Grubb effused. "It means so much. So far behind in my professional reading."

"Not at all, I completely understand. Once a scholar . . . good day."

With Grubb no longer part of the problem, Coyul addressed himself reluctantly to the ongoing burden of idiotic Booth, who brooded now in the center of his amber spot. "Wilkes, we're closing *Hamlet*. The women love it, yes, but even those loyal ranks are thinning."

Booth raised his head with its fine raven curls. "My finest role."

"With the imagination of the ages at beck, why always Hamlet?"

"Because he suffers," Booth intoned. "Torn by what he must do and cannot until too late—as I was torn between art and my country. As I suffered."

"Edwin suffered." Coyul turned critical. "Edwin *was* Hamlet. You were too busy drinking, wenching and having a darkly dramatic good time plotting against Lincoln to suffer for a moment. Please turn off that ridiculous light. Jake is the only man Below Stairs who broods with any depth. You look merely petulant or constipated."

"Though you wrong me, that is true." Booth dimmed his aura. "Jake broods like a definition of sorrow itself. But close *Hamlet*? For what, pray?"

"*Romeo*. There, Wilksey, was triumph unalloyed."

"Play again that puling Veronese adolescent?"

"By Thespis, not as *you* played him," Coyul reminisced. "Well do I remember."

So did the women among Booth's audiences, who still grew faint with the violence of his passion; so did his leading ladies, who usually sustained a bruise or two, and the hapless Tybalts, who had to fight in earnest to remain unmauled. Even Shakespeare, down for a weekend, was impressed: "There, sirrahs, is a Romeo with a scrotum."

"In your reading of 'she doth teach the stars to shine,' one could hear the undiluted hormones of a mating call." Coyul did not flatter in this. Edwin's brother was mad as a hatter but not without talent. But for his deplorable eleventh-hour politics, the world might have loved him as well.

"Close *Hamlet*," the Prince bargained, "and I myself will find a part worthy of you—or a vehicle, playing all the roles if you like. Sparing no expense for lighting, scenery, costumes or music."

Booth was skeptical but interested. "With love scenes and swordplay? Can I die?"

"In color and often. Strong men will weep and ladies faint."

"Don't they always?" Booth preened. "What is this role?"

Coyul had nothing in mind beyond getting back to his music—and perhaps wondering what Barion heard from America to trouble him. He tried to keep his people happy or at least short of revolt, slanderously called King of Liars because no one really wanted truth, Wilksey least of all.

"Do Romeo first," he hedged. "Make Edwin green. He was never your equal in the role. Then we will follow it with . . ."

"Nay, speak," Booth urged, hooked solidly now. "With what?"

"Well may you ask." Coyul favored the demented actor with a smile of pure anticipation, then dissolved in flattering, soft blue light. "The ages will remember you for it."

Booth stretched out a staying hand as to a ghostly father. "Stay and speak—"

"Remember thee for it . . ."

You had to stage everything for Booth. Like most actors, that was the only way it sank in.

Meanwhile the voices from America grew louder, uglier.

■ 6 ■

Slouching toward Plattsville

Barion rode the wind over desert and flatland, listening to the sound of American voices. Hovered over the steel-and-glass cities, drifted in autumn haze over gas station and 7-Eleven store crossroads, back and forth along the freeways of a country sliding down the long decline toward second-class nationhood while still the most powerful in a turbulent world. The voices he searched out would not be in the cities but out somewhere beyond them across a widening gap, among the have-nots, the small, the disenfranchised and vengeful. The common people toward whom Lincoln had presumptuously ascribed a large affection on Barion's part. As he turned east again, hunting with the concentration of a hawk, he heard the sought voices more clearly. He was coming closer.

Government? Sell us downriver like always. Give the country away to niggers and queers. Don't give a shit about folks like us.

Never had much school, but I know what's right. Liberry full of dirty books, Commoniss books. Klan got the right idea: kill 'em all.

Well, I don't hold with that, but you can't make a

39

living. Man can take a lot if there's enough to live on. Closed the plant . . . ain't worked since. Bad as '29.

Barion veered north now, closing on one place, one town where the voices resolved to dangerous coherence and—somehow known in the eons of his experience—a pivot point in American time. He knew that cry made up of many cries, remembered how it muttered through the sixteenth century, became an ugly but catalytic insanity in the eighteenth, an obscenity in the Germany of the 1930s. The place changed or the language, but not the voice. Coming from America now, from the great vindictive mass, always vocal but never heeded—ignored through the '50s, lampooned in the liberal '60s, polarized in the apathy of the '70s, returning now with ax-grinding leaders. True believers coming to the fore with the same old theme—*don't you make out you're better than us*—defining a narrow God by what they themselves hated and feared.

Contrary to American myth, Barion was no fonder of that nation than he was of Ghana or Finland; just that America bothered him more and more as the twentieth century grew old.

"Cash-register heart and a fairy-tale mentality," he fumed to Coyul in the early '70s. "Savage, sentimental and moralistic."

"Well, that's the thing about the Charmed Princess mystique," Coyul observed. "As often as they lose their virginity, it always grows back."

Barion's pulsing energy followed the great, rounded wrinkles of the Appalachians north. *We the people,* he remembered, recalling the look of the mountains when transplanted Englishmen wrote those words and few but Indians cut trail over the smoky ridges.

We the people, the ones who came first, turned out of England, Ireland, the Highlands for the sake of sheep; out of Newgate and debtors' prison scabrous and dying, but living long enough to sow an American seed.

Someone wrote a paper calling us free and equal, but no one made it stick.

Hard men and women, from Barion's firsthand recollection: not always thinking of God but seeing Him hard as themselves when they did. Their descendants much the same, not as hard but needing that peculiarly American form of religious ecstasy blended of poverty, ignorance, degenerated mysticism, collected injuries and the need for vengeance. Helped to some extent by social advances, unions and insurance, but somehow always at the bottom and the last in line.

The plant closed, relief checks run out. No more credit at the store. Sweet Jesus, Sweet White Jesus who wasn't never a Jew, give us—

A target!

"That's Roy Stride." Barion dipped sharply, shot down through darkness to the dim lines of light clustered along a highway. "Charity, are you there, too?"

Sweet Jesus, tell us who to blame, that's all. Give us a government with balls that ain't ascared of Russia or niggers, queers and Jew liberals. Give us the true faith of Jesus Christ.

All of which might have sickened Yeshua were he not grown used to it through the Inquisition, the Protestant Reformation and other outbursts of sanctity perpetrated by the true believers.

"What is this White Jesus nonsense?" he implored of Barion once. "They've spent two thousand years turning me into something out of Oxford or a Tennessee Bible college. *Both* my parents were Hebrews, I look like an Arab, spent all my life in the desert, and if they let me into one of their nice 'white' restaurants at all, I'd get the table by the kitchen door. What do these people *want?*"

"You know the lyrics," Barion reminded him. " 'Gimme that old-time revulsion.' "

Roy Stride knows folks that been buying guns, says

a day's coming when they send 'em all back to Africa or Jew-rusalem and sink the boats halfway.

The muttered threats, the idle talk, but the anger very real under it and the message clear even though no one listened. No one had ever listened.

Listen, you fuckin fat rich bastards: you cry over Indians and send money to Africa, but when you see our homes and farms going up for taxes, three, four generations of blood gone down under the gavel, that's just five minutes on the late news to you. Heart of your country gone, it's nothing to you but a few more cents at the supermarket.

Hey, listen good: we may be rednecks but some of us are rich rednecks now. You watch on TV what we say and do. Watch the folks in the TV tabernacle, plain folks come to hear the Word with their own kind of understanding—

Barion had seen them, the tears washing down the faces scarred with work and want, broken promises and broken dreams, pustulant with anger—

We got the TV now and a media voice. Think we'll go down without someone's to blame? Roy's got the right idea. Roy says . . .

The Plattsville town square with its ancient obelisk could manage no charm even in soft autumn dusk. A greenish plaque admitted the town's founder and age to an uncaring present. The World War I cannon's mouth was a trash-lined haven for transient birds.

"Depressed," said Barion. "In every sense of the word." His energy drifted like purposeful mist toward what remained of Plattsville's commercial area, past the closed and padlocked defense plant, the one movie house, letters awry on the worn runners of the marquee. Past the dark bar, sullen with slow-drinking men whose anger slammed at Barion out of the entrance along with the loud country-and-western music. Through the ship's graveyard of the failing used-car

42

dealership, no car that Barion saw less than five years old.

Prosperity was a brief, bright strip along Main Street. Very quickly the street ran to boarded-up stores. Like a garish gold molar in a row of bad teeth, McDonald's was still open for business.

Still early in the evening; McDonald's had a dinner crowd of families, work-tired husbands, house-tired mothers trying to get fast food into squirming, bickering children. Young people—brusque, callow young men munching hamburgers and wondering what, if any, excitement the evening might bring. More cautious girls with essentially the same question. Young couples . . .

Barion moved, invisible, through the loud babble and paused at one wall table. Roy and Charity. Their physical attitude at the table, close as possible though straining together from separate seats, told the story. They were in love—as they defined that agony—and physically possessive of each other.

Young as he was, Roy's face brought the word "ravaged" to Barion's mind: gaunt cheeks, thin black hair already receding swiftly, complexion scarred from acne. A mustache, carefully nurtured but of no specific character. Poor nutrition and worse circumstance, a face festered with violence that Barion knew from every riot or protest meeting since Imperial Rome. What character or statement there was resided in Roy's self-conscious costume: camouflage fatigues, jump boots and field jacket, a black beret bearing some insignia in pewter shoved through one shoulder strap.

Charity Stovall was even more poignantly familiar to Barion, who had glimpsed that face through Europe since the fall of Rome or even earlier, seen it suffer and starve under successive waves of Huns and Vandals.

I know this girl.

Charity Stovall died, raped and burned, under the westward sweep of the Visigoths; burned in her

thatched hut along the Humber or drowned in it at the
hands of Viking raiders. She searched the field at Hastings and after a hundred other battles to find her own
dead. Died in the Black Plague or survived pox-scarred;
burned for her Protestant faith in France, raped for her
Catholicism in Germany. Her face glared out of the
surge of doomed peasant revolts with a growing genetic
rage that carved its God and faith from bloodstained
granite. Rembrandt painted it and found a deep spirituality. Delacroix romanticized her, but Goya and
Breughel knew her better.

Her genes were worn out as Roy's, not much color
left to Charity Stovall, the blush gone from her DNA.
Below average height because her meagerly nourished
bones never lengthened to their full potential. Mousebrown hair and pale blue eyes, a cast of features the
superficial might call plain except for a blunt stubbornness and a set to her eyes that Dürer caught in one or
two canvases of German peasant women. Delacroix was
a damned fool, Barion reflected. He glorified that face
into a singing symbol of liberation. Not so. Mere survival. She hadn't had much of a chance to do anything
else for two thousand years.

Just now Charity Stovall's mind was muddled with
glandular longings, definitely ambivalent. Barion
paused to note the symptoms before digging deeper
into her psyche. Gazing fondly at Roy Stride, fingers
intertwined with his, Charity was torn between standards and inclination, a moral skirmish that her subconscious had just ordered her to lose as soon as possible.

Working swiftly through the convolutions of Charity's mind, Barion found more disparities. Mentally, Roy
Stride was average to the point of mediocrity. He would
never be more than he was, though his fantasies were
totally unfettered by reality. But Charity . . . here, in
this twenty-year-old woman, rusted from little or no
use, was an actual mind, capable but anchored like the
town-square cannon in the cement block of convention

and habit. The capabilities of that mind, its potential for many states, good and bad, went far beyond anything Barion would have suspected or Miss Stovall would ever need in Plattsville. Sooner or later, tied to Roy, that mind would ferment to bitterness. All this in predictable futures; right now the major decision of her life was: should she give in and go to bed with Roy?

He followed them out of McDonald's, table by table as they greeted young friends. They were the center of the energy that caught his attention in the first place, the names he heard and had to seek out. Now they paused on the sidewalk to embrace and grope at each other in a manner (it seemed to Barion) more urgent than pleasurable. Charity rested her chin over Roy's shoulder.

"Yes," she whispered, but her eyes were not that happily decided.

Futures and possibilities radiated from these two in this moment as surely as from Bethlehem.

Roy and Charity turned, still clinging to each other, and walked slowly up the sidewalk past the boarded-up stores to the lighted establishment known in better times as La Mode Dress Shoppe—now reborn as the TABERNACLE OF THE BORN AGAIN SAVIOR. Roy kissed Charity once more, almost conspiratorially, then they went into the storefront church.

Barion had known them as types through the ages. He needed to know their specific probabilities as individuals, all the more since he'd caught the message from Roy's mind just before the door closed behind them. The message that had disturbed Barion in the first place, the essence of Roy and so many like him whose combined frustration rose from them like the smell from a garbage dump in a long, hot summer.

We know the kind of leader we need. Give us a hero, Sweet White Lord. Someone to look up to who'll waste those rich wimps and Commoniss niggers and Jews without even thinking twice. And give us someone to

45

*look down on, too, the way so many look down on us.
Give us a victim, Lord, someone to hang from a tree and
pay us back. Before we find one for ourselves like we
always have to. Amen.*

Barion floated just outside the tabernacle entrance,
flashing a message to Topside:

BARION TO FELIM: RECORDS RETRIEVAL, PLEASE.

A brief pause only, then the answer burst on his
mind in a fervent rush:

ALLAH IS THE ONE TRUE GOD. ALL PRAISE TO—

BY ALL MEANS, BUT FOR NOW JUST GET ME PER-
SONAL AND FAMILY HISTORY ON ROY STRIDE AND
CHARITY STOVALL, THIS LOCATION.

A professional terrorist during his short life, Felim
had also been a hacker whiz who nearly accessed Israeli
intelligence computers before the Sabras punched his
ticket for good. He spent a great deal of time Topside
chanting and praying in his own custom-conceived
mosque, but his eidetic memory was invaluable in re-
trieving information on the spot.

FELIM TO BARION: SUBJECTS: R. STRIDE/C. M.
STOVALL. SPIRITUAL STATUS INFIDEL, MORE TO FOL-
LOW . . .

Barion quickly digested the information Felim
transmitted from Topside. When the flow ceased, he
absently materialized against a streetlight, tasting the
cool night air as he pondered the problem. He'd always
disapproved of Coyul's random interference in human
affairs, much of it from worry and guilt about his own
youthful mistakes. Leave bad enough alone, he always
said after that. Coyul had been right about propensities,
but bad enough could no longer be left to get worse.

"Well, why not?" he rationalized darkly. Govern-
ments and corporations used plumbers and played dirty
pool every day. Without working up a sweat, his little
brother was the master plumber of them all, and never
a greater need.

COYUL, CAN YOU HEAR ME?

The instant answer: WHAT'S THE MATTER? YOU FEEL WORRIED.

HOME IN AND JOIN ME.

Moments later, Coyul appeared in blazer and foulard, a camel-hair coat thrown over his shoulders to dashing effect. He inspected Barion's watch cap, pea coat and jeans gone ragged at one knee. "Don't you ever dress?"

"Only for ex-popes and defunct Episcopalians," Barion retorted brusquely. "Listen, kid—we're in trouble."

■ 7 ■

A conspiracy of princes

"Let's be unobtrusive," said Barion, dissolving.

Coyul followed suit. "By all means. I'd certainly not want to be seen here."

They passed like radiation through the tabernacle door. Inside the crowded store-cum-tabernacle, Coyul read the charged ferment of frustration like heat from an oven. Rows of people on metal or rickety wooden folding chairs, intent on the preacher on the small raised platform at the front. Taking Gomorrah as his text, Purdy Simco strode dramatically up and down, open Bible held aloft like a waiter serving dinner.

"Those are the Lord's words, my friends. That is what He said: that if He found twenty good men, He would not destroy Gomorrah for their sakes."

From a point just below the preacher's outthrust jaw, Coyul studied him. "Gomorrah's old hat. Why doesn't he pick on something timely?"

"Mr. Simco is a true believer, but no fool," Barion said. "He knows what he can play to his audience. You won't hear a word about war or an inflated defense budget. Their factory used to turn out missile components, and they'd like it back, thank you. They want to be saved but they also want to eat. Deviant sex is a safer bet and a hotter ticket."

Purdy Simco challenged his flock: "Did He find twenty?"

A ragged but fervent spattering of *no* from the faithful.

"And you wouldn't either in the Gomorrahs we have now, my friends. New York and Los Angeleez, places like that, places just down the road from us, right? Isn't it a Gomorrah that allows so-called gay rights? And lesbeen rights?"

Coyul looked to his brother for enlightenment. "For this I gave up an evening with Noel and Gertie? You said trouble."

"So I did."

"From what? The Classic Comics theology of Mr. Simco?"

"Smell the anger around you," Barion bade him. "The yearning, the frustration."

"I did. The whole place could do with a spritz of emotional air freshener."

"Pure explosive," said Barion. "I want you to meet the sparks."

Building to the climax of his excoriation of Gomorrahs past and present, Purdy Simco screwed his doughy face in mincing mimicry of his version of a city academic, his voice a nasal mew.

"He said to me, this college professor, when I spoke to him of the homa-sexuals and lesbeens I saw prancing down Fifth Avenue in their own licensed parade in that so-called great city of New York, he said to me: 'You have to regard this in its legal and social context.'"

Purdy Simco impaled his audience with a glare of righteous disgust. "Social context. I said to him: Sir"—straight face now, the soft, manly voice of Revealed Truth—"I am looking at it in the context of the most important text in the world. I don't care what it is in

49

your social context, it's an abomination in the sight of the Lord!"

The open Bible on high, Simco served dinner again, striding the platform, going for his cadenzas as the applause spattered about him like rain. "SHALL I HIDE FROM ABRAHAM THAT THING WHICH I DO FOR HIM? . . . WE WILL DESTROY THIS PLACE, BECAUSE THE CRY OF THEM IS WAXEN GREAT BEFORE THE FACE OF THE LORD!"

The applause mounted to fervor. In the front row, Roy Stride leaped to his feet, pounding his hands together. "With sword and fire!"

"There's our boy, Coyul. Roy Stride."

"Oh-h, yes," Coyul remembered. "That's one of the names I heard."

"Compulsive joiner. Used to be a Satanist."

Since the seventeenth century, Coyul had little patience with Satanists of any stripe. Beyond burning black candles and desecrating graveyards, most of them would be just as happy in the local drama club. "Rather inconsistent."

"Not at all. Read him."

Blending with the churning essence of Roy Stride, Coyul knew the extremes of Satanism and narrowly defined Christianity were not inconsistent at all in this case. Roy was looking for power and identity. He'd plug into anything that promised deliverance from helplessness and nonentity. All of it tangled now with a strong biological urge toward Charity Stovall—*there she is, that must be her.* Because young Mr. Stride's simpler motivations were overlaid with sentiment and a panting Protestant need for respectability, he imagined himself seriously in love with Miss Stovall.

"I tried to warn Luther about this: throwing morality back on the frail human conscience," Coyul reflected. "He threw his inkpot at me. They still show the splat to tourists."

"Roy has been trying to get it on, as they say, with

Miss Stovall for some time. Charity has rationalized it as love herself."

Coyul turned his attention to the young woman at Roy's side. "Meaning, I suppose, that she's found a way to reconcile what she ought to do with what she wants."

"Precisely. And tonight's the night."

Coyul was a study in indifference. "So?"

"They're the wrong people at the wrong time."

"So why do you need me? I'm just waiting for a bus, remember?"

"I sampled some background on them. Not the happiest. Please read Miss Stovall."

Coyul gave Charity another cursory glance—then a closer look. The flicker of interest was not lost on Barion.

"Shall I put time out of joint?" he offered delicately.

"Yes. Just for a moment."

Tableau in time frozen between one nanosecond and the next: Roy on his feet, Charity yearning up at him with the dazed aspect of someone who has found Ultimate Truth, too dazzled to examine it critically.

Coyul slipped into and blended with her mind. Where Roy was concerned, her mental and physical promptings were hopelessly muddled. Below that level, as Coyul had found with Roy, the years of deprivation, envy and inarticulate rage. Like Barion, he'd already detected the long, brutal history of Europe in her face. Nevertheless, even deeper . . .

She was like a person with a large house, living in only a few of the ground-floor rooms, the rest gone to dust and waste, although some oddments of emotional bric-a-brac here and there interested Coyul. Charity "guessed" she was in love with Roy because her painful Christianity would not allow physical gratification without the lapidary settings of true love and morality. In one room just off her mental parlor, not often used but not entirely abandoned, Charity had strong feelings for a young man named Woody Barnes, evidently the one seated on her left, a polished trumpet in his lap. Everything about Woody Barnes looked average—hair the color of sand, slightly wiry, freckled hands, blue eyes mild but observant, focused now in frozen time on Charity's face.

Sifting through the female psyche, Coyul paused at the Woody Room before passing on. Charity did not spend much time there. TV and romance novels had left their simplistic message. Woody was very close, but love was supposed to be an earthquake. Not a very intelligent attitude for the cortex he discovered, fine but unused.

"Not a bad sort," he judged, popping free of her. "A little cluttered, thinking with her glands. All the objectivity of a mating moose. Not terribly stable."

As he gazed down at Charity just then, Barion's expression was not unlike her blossom-bordered concept of him as Him. "I get millions like her. People with nothing to hang on to but a gnarled belief in cosmic cops and robbers, a hero and a heavy. Life as drama with themselves as star. Divine purpose as salvation, guilt for conflict. I thought dualism was only a stage."

"I told you so," Coyul singsonged.

"Yes, I know. I was wrong, but I won't compound the error. Coyul, we're going to work on this one together."

"Am I hearing right?" Coyul wondered. "Here on this cultural slag pile, listening to God Almighty suggest putting in the fix? The mind boggles."

"While you've *never* interfered," Barion shot back testily.

"Only in cases of exceptional talent."

"You read her: the girl's ten times smarter than she or anyone thinks, and a wellspring of possibilities, not all of them salutary. The miasma comes from imagining herself in love with Roy Stride. If she had a stronger sense of self, she'd just take this malignancy to bed and get him out of her system."

"Or just laugh him off." But Coyul knew her up-bringing didn't program Charity that way. "Just a moment."

He immersed himself in the essence of Roy Stride —measuring, analyzing—and emerged very quickly with the energic equivalent of nausea.

"See what I mean?" Barion divined his distaste. "If there was ever a need for a stacked deck . . ."

"Yes," Coyul agreed, still a little queasy. "Not quite like Hitler, but . . ."

"But very like some of his satellites in the early days, remember? Röhm and his SA troopers, some of those charmers in the Gestapo. I have background on Roy and Charity," Barion said. "What they came out of, what they are, what they might be. Blend with me . . . Coyul?"

Barion's brother seemed preoccupied and unchar-acteristically serious. Odder still that his mind was masked now. "Go ahead."

Filtered through Barion's mind, the data on Roy Stride were only a little less sickening. Age twenty-six, the ground-down descendant of ground-down ances-tors, unremarkable for anything but his smoldering rage and its classic symptoms. His own history was one of failure and frustration, a bomb looking for a place to explode. A compulsive joiner, evidenced in his belief-shopping from Satanism to Born Again Christianity without losing a beat, and his boasted affiliation with the White Paladins, the paramilitary group reflected in his costume. Roy had an armchair lust for Armageddon, for bloody and dramatic goals. With these went an over-wrought, distorted set of values and more hang-ups than a coat closet, including an agonized sense of purity where Charity was concerned.

There was more intelligence in Charity's back-ground but, as Coyul noted earlier, not much stability. Her grandparents had worked with religious tent revi-als. The anonymous couple who bred Charity and left her with the county stayed together for a while, alternating fits of Fundamentalism with others soaked in alcohol until they drifted apart. The father died in a distant hospital, bloated with cirrhosis, scribbling an ecstatic but incoherent history of human creation, convinced his pen was spirit-guided by John the Baptist. Charity's mother drifted to San Francisco and the last psychedelic love-and-flowers gasp of the Haight-Ashbury scene, where, in a microcosm not known for mental equilibrium, she earned the sobriquet of Franny the Flake. She OD'd on heroin in 1971 and was buried by the city when they could locate no relatives. Their daughter hadn't known much love in her twenty years; the mere possibility of it, of a chance to identify with *anything* beyond her loneliness, would fever Charity's blood like a virus.

She stood poised at the convergence of several paths; what happened tonight could send her down the wrong one. She'd go to bed with Roy because she was lonely. She would marry him because she was a "nice" girl by stringent Plattsville standards—and for the more banal reason there was nothing better in town or in her life already dead-ending to nowhere.

Barion's comment broke into the flow of information: *factor, Coyul. Both these families breed more boys than girls. Charity would have a number of sons. Statistically one would grow up with the worst of both of them in him.*

A son maturing in the damp fog of poverty, feeling hopeless and abandoned as his parents, raging at the world; who grew up with a paranoid warrior-manqúe father, racist and soured, a child literally weaned on hate. A mother frustrated without clearly knowing why, whose bitter, fermented energies would turn more and more toward this tabernacle or one like it. A child growing up with the rage and rotted dreams of both parents beating in his ears, making him quiver, making others see this malignant vibrance as charisma where it was truly a predatory instinct for the vulnerability of those around him.

The sort of man who gets noticed by people who bankroll Christian Identity groups, Barion's energy whispered to his brother. *There are avowed racists running for office now. This statistically probable kid would be a natural.*

Wholly possible, Coyul agreed, materializing to his brother again, lounging atop the battered piano. "You said there were millions of them. The same son could be born to a million sets of parents. Why these two in particular?"

"What I heard," Barion said in a troubled voice, "what led me to these people I've heard all through history when something was about to change. I was too inexperienced, too busy or whatever to take notice, but I always *heard* it. The sound of catalysts, Coyul. Cassius, Moses, John Brown . . . Hitler. I'm not sure. I'm never exactly sure anymore, but I've never heard it so clearly. Roy or his son. You read them. The odds are bad."

Leaning against the lip of the stage in his old pea coat, Barion awarded a loveless glance to Roy Stride, something of pity to Charity Stovall. "And there's this: you know they'll be coming for us someday. Sorlij or someone else."

Coyul nodded slowly. "I know," he said with unwonted gravity.

"And I'll get hell at home for the mess I've made here," Barion stated, and accepted the inevitable in a breath. "But I'm going to do something about this now. Whatever it costs. Help me, Coyul. Stack the deck, deal from the bottom, but *something.* Because if we don't, there's not going to be an America or a world worthy of the name."

"Well, it's always been a second-rate sideshow." Coyul tried to sound flip; for the first time in his very long life, he failed utterly. "Aren't you overstating?"

"You think so? This country has gone to the right

before but always with a balance to straighten them out. The balance simply isn't there anymore. The middle class isn't that secure, the same as Weimar Germany in 1932. Look around, Coyul. These are the people who'll call the shots if this country swings to the extreme right. Look at these faces. You think they're *kidding?* Look at me," Barion concluded in dry disgust. "I wanted to win a prize. You told me not to tinker. You were right. Nothing but a mess, five million years of mess—but *this* one I'm going to clean up before it spills."

"Don't wallow in self-condemnation," Coyul admonished with surprising gentleness. "You've had some fine moments."

For one instant, before his brother's mind curtained itself behind the habitual cynicism, Barion caught an unusual emotion from Coyul. Something like guilt.

"Well." Coyul fluffed out his foulard. "What do you require of our hard-breathing heroine?"

"To marry someone else."

"Anyone in mind?"

"Anyone would do." That was secondary to Barion. Perhaps Woody Barnes, whose most incendiary ambition was to work as a jazz sideman at Jimmy Ryan's or the Blue Note in New York. Woody had more talent than drive, but a musician, even a poor one, was preferable to a fanatic. He could only assault the ear.

Coyul studied the three, ruminating, one knuckle to his lips. "If you're in trouble, so am I. Two rowers in a sinking lifeboat telling each other 'I told you so' doesn't keep either from drowning. I don't know . . . there *is* an element of creativity in all this."

"Carte blanche," Barion promised. "No questions asked."

"Perhaps that's best," Coyul considered honestly. "It *just* so happens that certain friends of mine need something to keep them out of trouble and my hair. I'll need complete Topside cooperation."

"Got it," Barion responded staunchly, already see-ing daylight at the end of a long, dark tunnel. "As for Woody Barnes, I have a few ideas for him. He's a friend of a friend. So, deal?"

"Deal. And I'll probably live to regret it."

Barion's hand arced in a peculiar gesture—

—and Purdy Simco's hand descended with the Bi-ble, the congregation stirred, Roy's hands went on ap-plauding his idea of magnificence.

"While Roy takes up our offering," Purdy Simco crooned to the faithful, "let us sing together. Sweet Jesus, hear our lifted voices and the need in our hearts."

Charity climbed the precarious steps to the plat-form stage, Woody close behind with his trumpet. Char-ity seated herself on the old-fashioned round piano stool and struck the first chords of "Amazing Grace." The instrument was badly out of tune. Coyul winced in ac-tual pain.

"My God, they mean it." He retreated far as possi-ble from the offending sound while Purdy Simco and his congregation assaulted the hymn like amphibious ma-rines.

"A-*maz*-ing Guh-*race*—" In support of their attack, Charity played determinedly, which is not the same as well. Woody's horn had more encouraging overtones for Coyul. There was a quality to his style, hard to pin down but interesting. Too good to waste here.

"When Luther broke with Rome, the Church kept all the good music. This does nothing for theology or the muse. Shall we wait outside?"

"No, wait." Barion stayed him. "Stride: I want to catch this."

While Charity and Woody reprised the hymn, Roy took a small basket from the platform and flourished it before the congregation.

"Offering time!" he called in an abrasive but com-pelling voice. "You all know what the tabernacle needs. We all know how hard it is, don't tell me that. Don't show me silver, show me green! The tabernacle's important as meat on the table, because we are the people, yes we are. Ain't nobody gonna save us but us. We been down, but we're going UP!"

Roy moved from row to row with the basket. To a balding, florid-faced donor: "Mr. Beasley, you just put fifty cents in this basket. Ain't you ashamed? I *know* you got a dollar, 'cause I seen you break a five in McDonald's. There you go"—as the extorted and sheepish Beasley produced a limp single—"never mind the fifty cents, it won't get lonely."

Roy's challenging finger swept over the congregation. "Do you trust the government? Hell no! You feel sold? Betrayed? Do you hear the true word of Jesus Christ in your heart? Lemme see the green, then. New day coming, hallelujah! New day coming when the people rise up. Don't trust Washin'ton. They sold out the farmers, closed the factories, sold mosta New York to the Ay-rabs. I read that in a book, you can look it up. But the people will rise—thank you, sister—the people will rise in a triumph for Jesus, a triumph of the will!"

"See what I mean?" said Barion darkly. "A catalyst looking for a disaster. We can go now. We'll meet them at McDonald's. They'll probably stop there when this is done."

"Already our plot shows its darker side." Coyul steeled himself. "McDonald's, then. If we must."

■ 8 ■

The hero is the one who just
wants to finish his drink
and go home

The garish orange and Formica decor of McDonald's appalled Coyul, as did the notion of fast food or the amounts of it humans could ingest without mishap.

"Do you see what they call a well-done hamburger? Looks like it was dragged too late from a burning house."

"Very popular place," Barion remarked. "Some of my people want a franchise Topside."

"Shoot them."

"Business at hand, remember? Shall we proceed?"

Reluctantly Coyul turned his invisible attention to the three young people at the table: Roy and Charity against the wall, Woody sprawled back on the outside seat, fitting the mute to his trumpet. With his leg rubbing against his woman's (the possessive notion excited him), Roy told Woody, "Get us some more napkins, okay?"

Charity held hers up. "We got napkins."

"Yeah, but they're all wet. And Charity needs a new straw."

Woody went obligingly for the setups. Under the table, Roy added bourbon to his Coke. "You want a taste, honey?"

"Gee, I don't know. Does it go with diet cola?"

"Goes with anything your heart desires. Come on, ain't polite to let me drink alone."

"Well . . . just it's cold outside," Charity accepted with a prim giggle. "But you tell me if I start to get bad."

She slipped her plastic glass below the tabletop and Roy hardened it a little. "Sort of a wedding toast," he said, smiling at her. "Tonight's our night, honey."

—while Coyul sighed with the burden of the duty-bound. "I regret this already. The dialogue's as bad as the drinks."

"Be a little kind," Barion admonished. "This is going to be Charity's first time and very important to her. Actually, she's readier than he is. Why don't you read Roy; he's sending signals pertinent to our case."

Charity's all mine—Roy glowed with a flush of ma-cho. *Nicest girl in town and she's all mine. Thought once it might be Woody. I like Woody, like the way he does what I tell him, long as I make out like I'm asking, but that just shows you the difference. I'm a leader natural born, Woody just ain't aggressive at all. Even in the Marines he barely qualified with a rifle, he told me. Wouldn't touch the piece I got under the back seat. Just looked shit scared when I showed him the ammo and grenades for the Paladins. Threw him one: he caught it all right but just gave it back and looked sick. Ought to come out and join the Paladins. We need good boys been in combat, even the little bit Woody saw. Couldn't be much, he don't never talk about it, just mostly about some Jew bastard he knew in the Corps. He don't think right. He's pure White American like me and we need all we can get, being a minority ourselves now.*

For sure it's tonight for me and Charity. Man, about time something worked out right in this shit-ass life. All three of us out of work, and we deserve just as much as the Commoniss niggers riding in Cadillacs in Washington, which, hell, it's all black now anyways. I read that in a book. President steps off the White House lawn, must feel like he's in Africa.

We Paladins gonna take this country back someday, and I'll be there, breaking bad and spitting lead, a natural leader. Gonna be blood spilled, the only way, gonna take America back for God and the Aryans.

But tonight I'm gonna take a little for myself—except, shit, I hope I don't have the usual trouble. No problem at all with some old whore, but somebody nice like Charity . . . you can't fuck goodness and look her in the eye at the same time. I mean, that's a problem. She's the girl I'm going to marry, and I wouldn't be spiking her drink except I'm nervous. Only time it was ever super good was in that whorehouse in that hunky town near Pittsburgh. Big Polack whore didn't give a damn what you wanted done, she served it right up. Just you can't go on paying for it to get what you need, that ain't the way for a man to do. Maybe another shot in this lousy Coke, just enough so I won't worry . . .

Coyul snorted: "If this tumor had a brain, he'd be neurotic."

"Think what his son will be with the same problems and more intelligence," Barion urged. "Does it suggest an approach?"

For a moment, Coyul's expression came close to his popular image. "There could be some good dirty fun in all this. Being a son of a bitch in a worthy cause."

"*That's* my little brother."

"Woody." Roy nudged him under the table. "How about getting me another Big Mac?"

"I just went," Woody protested mildly. "Whyn't you go yourself?"

"Because I'm all tucked up with my woman and I ast you nice."

61

"Okay, okay. In a minute."

While Roy rubbed up against Charity, Woody tried to be cool about the whole thing and not notice. He took a deep breath and let it out through the muted horn in a long, sleepy, drawling phrase like Winton Marsalis on "Melancholia," or the other jazzmen whose records he could seldom afford. They made a whole new language with the horn, not playing the melody but knowing all about it anyway in that special tongue.

"What you doing with that thing?" Roy wondered.

"Marsalis. Blows a good horn."

"Yeah, I read about him." Roy was always talking about what he read, although Woody never saw any books in his house except *Soldier of Fortune* or *Guns and Ammo.* "Smart nigger, thinks he got all the answers. Whyn't you play like a white man?"

Woody put down the trumpet. "Char, you want anything?"

"No, I'm just fine." She wiped her lips too daintily. "I like the way Woody plays."

"Nigger music. Listen, Woody: you come to the next Paladin drill with me. They'll straighten you out. Old marine like you, we need guys with combat time."

"No way."

"You always say that. I'm serious, man. Why not?"

"I'm a pacifist," said Woody Barnes.

"That's what the Commonists like," Roy asserted with the air of an insider. "That's what they want when they come marching down Main Street. Where'd you get to be a pacifist?"

"In Beirut." Woody drained his Coke and slapped the paper cup on the table, rattling the ice. "What you say you wanted?"

"Big Mac again. Extra French dressing 'n' pickle." Roy splayed a couple of dollars on the table, mostly change. "Hey, you see how I took up the collection tonight? I know how to squeeze it out of 'em."

"They know five percent of what you squoze gets back to the Paladins for guns and ammo?"

"Hey, not so loud." Roy glared at Woody, then glanced at Charity to assure himself the effect wasn't lost on her, then around at the nearby customers with overdone caution. In a tense whisper: "We got enemies."

"Just a passing thought," said Woody.

"Well, you just go on and let it pass."

"Positively wallows in the role of conspirator," Coyul remarked.

"To the hilt: the drama, the air of danger. The Paladins can't afford much ammunition," Barion recalled from Felim's briefing. "They have to be very good shots, although so far they've only destroyed a few paper targets and someone's window. But they feel terribly clandestine." To Coyul's appreciative smile, he amended: "I'm sorry. I shouldn't joke about him."

"Difficult not to."

"Just so. The Nazis were a joke to Germans in 1925, remember? The upper classes found them a never-ending source of amusement." Barion looked toward Woody at the counter. "Let's read Mr. Barnes in his heart of hearts. It may be of service."

All right, Woody thought, that's the way it is. Roy's gonna score with Charity at the White Rose. He shouldn't take her there, that's the best-known make-out spot in ten miles. And talking about it all week; some spy he'd make. We've been friends since eighth grade; when I went into the Marines, he enlisted in the Air Force. Gonna be a top-gun jet pilot. Except his eyes weren't good enough or his teeth or his education or anything else. This town doesn't grow a lot of college graduates. We used to have more to talk about, but now listening to Roy gets real old. It's all one thing, race and politics. Last couple of years, he's got a hard-on for

▪ PARKE GODWIN ▪

niggers and Jews, all he can talk about, and he can't understand why I keep remembering Milt Kahane so much. More like I can't ever forget. Milt and that old black man.

I was in New York with Milt before we shipped for Beirut, three straight nights checking out the jazz joints. The last night we found that place where drinks were mucho expensive but the combo—oh, man, they were worth it. That old black man with a lifetime in his horn. The way he talked to me between sets: not polite at all, just an old-timer giving it straight to a kid. Shit, he didn't *think* he was good as me, he knew he was better where that horn came in, and damn if he wasn't right. Thought a lot about that old man in the hospital; about him and Milt Kahane. Still thinking about them, but everything gets mixed up together, like will I ever make it back to New York where it's all at or just sit around here forever, wondering if I want Char enough to do something about it? Or if I'll ever be good enough to even play backup for that old man who knows it all.

Milt was that good. That's how we got together, rapping music at Parris Island. Too damned good to go out fragged and bagged in Beirut. He talked about the Israelis like they were a separate people he didn't agree with, like the way they sent in Lebanese Christians as hit men at Beirut. That bothered him, but when he got it squared away, he said to me, Barnes, I have planted my last fucking tree in Israel, and I'd like the last one back.

I said, Hell, ain't you sticking up for your own people? What people? he asks. I'm a financial analyst from Long Island, or I will be if I ever finish at NYU. Just don't want to hear any more Zionist bullshit.

I remember: that was at chow the day he got zapped and damn near me, too. We sat down in the shade of a half-track, eating corned beef and carrots and fruit cocktail. Milt bummed a cigarette from me, angry not because he couldn't figure it out but because he had.

64

Barnes, he said, countries are just like women. Sooner or later everyone loses their cherry and gets to be just another broad on the block. I don't know if I'm a Jew anymore.

What do you mean? I said. You were born Jewish.

You were born dumb, Barnes. That mean you gotta stay that way?

We pulled detail after chow, humping ammo to the M-60. Not expecting trouble; didn't even see that grenade come out of a window until it fucked us up good. Milt got most of it, but there was enough left over for a nice road map across my stomach. So Milt Kahane went home on the same hospital ship with me. I got a bed, he got a box in the hold.

When Roy mouths off about Jews, I see Milt eating those goddamned peaches and smoking my cigarette, asking questions and not liking the answers he got. Me and Milt and that old black man with his trumpet, I guess we're pacifists. Once you're nearly blown away, you get real picky what you'll die for. Roy really got off on the scars where my belly button used to be. I said they were religious medals, not that he'd understand. Roy never wasted anyone but he'd sure as shit like to. Going to declare war all over Char tonight.

Wish I knew what the hell bothers me so much about that. Maybe—hell, no maybe about it. Char deserves better than what Roy's turned into, but I'm not fool enough to say so. Already did my gig in somebody else's war.

"Not a bad sort." Coyul watched Woody carry the fresh tray back to the table. "Eloquent in his way. The ones who've done the bleeding always have a great respect for peace. Attila, for example. Very keen on animal husbandry now. Goats, that sort of thing."

"They'll be off to the White Rose soon," Barion said. "Will you be ready to take it from there?"

"Of course. I'll make an appearance."

65

"Let the blandishment fit the time," Barion advised. "Don't think about them, think *like* them."

A crucial aspect, as Coyul knew. In a careless moment a few years back, he'd appeared in slacks and an Izod shirt to a cult of California Satanists. They threw wine bottles at him. Charity Stovall would be no less hag-ridden with stereotype. You couldn't hurl new ideas head-on at old notions. It never paid.

■ 9 ■

H hour minus one

Charity liked riding in Roy's car the way the three of them always did: holding hands with Roy in the front seat, old Woody in the back talking softly to himself through the muted trumpet. The old car was like a house and they were the family, the realest she ever knew. Roy in his old field jacket and that black T-shirt with the skull and KILL 'EM ALL. LET GOD SORT 'EM OUT on the front—which she really didn't believe in that, it was just Roy's sense of humor. Beer cans rattling around on the floor and over the tire iron. Big sponge-rubber dice hanging inside the windshield and the two tiny baby dolls banging suggestively against each other.

So tonight they'd do it. That troubled her more than a little, but yes, she did love Roy. Especially tonight in the tabernacle, the way he made those folks dig down a little deeper for Jesus.

I wonder if Jesus will call tonight a sin. I couldn't do it unless I loved Roy and was going to marry him, which we'll do it as soon as we can afford to, and live our lives in Jesus anyway, so maybe He won't mind if we are a little ahead of time.

"Night, Woody," she said when they let him off at

his house. She liked the way he leaned in through the window to kiss her on the cheek like family.

"Take care of yourself, Char. Don't do anything I wouldn't."

Wouldn't you, Woody? What did you mean by that? I know you like me, but you don't know about tonight because Roy certainly wouldn't talk about it. Good night, dear Woody. When you see me tomorrow I'll be a whole different person—

"Quite," promised Coyul from the back seat.

—married in the sight of God, kind of, but I'll always think of you as family.

"Of course, the tasteful Mr. Stride has been bending Woody's ear about it all week." Coyul remarked.

"He's on the intelligence team for the Paladins," Barion noted, "usually disseminating more than he gathers, but then you have to realize, as the current phrase has it, where Mr. Stride is coming from. Drama is essential. He and Charity are true lovers silhouetted against the fiery backdrop of strife-torn Plattsville and the Cause. Like the motorcycle he couldn't afford: one way to put some kind of power between his legs."

After Woody's door closed, Roy pulled Charity closer to his side for a long kiss. Charity felt the warmth and roughness of his cheek against hers and the slight thrill of knowing Roy was always a little dangerous. You never could tell what he'd do.

I said yes and I guess I meant it, she thought. *Face it, I'm twenty and it has to be sometime, so might's well be with somebody I love. Just I wish I knew if it is the right thing to do. I'm glad Roy didn't let me put Jesus on the dash when I wanted to. He'd be looking at me now, maybe making me change my mind, maybe damning me to hell.*

Just that I hate going to the tacky old White Rose, which everybody knows about it, but we can't go to his house or mine, and the car's okay for fooling around but too damn uncomfortable and cold for anything else

. . . boy, when I set out to be bad, I am really a New York Saturday night.

Roy drove without haste, not wanting to seem like he was rushing her. Charity wished he'd hurry before she changed her mind.

"Until later," Barion excused himself to Coyul. "I must see to Woody."

"You always get the nice jobs."

"Woody's on my end. Never in the world or even in the fevered indulgences of Wilksey Booth has there been such a need for careful casting. Have a nice evening."

"I just might," Coyul predicted. "For Charity, an education. For Roy, enough rope."

Charity stayed in the car while Roy got the room. Coyul drifted in after them like the night chill before they closed the door.

"Well, hey," Roy bluffed to cover his awkwardness. "We finally got here. Let's get comfortable."

With elaborate casualness, he took off his jacket and hung it on the rack near the door, then took Charity's coat. Charity made an instinctive female assessment of the room and sat tentatively on the bed, an acknowledgment of their purpose, though still tensed to fly.

There followed a strained interlude while Roy tried to hide his nervousness. Charity opted for demure silence to cover moral panic, spending much time in the bathroom and in finding the right music on the small FM radio. Finally Roy sat down on the war-worn bed beside her.

"Well," he said by way of prelude, "I guess."

Coyul tactfully removed to the unlit bathroom. Behind him, the lights went out. Murmurings, the rustle of sheets and blankets. Neither of them noticed the soft closing of the bathroom door.

Coyul knew to its core the essence of Charity

Stovall, who had lived her twenty years in the lower echelons of Christian belief, a lurid topography with no middle ground. Her theology was banal but rendered in full color, a Caucasian *Green Pastures* at one end, smoke, fire, pain—the whole Faustian, *Exorcist* claptrap at the other.

Coyul conjured a soft, indirect light over the bathroom mirror, admiring his makeup and costume—impressive mustachios and spade beard, cruel, chiseled features. He added a fastidious pat of Givenchy to the gaunt cheeks and gave serious thought to his scenario, flashing an urgent message—

PRIORITY, WILKES: DROP EVERYTHING.

The classic figure of Booth took shape at Coyul's side, cloak gathered and draped over one arm. "I love the beard, Prince. You are Lucifer, point-device! What's to do?"

"I promised you a great part. I have one: a zinger, possibly the keystone in the vaulting arch of your career."

Booth bowed with panache. "Your servant, sir."

"A role with range and depth," Coyul embellished. "Exquisite suffering, color, your own choice of music."

"Steiner," Booth opted eagerly. "No one scores drama like Max—if we can ask him of Topside."

"It can be arranged." Coyul admired his finished Luciferian effect in the mirror. It would scare them to death. It scared the hell out of *him.*

"Our drama?"

"Damnation."

Wilksey Booth's eyes flashed like black diamonds. "Jesuit or Joycean? Something medieval?"

"Beyond that," Coyul urged. "Beyond Doré, beyond De Mille. They're Born Again. You may indulge."

"Ah! A moment, if I may." The handsome actor assessed his image in the bathroom mirror. "God, I am magnificent! Perhaps in the future a surprise appearance on *Dynasty?*"

"Wilksey, we are gentlemen. The shlock is for the customers."

"A passing thought, no more. Watch!"

"Oh, Wilksey—that's good." Coyul observed with admiration as Booth's fine head became something foul, green and misshapen, medieval in its darkest concepts but with an obvious debt to George Lucas. Charity Stovall would—oh, it was to quiver!

"Remember me, Prince," the green thing rasped, "when thy sublime brothers find thee. Also that my name appears over the title and in larger type."

Woody had a cup of coffee in the kitchen with his uncle before going up to bed. Still not terribly late, but there was nothing to do in the morning except wait at the unemployment office for a job that wouldn't be there, wait for his union relief check and maybe clean up the yard.

Climbing the squeaky stairs, he thought on Charity, Roy and himself with some sadness. Since the Corps, he had more of his shit together, enough to get sour knowing he'd never make it back to that uptown club in New York unless he had the price of a bus and a drink; that Roy would never make it anywhere, just go on boring the shit out of everyone about the coming racial wars. And Charity? Hell, she'd never see anything until she woke up twenty years from now, still in Plattsville, making dinner for the same Roy but with a beer belly and four kids mean as their daddy.

He shouldn't take Char to the goddamned White Rose. Everybody driving by knows who's inside just from the cars. Am I feeling sorry for her or just wishing it was me instead of Roy? Me that don't even know where I'm going myself.

"A long way, Barnes."

He couldn't tell if he'd heard an actual voice or his own thoughts, but it sounded like Milt Kahane. Woody opened the door to his room, threw the down vest

71

where his old easy chair would be, snapped on the lights and felt his heart stop.

Milt Kahane lounged on his bed—beefy, vital and sardonic, crisp black curly hair, wearing the same wild Hawaiian shirt he had on the night they made it to the jazz club. "Hey, Woody."

When Woody's heart jump-started up, he backed against the undeniable reality of the door. "Milt?"

"Uncle Milty, live and in person. More or less." Milt grinned expectantly. "Dummy, you can't say hello?"

"Uh . . . hi, Milt."

"Semper fi, Barnes."

The groan of his unoiled clock was conspicuous by its absence, the second hand petrified just short of 2. "Milt, is this really happening? Aren't you . . . you know?" Then, in panic: "God, am I? All I had was a burger and—"

"Relax, it's not the big one." Milt laughed, swinging his legs off the bed. "Got us a gig, that's all. See your vest?"

The garment was an impossible still life where Woody had thrown it, one edge caught mid-crumple, the rest still defying gravity over the chair.

"That's—interesting."

"Boss calls that trick time out of joint. Lets me prove my point without a lot of *Topper* dialogue."

Woody swallowed hard. "Yeah, well, I definitely believe it."

"Just like the Corps, Woodrow; the Boss is looking for a couple of good men on brass who can also bullshit a little in a good cause." Milt raised his horn and spurted a clean run up to high C.

"Haven't lost your lip, Milt."

"Never." As usual, Milt Kahane looked like he was thinking something funny and sad at the same time. "Why do you hang out with that putz Stride?"

"Roy? I dunno," Woody hedged, hands in his pockets. "We grew up together. He's kind of crazy, but—"

72

"But he loves his mother, yeah, I know. Personally I'd like to give him a briss from the neck down, but the Boss works in mysterious ways."

"What you got against Roy? You don't even know him."

"I've known that shmuck for two thousand years," Milt said. "And you just follow him around. A natural follower, Barnes. You were following me the day that Shiite mother fragged us. Our fire team got him a few minutes later. Man, was he surprised to see me! Don't ask." Milt Kahane chuckled. "Tell you about him sometime. Roy Stride in a polka-dot headdress."

Milt rose, tucking the trumpet under one arm. "Time to ship out, Barnes. Travel and adventure! The Boss wants to brief us."

"The Boss?" Woody hesitated, still trying to get a handle on all this. "You mean—"

"Numero Uno," Milt corroborated with a bright smile. "But most of the clowns Topside don't know it. He keeps a very low profile. I said *relax*, Barnes. This is no shit detail. He's a cool guy, very laid-back. Doesn't come on or anything like that."

The walls of Woody's room began to blur, fade, darkening to the midnight blue of infinity.

"First time I saw him," Milt remembered, "I thought he was some shlub from California."

■ 10 ■

The woman taken in adultery,
and other set pieces

Roy was very still beside her. Charity thought he might be asleep. They had to go home soon. Late she could explain; all night was pretty obvious.

When Charity sorted out her feelings as a retired virgin, they resolved to disappointment. Nothing specific; she couldn't make any kind of comparison because she wasn't that kind of girl. All the same, this was what all the shouting was about? Her expectations had come mostly from a little petting in Roy's car, mostly from the movies and TV. Reverend Falwell was right: certain things just shouldn't be brought right into your living room where you might have company or children. Movies went even further, soft lights and softer music with the man and woman photographed from the shoulders up, and you knew what they were doing and that they enjoyed it. Transports of joy—that was the phrase she heard somewhere, except she wasn't transported at all, just stayed there.

Roy seemed to have some kind of trouble, she couldn't tell what, but he acted embarrassed even after the lights were out. The whole thing was over in a hurry, just when she was beginning to relax and enjoy it. Afterward he asked if it was special for her. She said yes.

Charity stared up into the darkness with emotional second thoughts. They had sinned—well, not much since they were practically married, but still a sin. Come down to it, she wasn't sure bad girls got punished all that much. What they got were children.

Which it's just about the same thing in this town. I love Roy, I guess, so it'll be all right when we're married.

How? How would anything be all right or even different? She had married friends; when did anything change for them?

The though was so clear and frightening that Charity blotted it out, shifting closer to the warmth of Roy beside her. There were a lot of thoughts like that in the last year that she kept from Roy and Woody, notions she barely had words for. Like Reverend Simco saying most of the world was unsaved. That meant a lot of people. All those people and the way they lived, were they *all* wrong? Like, when you were poor, you couldn't afford to waste anything. Saving got to be a part of you, so God must hate waste as much as she did.

So would he waste all those million-billion people just because they're not exactly like us? Gol-lee, that's like chopping down a whole forest just to get one toothpick. If I got better sense than that, God sure has.

Roy lay on his side facing her. In the dim light she could just see the dark smudge on his shoulder that would be his White Paladin tattoo with the skull. He got more excitement out of belonging to the Paladins than anything else. All those secret communications with groups in Alabama and maneuvers in the woods, when all Charity could see was a bunch of out-of-work hunks who liked to play with guns, drink beer and talk about the "coming Armageddon."

They ought to get up soon and go home . . .

She must have dozed. Charity was suddenly aware

75

of Roy turning over. The air in the room smelled horrible. Roy sniffed distastefully. "What's that?"

"Like sulphur." Charity tested the air. "Ten times worse." Besides the intolerable odor, something else. "Roy," she quavered. "L-look."

"What?"

"There," said Charity, terror rising like a tide. "There!"

"Where? There ain't any—"

"Look!"

The darkness around them had taken on the hue of blood. As Charity stared, numb with fright, the blood resolved to a smoky, infernal scarlet. With a deafening *whoosh* the room seemed to implode. The light went garish fire engine red as the far wall sprang up in a solid barrier of flame.

Charity screamed. Roy tried to.

Against the wall of fire, amid the choking stink, two nightmare images were silhouetted. One of them Charity knew in every detail from God-fearing childhood: the horns jutting from the narrow, saturnine head, the pointed beard, eyes like hot coals. The lashing tail and hooves. Her deepest fears incarnate.

"Heel, Damocles!"

The huge figure of Satan jerked at the chain wound on his wrist. Straining at its check, something scaly with large bat wings gurgled uncleanly and slavered at Charity. As she and Roy cringed on the bed, Satan stroked his beard with the back of one claw and smirked at his leashed minion.

"I call him Damocles because, like the mythical sword, he hangs over wretches like you." An exquisite sneer. "Just waiting to fall. And you yourselves have cut the thread."

Charity felt for the silver cross around her neck. It felt hot. "Please . . . God in heaven, please . . ."

"Too late for that," Satan told her in tones that

would have thrilled Bellini or Gounod. "You're both dead."

"Dead?" Roy found his voice somewhere. "We're too young to die."

"Coronary, you clods. Both of you. Unusual in humans so young, the more so during a fornication not rigorous enough to tire a terminal emphysemic. Nevertheless, dead in the act."

"With no relish of salvation," the scaly demon paraphrased in a voice that made the *Exorcist* demon sound like Linda Ronstadt. Damocles' leathery wings flexed with impatience. He ravaged the rug with his foreclaws.

Charity and Roy were jolted upward from the bed like shells ejected from a rifle breech to hang suspended and nude in midair. Satan gestured negligently at the bed, where two forms gave a convincing impression of very dead.

"Dead and damned."

"We can't be," Roy attempted pathetically. "We're members of the Tabernacle of the Born Again Savior. Good Christians."

Damocles chuckled, a sound like scratching on a coffin lid. "Our favorite kind."

"No." Roy groped for the nearest part of Charity to hang on to. "My White Christian God—"

"Oh, shut up. Where do you think my authority comes from?"

Roy found a vestige of his courage. "You ain't no Christian, never were. You look like a lousy Jew."

"A touch of the Levantine." Satan bowed. "Beelzebub and all that. A touch of the Egyptian as Set, various Etruscan and Roman . . . this is really a set piece. Benét did it so much better. In the main, Mr. Stride, a Wasp like yourself. Hit it, Damocles."

Damocles pointed a foreclaw at the two shuddering wraiths. "You have the right to remain silent—"

"Never mind the Miranda," Satan prompted. "Skip to the appeal."

"All right," Damocles sulked. "You get a phone call."

Floating helplessly, hanging on to Roy, Charity stammered, "Wh-who can we call?"

"Why not God?" Satan suggested. "You've been bending His ear for the last few minutes. Give Him a buzz."

Charity did. "God! Please help us!"

The air tore visually, like something out of a Cocteau film. An imposing patriarchal figure blossomed out of nothing, brilliant white against the crimson nightmare, very much like Charlton Heston in *The Ten Commandments.* He inspected Charity and Roy like smudges on glassware.

"Forget it," God said, and disappeared. Damocles' wings flared in triumph.

"Ha! Ours!"

"Appeal granted, heard, denied. Damocles, the lady was thinking of transports. Give her one."

Foaming from an obscene mouth, Damocles plucked the two gibbering forms out of the air and tucked each under an unpleasant arm. Charity had just enough mind left to see Roy, eyes bulging and mouth working in a silent prayer, before the dark came down on her with a last sensation of falling . . .

"Don't slaver so, Wilksey," Coyul remarked as they descended. "They've got the gist."

"Oh, but, Prince, how often do we have the chance for such good trashy fun?"

"Don't get carried away. You have a makeup and costume change. Mr. Steiner, Mr. Shostakovich—cue music, please. The damnation bit."

11

THE EDUCATION OF CHARITY STOVALL

■ 11 ■

One man's media . . .

Dead and damned. Alone. Roy, the world, life gone. Dead and damned.

Stunned.

Charity couldn't make a sound beyond a pitiful squeak forced out between chattering teeth. No sense of time. She couldn't tell how long she'd huddled naked in the limbo of oily fog. Any attempt to think trailed off in whimpering terror.

Gradually she became aware of her surroundings. Limbo resolved as the fog sank to a thick, writhing carpet. No color, only barren black rocks jutting here and there. No hellfire as she'd learned from childhood and bad dreams, only damp cold and the fog coiling about her bare legs. Here and there, plumes of dark, stinking smoke rose out of the fog into a gray sky. Naked and shivering in a hell not cold enough to kill the sickening stench from the oily pools surrounding her.

And the sounds. She wasn't alone. Even gratitude for that had to be fumbled at before she could be sure of it. Thin, piping agony floated eerily on the fetid air. At last Charity dared to stumble toward the nearest sounds that might at least mean companionship.

Incredibly, there was music, deep, booming and grim, of a piece with the total absence of color. Charity hugged herself tight against the chill. As she groped forward, she heard a shift in the music, a definite beat to it now, stroked on deep bass strings.

She moved timidly, expecting demons behind every dark-rearing boulder. "Oh!"

She started; a naked arm thrust upward out of the mist just in front of her. She felt herself beginning to sink in clammy ooze. The bog's obscene odor clogged her nostrils. Charity scrabbled backward to firmer ground. The arm became a shoulder and then the head and torso of a man covered with numbers in red dye.

"Help me," he moaned. "Mercy! A good pilot, anything. I lived by the media and died by the rating."

The pitiful wretch went down again before Charity could summon the courage to help him. There were reaching arms all about her now, dyed with numbers, faces rising a little way out of the mist to implore her aid before falling back.

Charity wondered aloud, "Is this the hell for fornicators?"

"No, not quite."

"EEEE!" Charity jumped as if she'd been goosed with a cattle prod. To her left, seated on a mountainous stack of *TV Guide*s, a monstrous thing with television screens for eyes and a speaker mouth hulked over two tiny men cavorting between his cable cord legs. One gesticulated continuously. His head was no more than a huge mouth that worked furiously without sound but produced a constant shower of popcorn. The other puppet-thing giggled and gibbered, rocked back and forth with the edged inanity of an idiot brushed for one terrible moment by the truth of the world.

"This section is for the abusers of media," said the electronic nightmare. "Actually designed for romance writers, but our place isn't ready yet. What are you?" The blank eyes peered at her. "A televangelist?"

"No, I—" Charity shivered with the damp cold. "I'm just me. Charity Stovall."

"Mm-hm. Don't look smarmy enough, in any case. Now *this* one." One jack-plug finger tapped the popcorn purveyor between its spindly power-cable legs. "He was a Fundamentalist politician who proclaimed himself God's candidate." The jack finger flicked at the laughing fool. "This one believed him."

Dumb as the popcorn man, Charity backed away from the horror, remembering how she'd rung doorbells for the same cause in Plattsville.

"This, as you've noticed, is a rather Brontëan neighborhood," the monster said. "It's for gothic writers. How can you be gothic without bad weather? Ahhah! Hear that? Please stand by." The ugly head swiveled on its circuitry neck. "They're coming for you."

"Me?"

"Listen." The voice trailed off in speaker hiss. "Lissen . . ."

Under the sobbing wind, the strange deep music resolved to a descending motif of three notes in the strings. Long, short, long under a haunting human voice.

Charity. Char-i-tee . . .

"This also is reality," the speaker voice informed her.

"It's not real!" Charity wailed. "I'm supposed to be in hell, punished. This is crazy."

"I didn't say whose reality. The popcorn always suited you. You never asked for anything better."

"Who's following me? Tell me that much, will you?"

"In this place," said the TV creature, "most likely the last person you'd want to meet. Unless you care to remain for my editorial—public service, carefully laundered of damaging inference, station not responsible for content—you'd better run like hell."

Amid swirling fog, ominous music and the inane cackling of the true believer, Charity Stovall fled away.

■ 12 ■

Prometheus in Dolby

The pursuing voice faded, but she heard another just ahead. A man's voice like a clear trumpet, like Richard Burton in *The Robe*. One fearful glance over her shoulder, then Charity found the courage to call out.

"Hey! You out there, where are you?"

"Here!" the voice summoned. "Here, come to me, whoever you are. Now, you nighted ranks, you host of villainous shades, do I yet defy you! Time and again, though you pursue and yet I strive, and to your darkness give the lie—it is not the winning but the quest that raises me anew from your defeats."

She didn't know what he was saying, but the quality of that voice galvanized Charity in a place untouched before: powerful and heroic, yet vulnerable, racked with anguish of spirit.

The mist shifted slightly and she saw him, spread-eagled against a huge boulder by chains spiked into the rock. Not embarrassingly bare like herself, but his black tights and sheepskin vest set off a body heroic as the voice: slender, tight-muscled, smooth chest heaving under an open linen shirt, the finely shaped head crowned with unruly black curls.

"Come, child. Free me."

With her hands a poor makeshift for modesty, Charity approached the pinioned hero. Black eyes pierced her through out of the pain-drawn face. Under that gaze Charity knew, dead or not, she was still female.

"Uh . . . hi."

"Take the hammer, girl. Free me."

"Hammer?"

"Even there by your foot." He laughed bitterly. "That with which they pinned me to this rock thinking none would have the heart to help."

Groping under the carpet of fog, Charity found the heavy sledgehammer. "Batter at the spikes," he directed. "If my arms are free I can loose myself from the manacles. Haste you."

As Charity lifted the heavy hammer, the ground trembled and shifted beneath her feet with an ominous rumble.

"Quickly," he urged. "This ground is perilous."

She could barely lift the sledge at first, but spurred by fear and the quaking underfoot, Charity drove it faster and faster at the prisoning spikes. The first of them came loose with a hollow clang. The earth shifted sickeningly. Not far away a great gout of flame shot up through the mist, showering them with fiery needles of pain.

"Hurry, girl!"

His voice drove her to pound maniacally at the remaining pinion until it fell away. The young man brought his lacerated hands together with a concentrated energy fierce enough for Charity to feel. The entire charisma of tension and conflict in him focused in the hands as he grasped one manacle and writhed his wrist through it. The skin tore and bled; his lips drew back in a grimace from the effort.

"Careful, you're cutting yourself."

"The blood will—ease—the—passage." One lacerated hand sprang free as the ground beneath them palpably sank and heaved again. "Hold the chain, girl, it's coming . . . there!"

He stood a moment, flexing the torn hands, then allowed her a fleeting, distracted smile. Considering their plight, Charity could still find it devastating.

"Dane." He bowed his head briefly. "Once heir to a crown, now but a poor, tormented shade like yourself. Though not so poor that I lack thanks, nor so dull"—his smile turned warmer—"as to overlook your dire need of costume. Allow me."

Dane shed the sheepskin vest and draped it about Charity's shoulders. With considerable gratitude, she found it large enough to cover the conventions.

"Th-thank you." The ground surged again, throwing her against him. "My name is Charity Mae Stovall from Plattsville, 'n' can we please get out of here?"

"The wish is the act." He grasped her hand. "Come."

They set off at a jolting trot across the dreary landscape, Charity clinging for dear life to Dane. The rumble of the treacherous ground grew to a roar. To their left and right the earth ripped apart, belching flame and ash into the sooty air, pushing back the mist in hissing retreat from blackened heath. Charity caught a glimpse of some hapless creature disappearing into the flaming maw.

Still Dane hurried her on, dragging her over rocks, guiding her surely toward some distant goal she could only guess at, and always the music under the roar of laboring nature. In a lull between quakes they stopped to rest. Charity wilted to her knees, panting. Dane knelt beside her; even through the sheepskin his hands were a comforting human warmth in the middle of chill horror.

"Just a jot further, Charity." He pronounced her name in a way that made it sound noble, full of meaning.

"Someone's following me, Dane."

"And me," he said. "There's always someone. And he will find me. Come, the ground's not safe."

"Not yet," she protested. "I can't even get up. Where are we going?"

"Where I must." Dane paced forward alone. Blinking through her fear and exhaustion, Charity saw something about him that escaped her before. Dane moved in a definite light that defined him from his drearier surroundings. It must be his goodness, she thought. Just like a spotlight on Bruce Springsteen. *Gol-lee, he must be important.*

"We go to all that should have been precious to me." His sadness was audible. "All I should have clung to, honored, but never did." He swung about to Charity. The mist swirled between them, and the poignant music. "And you? What condemned you to this place, child?"

"I wish you wouldn't call me child. You're not all that much older than me."

"Hurrying the pleasures of wedlock?"

Charity found she could still blush. "That's kind of personal."

"Be not amazed that I can so divine; your namesake virtue's written in your eyes. No sins I find but they were writ by love."

A little hard to understand, but he certainly said it real nice. "Well, I guess modesty don't cut much here. That was it. Just . . . I wish I could've enjoyed it more. I mean, long as I had to get a heart attack. Boy, who could've figured on that? Is that your sin, too?"

"No." Dane's sorrow emanated from a great distance with an underlying rage that drew it taut. "Far worse, Charity. In the terms of the world, you only crossed a boundary without the passport of Grace. I . . . ran from all meaning. So now I must ever run toward it, fight and lose. In the matter of *hell*"—the magnificent voice hurled the word like a missile at a dull gray sky. "Demons, you lack imagination!"

The organ tones thundered away, mocked with echoes and the growing roar of the earth itself. Charity was flung backwards as the heath writhed up under her and opened in a great rift between her and Dane, belching fire and black smoke to dirty the mist.

Dane held out his arms. "Jump, girl. I'll catch you."

"I can't, it's too far."

"Try."

She scrambled to her feet, moved back from the yawing chasm already widening as she crouched for a running start.

"Now, ere it's too far."

With a quick prayer—not certain to whom under the circumstances—Charity churned toward the rift. She leaped, felt empty, scorching air on her bare legs—then nothing, no solid ground to meet her descent, hands scrabbling in panic at the lip of the rift, the rest of her dangling over searing void. Her fingers lost their grip, clawed, slipped, then Dane caught her and drew her up onto solid ground.

"The whole moor's sinking," he shouted over the thunder of chaos. "Tearing itself to pieces. Come on."

He dragged Charity after him toward a barren promontory rising high over the mist. "Take heart: even surviving is an action. To choose and act, even in hell, we are alive."

"How can we be alive?" Charity ran a dirty hand through her hair stringy with damp and singed ends. "We're as dead as you can get."

"Life's not state but quality. Here, this will help." Dane drew the lace from the front of his shirt and tied back Charity's hair. "In the far kingdom of Plattsville, would you ever know a day like this?"

No, Charity reflected honestly. I'd be working in the kitchen or just riding around with Roy or watching dumb old TV. Scary as this place is, and for all his weird talk, Dane is the beautifulest man I ever saw.

"Now you get down to it," she allowed, "things could be a lot worse."

"So they could." Dane swept her clear off her feet and kissed her. Charity's heart definitely missed a few beats. She felt his kiss down to her dangling toes.

"Just a little further now."

At the summit only a vast blanket of white fog lay before them, dirtied with smoke and reddish ash. The rock beneath them trembled. When Charity looked back, she saw the earth convulse once more in a scream of sundered stone. The last spasm subsided in echoes that stumbled away across leaden skies like fading timpani. "Is the weather always this bad here?"

"No. Quite oft it turns truly foul." Dane touched her cheek. "You're a brave lass, Charity Stovall. And very lovely."

Charity gulped. He said it easily enough, as if a little surprised at the discovery. No one had ever called her lovely. Now, suddenly, she felt that way. But Dane was pointing, a gesture weighted with more doom than hope.

"There. My father's keep."

■ 13 ■

Yonder lies the castle
of my father

From somewhere, dry strings swept up to be capped by a single piano note from which a chilly figure shuddered away in woodwinds. The mist eddied and parted to reveal a brooding castle of black stone rising from the heath. Over the single tower a banner turned in the wind.

"There's a flag, Dane. Someone's home."

"No one is there. But one will come."

The ubiquitous music turned rhythmic as they jolted down the last slope and on toward the drawbridge. They crossed it, passed under the portcullis across a cobbled courtyard and up a spiraling set of damp steps, Dane's boots ringing on the stone. They moved down a long, gloomy corridor toward a widening flicker of light.

"Told you someone's here."

"There's always a light," Dane answered. "And someone always comes."

"Your folks?"

"No."

The vast hall stretched away before Charity, an

91

ocean of dark with one small island of light from a wall
sconce. Dane took the torch and set it to logs and kin-
dling laid in the huge fireplace. With more light came
welcoming warmth. Giant shadow snakes danced up
the high walls. Charity could see the size of the hall
now, big as the Plattsville High School gym. Over the
mantel a single lion's head glared at her in bas-relief.
Just under it, Charity caught the transient gleam of
light on cold metal. All of it gloomy and depressing; yet
that odd, steady light followed Dane. Like the music, it
must be awfully annoying, but Dane seemed to accept
it as part of himself like Roy's camouflage fatigues.

"We sort of never get hungry here, do we?"

"No. Not for food." Dane left her by the fire and
vanished into the gloom. He emerged again carrying
something, which he held out to Charity: the most gorgeous pearl-gray velvet gown she'd ever drooled over
in a movie or on the cover of a paperback romance. She
thrilled to the sensual crush of the material. The neck-
line alone was illegal. "It's beeyootiful! Where'd you
find it?"

"My mother's."

"Oh, Dane, I couldn't."

"Of course you can. It's yours."

"All right. Turn your back and I'll give you back
your vest." Charity let the luxurious weight of the velvet fall about and caress her body. What could be so bad
for people who can dress like this? she wondered with a
shade of mean envy. At least they had fancy problems.
"Oh, it's really *neat*, Dane. Thank you very much."

"Stay by the fire. Stay in the light." Dane prowled
the shadows beyond their fire, the musical voice coming
out of gloom. "This was my father's house, seat and
symbol of that honor to which he hoped I might aspire.
Remember me in your prayers, Charity. Say that when
I might have mattered, I would not. That even now I
need to act and choose when action mocks me with
futility."

All that was pretty, but she did wish he could talk a little plainer so she wouldn't feel like a fool trying to answer what she could barely understand.

"Do you know poetry, girl?"

"Just what we had to read in school. Woody Barnes gave me a book of poems for my birthday once." By Rod somebody, she recalled imperfectly, though one of them was enough. It was about a man in love with a man, which she didn't approve of that at all and didn't bother with the rest. Anyway, why was Dane going on like this, so far away from her? "Come sit by the fire, it's real toasty now."

Dane knelt by Charity. Even kneeling he conveyed the effect of a taut athletic effort, like Gene Kelly. But now Charity could see the firelight dancing in his eyes and understood very well the feelings they stirred.

"There was a poet of Italy," Dane said, "who wrote of hell for those who changed allegiance or had none. Ever must they pursue, this way and that through a mist, one banner that ever eluded them. In this place I should have honored am I damned ever to find it empty, ever to lose and know too late what winning might have been." The fine head bowed over his knee. "Pray for me."

His voice was like an open wound. Charity's heart opened and reached for his pain, closed tight around it. "Dane, I'm sorry."

He flung himself on his back, searching the darkness above for a hope that would not be there.

"You're crying. I never saw Roy cry." He would have let himself be run over first, though tears took nothing from Dane's manhood. "He was my boyfriend."

"The boy who loved you?"

"Yes. Well, just that once."

"Oh, there's the sin." Dane wound his fingers in her hair. "That such a woman was loved only once."

When he drew her down to him, Charity knew the

meager statistic was about to rise and loved the whole notion. She slid her arms around Dane's neck while the violins overhead haunted them with melody. "I don't want you to hurt, Dane."

"Or I you. We'll help each other." His body moved against hers, sending a different heat through every part of her. This was a fringe benefit she hadn't counted on.

"Can we? Even dead and all?"

"Why not feast on the lamb?" Dane chuckled with the dry ghost of humor. "We've already been hanged for the sheep."

"Sure enough," she whispered against his lips. "Way I figure, they owe us."

14

Enter Nemesis, pursuing

Something woke her.

The fire had burned low. She lay with her head on Dane's arm in a soft glow from the embers. Then Dane gently slid his arm away. She felt his movement. When she turned over, he was dressing rapidly.

"Did you hear it?" he muttered.

"Something woke me up."

"Yes." Dane threw on the sheepskin and thrust his feet into boots. "They have found me. They will not do't in the dark." He threw another log on the fire in a shower of sparks, then came back to Charity. "Stay in the shadows. Do not speak or cry out at what you see. All was foreordained." He handed her the gown with a remembrance of their earlier tenderness. "I should have known you in life. But it is enough."

"There wasn't anybody like you in Plattsville," she blurted—an admission of wonder and regret not unmixed with a certain relief. Dane was pure electricity, ten times what Roy would ever be or even Woody, but a woman could get very tired loving a raw wire. Roy and Woody she understood; besides, he might not even be Protestant.

"Well, then, come on," Dane challenged the dark.

"Come and make an end." His hand swept over the mantel and came away with a magnificent rapier that flashed in an arc of light. *"Listen!"*

Hurrying into her gown under a muted cadence from plucked bass strings, Charity heard the hollow echo of a male tread over the courtyard stones—up the stairs, striding toward the hall. Illumined in his own light, Dane bounded across the vast chamber onto a low dais, whirling, rapier held high.

"Nemesis, come! And you unfeeling stars, I hurl defiance for reply, and cast into the balance for the world to see, my soul 'gainst thy insensate cruelty."

As Dane's ringing challenge died away, Charity started at the answer, a blast of horns descending in a minor mode. Another spotlight revealed a figure leaning, negligent but coiled, against the entrance arch. Even in apparent relaxation the black-clad stranger had about him the same dangerous energy as Dane. His sardonic laughter echoed off the stones.

"Bravo, Dane. Pentametric to the end." He lifted his rapier. "But I have found you."

A stifled scream of tension tore from high-pitched strings. Muffled timpani measured the intruder's cat tread across the hall as Dane stepped down to meet him.

Charity swallowed hard. *Oh, man, it's Darth Vader.*

"So you have," said Dane. "But think no more to follow me. Here upon my father's hearth, with all he left me, this sword, I spced you home to the deeper hell that spawned you." The sword cut a hissing swath through the air. "Come, sir."

Moving in his own light, the stranger's blade crossed Dane's with a chilly *ting* and slithered along its middle third. The two slender threads of steel were no more than moving light, flashing about each other. The two men circled like lethal dancers, the nasty *ting-tack!* of the blades a deadly dialogue. The steel threads wove about each other, crossed, disengaged, beat with resonant echoes over the inexorable trombones that measured them.

Then in a blur too swift to follow, the dark little man thrust and lunged like a striking snake. As quick, Dane parried overhand with a twist of his wrist; the blade streaking for his heart swerved far aside, tore from the attacker's grasp and clattered on the stone floor. He stepped back.

"Your father taught you well, Dane."

"Had he schooled me so in honor, or were I pupil apt, I should be with him now. But as to sword—" Dane speared the fallen rapier guard on his own point and launched it toward his enemy's grasp. "Well enough. Come again."

"You should not lend me mercy I may not repay." The stranger leaped at Dane again in a slashing attack, closed and tripped him. Dane lost his balance and fell. The dark man's blade whirled in a circle of light, came down just as Dane rolled aside and sprang to his feet. They closed again, beat, disengaged; then the smaller man slipped under a slight miscalculation in Dane's guard and lunged.

Dane faltered; the sword dropped from his fingers. Charity cried out as he sank to his knees with a strangling cough and fell on his side. His enemy regarded him with remote pity as the music melted to poignant strings.

"Victory," he pronounced with no joy in it. "Rest, most noble among the damned."

Dane lay in his light, a stain spreading over his shirt. With a sob, Charity ran to cushion his head in her lap.

"Dane. Dane!"

His eyelids fluttered open. "Aye, Charity. Well enough."

The grave, tender music brooded over them, a repeated figure in muted brass. Dane listened with a wan

97

smile of satisfaction. "For the time . . . you made me very happy."

"Oh, Dane. Honest, for all the trouble, I was never so happy in my whole life." A rage welled up in Charity, a fury with a virulence to frighten her. Even her voice was different when she turned on Dane's killer. "You son of a bitch."

He stepped back, offended. "Madame, please."

"Pardon my language, but damn if I don't wish I was a man for two minutes. I'd take his sword and shove it where the sun don't shine for what you done."

"For what you *did*," Dane corrected weakly. "So please you . . . a little of your namesake for our mother tongue."

She hugged him close, desperate. "I don't want you to die."

"I must." Dane's hand faltered up to touch her lips and hair. "My father's waiting. My . . . spirit fails. But I did love you. That . . . makes fair end."

"Please don't die. It ain't fair!"

"Don't blame this churl; he's but transport. He sends me home. Oh, Father, I stained your life. For earnest, take . . . my death."

The somber music faded to silence. Dane lay still in Charity's arms.

"Oh, Dane." With infinite tenderness, Charity eased his head down onto the stones and bent to kiss the stilled lips. "I should have gone with you. You were a man to die with."

"You are worthy, child." The stranger sheathed his sword. "The sentiment becomes you."

Charity was a little impressed herself. She'd never felt that depth or voiced anything like it in her life.

"You must go now."

"Go where?" she asked listlessly over Dane's body.

"Where you will, but with dispatch. Hark!"

The wind had risen outside, a pitiful moaning sound, bleak as her own sorrow, and a voice rode on it.

Char-i-tee . . .

"I came for him," the dark man said. "They come for you. His ghosts o'ertook him; yours will come betimes. Quickly begone."

With a last adoring look at Dane, Charity hurried away from the hall, down the worn steps and across the gray courtyard while the wind cried with its terrible summons.

Charity?

She fled across the drawbridge into the fog.

In the gloomy hall, the victor gazed down at the body graceful even in death—and signed plaintively. "Wilksey, your pauses are interminable."

One baleful eye opened and impaled him with accusation. "That is the way to play it, Mr. Kean."

"Indeed." Edmund Kean snorted with dry disgust. "Is there no o'erdone reading, no tattered cliché, no cheap effect to which you will not plummet?"

"You amateur!" Wilksey Booth shot to his feet like a jack-in-the-box released. "You charge me with overplaying?"

"Amateur? I was playing the Bard before you were born."

"Precisely, Ned. One wouldn't mind your Shakespeare lit by flashes of lightning—"

"Just so." Kean's intensity softened with satisfaction. One's better reviews were delights evergreen. "Coleridge did say that."

"Were it not for all the darkness in between."

"Take care." Kean's sword flashed again from the scabbard. "I might school you in earnest."

"You?" Booth derided. "The bawdy-house school of fencing?"

"Oh, did I tax you beyond competence?"

"Beyond patience, Kean. You know the disengage one-two-three always comes before the parry-quatre-thrust-lunge and you *always* forget. Not to mention that you lunged when I was out of my light."

"Allowance must be made for colonials. Let us rehearse once more," Kean said. "And whilst we do, remember who was called in his day the very Sun's Bright Child—and who merely assassin."

"Oh, base prompter's boy!" Booth recoiled, wounded. "Come you over me still with that? I shot *one* Republican. Have at you, villain."

Ned Kean crouched *en garde*—then lowered his point. "Stay, it's no fun without an audience. She sorrowed with heart, that girl, and raged with natural fire. But that accent . . . ?"

"Allegheny," Booth agreed. "Eerie, isn't it?"

"Nor did I recognize your death music."

"Oh, that? Walton: the passacaglia from the film *Henry V.* Falstaff's death."

"The death of a clown; how apt," Kean sniped. "Now my choice was Shostakovich."

Booth sniffed. "Bit much on the kettles and brass."

"It likes me well. The ghost and duel music from *Hamlet.* Ah, those minor thirds in the horns—ominous, fated. I say, Dimitri?" Ned Kean petitioned the dark overhead. "Could I hear my entrance again, old boy? Rather fancied it. And, Wilksey, do shorten those pauses when you die. One tends to nap."

Together in their universe, the circle of light, the actors listened to the reprise of music and were stirred.

■ 15 ■

Aryans in the fast lane

No pain, nothing clear except terror.

When Roy could think straight, he found himself in a small chamber inviting as a dentist's waiting room. Table, lamp, modern chair, a copy of *Soldier of Fortune*, a worn book with no dust jacket—and to Roy's huge relief a cotton bathrobe hanging on the coat rack. He put it on immediately; he found it hard to feel secure fully clothed, but naked was unbearable.

Time, if there was such a thing for him now, passed and kept on passing. Nothing. No sound. No one came. His tension began to ebb to the point where he could relate to his surroundings. Dr. Corbett once had a waiting room just like this, and the magazines were just as out-of-date. The copy of *Soldier of Fortune* was six months old. Roy paged through the book's first leaves. *Mein Kampf* by Adolf Hitler, who was one of his gods along with George Lincoln Rockwell and Rambo.

"Never knew he wrote a book."

He tried a few pages and gave up. Hitler was an unappreciated hero of the race struggle, but whoever wrote it in English made it boring as hell. Suffice to say, Roy never spent an evening trapped with the inexhaustible Austrian.

More waiting. Roy thought of Charity: where did they take her? More to the point right now: what would they do to him?

The very silence was oppressive. "If this is it for eternity," he judged aloud to shatter it, "I think I can handle it."

When the door opened behind him, he jumped clear out of the chair, clutching the bathrobe around him.

"Roy Stride? I'm Drumm."

"I didn't do anyth—"

Roy caught himself, not knowing whether to be scared or plain laugh. A squat, unimposing little man, Drumm was decked—stuffed, rather, into the dress finery of the White Paladins: tailored camouflage fatigues, white silk scarf and red beret, web belt under a double strain to contain his girth and support the heavy Magnum revolver in its tooled holster. With all the authority these might have lent, Drumm didn't make it. His paunch betrayed the military intentions of his blouse. His glasses were thick enough to make his eyes look like small, distant clams within concentric rings. The vague mustache added no character, merely coexisted with his upper lip. Drumm removed his beret with the care of a cardinal divesting after Mass to reveal a toupee neither subtly matched nor firmly allied with his sparse indigenous hair. He greeted Roy with the fervor of adoration.

"At last the day. We've been waiting, sir."

Roy backed away, trying to keep the bathrobe closed. "Hey, look, I just got here."

"On a trumped-up charge."

"I'm innocent . . . who are you?"

"My cause is yours," Drumm said with dramatic urgency.

"You with the Paladins?"

"We're everywhere." Drumm patted the toupee for evidence of wanderlust since last contact. The two

102

clams fixed on Roy. "We know you; we intercept the dossiers. And Charity? Was she pure?"

"We're gonna get married," Roy maintained, but the tense was obviously wrong. "Were gonna get married."

"I mean was she Aryan?"

"One hunnert percent pure White American Aryan like me. The purest."

"And like so many capable men, you are here through the judgment of inferiors." Drumm rubbed his pudgy hands together. "As myself. I was with Rockwell in Arlington."

Roy regarded Drumm with new respect. "The American Nazi Party." The last of his fear vanished. Drumm was no threat but an ally with major-league credentials.

"With me to guide him, George Rockwell formed and headed the ANP. He saw the merit and the truth in the plays I wrote that no one would produce; that no one *here* will do anything but throw back at me, thanks to Jason Blythe, our pristine prime minister. The truth of the world was in my work, Roy Stride. And that truth is the God-ordained and inevitable supremacy of the White Race."

Roy even found the composure to grin. "Right on."

"Your hand, sir."

"Gimme five."

"There are those who guide, those who lead, many who follow. I am a prophet; you may be much more than that. Wait." Drumm peered suspiciously about the chamber with an air of habitual caution, bent to inspect the inside of the lampshade and under the table, ample rump presented to Roy, who quelled a profitless urge to boot it.

Satisfied, Drumm beckoned him close. "I don't think we're bugged, but Blythe's spies are everywhere. All of us are marked. We must move soon. You may be the leader we have waited for. Rockwell was shot, cut down in his prime. His followers wait even here to carry on his cause, needing only the day and the man. Are you fit for it? A leader seizes the moment. Will you?"

Will I? Roy felt ambition surge in him like a shot of whiskey. *Damned, no chance at all, call that a trial we had? All of you just watch. Just one chance, all I ask, and he's handing it to me. Get set up, find Charity, and won't be any son of a bitch on two legs big enough to fuck me over anymore.*

"Okay. Your people ready?"

"And waiting. A coup," Drumm said. "A purge. One lightning strike."

This wasn't hell but heaven. "Weapons?"

"All we need, the latest. AR rifles, ammo, C-4 plastic, LAW rockets, men in the right place ready to move. The government has a rotted will; the danger is in fanatics and interference from Topside. But the time and stars are right, Roy Stride!"

"Lead me to it." Roy felt marvelous—until second thoughts nudged him. "No, wait. I gotta get some decent clothes." Not even Hitler could conquer in a bathrobe.

"Before all else." Drumm clicked his heels and flung open the door. "The Whip & Jackboot will furnish all you need. Run by a nigger and a Jew, but we can't purge them all."

"Yet," Roy corrected with the first overtones of authority.

"Well put, sir." Drumm motioned Roy first through the door. "I was not mistaken in you. You show genius."

The Whip & Jackboot: the glories of the display window alone convinced Roy that Drumm knew his taste to a T, his brightest fantasies. Within the window there were many metal-studded styles and a great deal of leather.

"I'll leave you here." Drumm searched the mall both ways with his perpetual air of secrecy. "Remember, you're being watched. I'll get word to the others and to you when it's safe to meet."

"Yeah, cool." Roy wanted to get off the sidewalk. The bathrobe didn't do anything for a man of destiny.

"The code word for the takeover is Case White. Leader, the pistol is cocked." The metaphor pleased Drumm. "You will pull the trigger. *Auf Wiedersehen.*"

"Stay cool. No, wait a minute." Roy found he was thinking clearer and more confidently with each passing minute. Never mind the people on the sidewalk; they didn't seem to think a man in a bathrobe was ridiculous or even interesting. Looked like a bunch of stuck-up yuppies, didn't know their ass from a hole in the ground. "You said you know everybody that comes here."

"Everyone," Drumm confirmed. "We make it our business to know. Not hard, a few favors here and there. Now and then for the right person an agreeable girl in the right motel. I mean—that is to say . . ." Drumm looked away, awkwardly conscious of a gaffe. "Excuse me, Leader, I—"

"That's okay, just watch it. Pass an order to the troops."

Click! "Immediately, Leader."

"Find Charity Stovall for me. I don't give a shit who you put in what bed with his own mother even. Charity's my woman and I want her, understand? That's General Order *numero uno,* got it?"

"Sir." Click! "Until then, may I suggest A Son Goût, just down the mall? Adrian the sommelier personally extends his invitation."

"Adrian the what?"

"In charge of the girls." Click! "Until later, my Führ —my Leader." Drumm bustled away. He had very little military bearing and digging in his nose destroyed that.

Roy entered the Whip & Jackboot. Before him stretched rows of gleaming, studded jackets and matched uniforms, shelves of precisely arranged peaked caps like a squad on parade, racks of leather whips, whole tack sections of leather strapping. Midway down one row, a balding black man with bulging eyes and enormous white teeth fussed over an item on a rack. Seeing Roy, he shuffled forward with a servility that warmed the customer's heart.

"Mistuh Roy Stride, suh! Lan', it *good* to see you in a gent'man's shop where y'all belong."

Roy felt better already. He straightened up. The demeaning rag of a bathrobe took on regality. He liked a nigger who knew his place; didn't have anything against that kind at all. Tell them a Mandy and Rastus joke, they'd laugh hard as you did.

"Well, now, first we gone take you back to this li'l old booth, get you some trousers and shirt while Jacob measures you. Come 'long, Mistuh Roy."

The black man shuffled classically, using a great deal of graceful effort to cover very little distance. Hell, they all had rhythm.

"What's your name, boy?"

"Washington Moonlight Jones, suh." He revealed again the vast expanse of gossamer teeth. "Mama call me Moonlight 'cause that when Daddy done his bes' work among de neighborin' stills."

Roy swelled with pleasure and ventured a Rhett Butler grin of roguish but patrician understanding. "Moonlight, you black rascal, give me the best you got."

"Don' fret. We gone get you lookin' fine."

In a few moments Roy was in and out of the booth, the silly robe traded for shirt and trousers. There were several small holes in the shirtfront and faded stains around them, but he wouldn't have them on for that long.

Moonlight gestured like a majordomo. "Now, y'all come 'long with me in the back. We got Jacob. He trash but he do know what a mil'tary gent'man need for wear. Ja-cob? Gent'man need some outfittin' right now." Moonlight lowered his voice in confidence. "He try to Jew you on price, old Moonlight set him straight. Been took care of. Jacob?"

Moonlight thrust aside a curtain. "G'wan in, Mistuh Roy."

The dingy back room was rack-lined with uniforms in various stages of completion. At the end of a long table, tape measure draped about his oddly twisted neck, a bearded Jew of indeterminate age hunched over a thick book. Bespectacled and ringleted, the fringes of a prayer shawl splayed from beneath the hem of his shabby vest.

Roy sneered: a real one, all right. "Work hours, Ikey. You praying to Moses on company time?"

The tailor gave Roy an unhurried inspection before closing his book. Somehow, under that gaze, Roy recalled the factory worker he bad-mouthed in a bar once, a man who stood much bigger than he sat. Roy had the same second-thought prudence then as now. Jacob exuded an undefinable force that belied the humble appearance. In a dark alley, he might be dangerous. Though his head canted at an unnatural angle, his gaze was pitilessly direct.

"Not prayer, no. Thinking on the nature of belief. Like the Talmud, a preoccupation of mine." Jacob clapped his hands briskly and rubbed them together; the image of quiet strength vanished. "But business is business. It's good you come by my shop. Something in a uniform, yes?"

Jacob undraped his measure and subjected Roy to professional scrutiny, tugging at one ringlet. "It wouldn't need to be made special. From looking alone, I can suit you from stock."

He puttered about Roy, measuring fore and aft, up and down, noting the results on a greasy slip of paper. When he stooped to gauge an outseam, Roy saw the livid rope scar that ringed his neck.

"The *shwartzer* says I must always measure. Feh! Who has been a tailor so long? Go give advice but leave to me clothes. So: didn't I say? A perfect size forty all around. Wait, I will bring it all for approval." Jacob vanished into another dark recess and shortly reappeared with an armload of boxes. "You will try them on and say I know my business?"

Dressed before the full-length mirror, Roy palpitated: what approval was needed for sheer magnificence? Black the uniform, stern black and cut in SS style with silver buttons, even a death's-head ornament on the peaked cap. Flared riding breeches fitted perfectly into high, polished boots perfect for striding over a conquered city. *Too much, oh, Jesus, too much.* In the mirror the magic uniform converted his whole image to strength and dominance. With a sense of ritual, he centered the cap on his head, tried a rakish angle, straightened it again and patted the heavy Lüger at his hip.

"Gotta hand it to you, Jacob."

"Only wait." A protesting hand. "Something is missing, I think."

"Hey, what?" How could perfection lack?

"Maybe a swagger stick like the Englishers? No, they are not a generous people. How long before they gave back Jerusalem? Who needs the English? We will keep it good and German. Moonlight! Bring to me, *bitte,* the Gauleiter Special."

From the remote front of the shop: "Comin' fas' I can." Followed by a considerable hiatus.

"Which means, we can hope, sometime before evening prayers." Jacob lifted his eyes to Jehovah. "Meanwhile we will settle on the price."

"Don' you fret Mistuh Roy with no bill, you trash." Moonlight hovered, stern, between the parted curtains. "All took care of by the Paladins. Here you is, suh: just what y'all need."

Now, truly, perfection was improved. The black whip coiled in Roy's hand with the lead-weighted feel of authority. He cracked it once; the sound was music. *All right, you motherfuckers, come on.*

Jacob beamed approval. "You should wield it in good health. Maybe on the Arabs."

With what he meant to be a superior smile, Roy nodded curtly and stalked out of the shop, cracking the whip. When the front door slammed, Moonlight and Jacob went through profound metamorphosis. Moonlight stood much more erect, chuckling as the whole cast of his features shifted.

"It's impossible to insult them or overplay, Jake. New York, Harvard or the boonies: a nerd is a nerd, world without end, amen."

"Yours to shuffle, mine to cringe and fawn." Jake divested himself of the grizzled wig and spectacles to reveal youthful black hair. The gabardine, vest and prayer shawl added to his discards. He slithered quickly into a work shirt and corduroy trousers. "Honor thy stereotypes, the authors of thy thinking, for without them, thou wouldst have to see."

"You dig El Shmucko with that whip?"

"He's a fish," Jake said with cold contempt. "And he's going to get everything he always wanted."

"What's his bag?" Moonlight wondered.

"Power. The Prince is going to give him all he ever longed for."

"He must be pretty rotten."

"No more than most; just hungrier. The world shut him out. Never turn your back on a small man," Jake said with conviction. "We're a dangerous breed. Catch you later. Got a call on my cab."

■ 16 ■

Problems of the whore/madonna syndrome (Aryans at half-mast)

Mirrored dramatically in A Son Goût's polished window, Roy let his own image ravish him. From cap to boots and whip, he had never felt so tuned to his inner essence. He felt secure and strong, a man with an identity and a destiny at last, seduced as Narcissus.

When something else could intrude on his rapt self-admiration, the displayed pictures and X-rated toys in the window told him this was a place for kicks of a very special kind. A small rubric lettered low on the glass— CATERING TO YOUR REFINED NEEDS—confirmed the impression. Drumm had steered him right.

Entering, Roy found himself in an opulent anteroom done in red velvet plush. Two young men in White Paladin uniforms, on their way out, snapped to rigid attention, puzzling Roy until he realized he was the recipient of the courtesy. Good enough. He touched the whip to his cap bill.

"As you were. I was enlisted once myself. Carry on."

"Good *day*, sir!" A distinguished older man in tux brushed through beaded curtains at the rear, menu tucked under one arm, manner silken. "We hoped you might honor us with a visit. Welcome to A Son Goût, Mr. Stride." A slight but impeccable bow. "Adrian at your service."

"Heard you had a real nice place here. Take care of, uh, special needs?"

"Absolutely," Adrian assured him quickly. "A Son Goût has earned its reputation: purveyors of the best and the unusual, an oasis to the male libido athirst."

"Huh?"

"My own little joke." Adrian waved it away. "This way, sir."

Roy followed him through the beaded curtains to another room in the same plush with more gold trimming and tables covered with crisp white damask. Adrian seated him with a flourish and opened the menu with a practiced twist—frowned and closed it again. Kind of a queer, Roy guessed, but he had to admire the flashing choreography of the white hands. Strictly class. Adrian reminded him of that guy who used to advertise expensive booze in magazines.

Adrian snapped his fingers. "Esmeralda?" A rear door opened and a thin girl of about eighteen skittered into the chamber. She looked passably slutty to Roy; he could make it with her in a pinch: thin hips, way too skinny, in ratty black tights and a leather miniskirt. The pouting face with its carmine mouth, green eye shadow and frowzy, peroxided hair over dark roots might interest him on an odd night—but not special. Too punk rock.

"Esmeralda, this is yesterday's menu. Today's please." The girl changed them quickly and slipped out after a sultry glance at Roy.

"Esmeralda is one of today's specials." Adrian pursed his lips over the current bill of choices. "We are expecting a party from SoHo." He beamed at Roy, hands laced. "Do we have an appetite today, sir? Truly lustful? A full repast or just something to pick at?"

111

"The full treatment." Roy settled back. "Best you got."

"Good, sir."

Roy twitched his whip. "No spades or losers, you got it? That special don't look so hot. And no Jews."

Adrian stiffened. "But of course not, sir. We prepare to order. Esmeralda was prepared for the disco trade. We offer as well an *haute monde* selection, very popular with the New York set. And for the palate beyond astonishment, an anorexic double amputee. Then there is the consideration of vintage. For example, the '67: an excellent year but still a trifle young."

Roy whetted to the prospect. "I like 'em young."

"And the '70," Adrian ventured. "Naïve but a fun libation." The delicate turn of a pale hand. "Though for a true Sauvignon complexity, may one suggest the '54, which should be superb now. And absolutely Wasp, sir."

Roy nodded. "Now you got the idea."

"Untainted with, shall we say, Mediterranean influences."

"Pure blood is very important."

The white hands described a precise sine qua non. "To the discriminate, quite everything."

"That's what I want. But, you know . . . kinky."

"Kinks, sir?" Adrian managed to correct and reassure in one breath. "Proclivities, rather. By a miracle of serendipity, we have a selection of two today, each a masterpiece." The sommelier's gift for description grew to rhapsody. "Ms. Eleanor Padgett-Clive, vintage '60. Niece to an earl. Down from Cambridge, firsts and blues. An enormous, one might say legendary, appetite for men, curbed only by her breeding and the restraints of civil law."

"Hey, a real nymphermaniac?"

"With frequent relapses," Adrian blandished, "which allow us to feature her as a selection of rare value. And—if it is not redundant to observe—dying to meet you, Mr. Stride. Are we tempted, sir?"

"Right on!" Roy bumped back the chair. "Lead me to it."

Adrian wheeled with the precision of a sergeant major on parade. "This way, please."

The bedroom was something out of old movies, done mostly in merciless scarlet and electric blue. To any taste but the most diseased, the colors alone might have precluded sleep or even relaxation; for Roy they were Uptown.

"Bon appétit, sir." Adrian withdrew.

If this was hell, it was definitely the high-rent district, and why not? Damned for making it just once with Charity, and that once not all that good. Face it, she didn't know much, and he had his usual troubles like with any respectable girl. Why shouldn't he land in clover just once: power, girls, every dream about to come true? He could really get comfortable here, make it every time with the right kind of woman.

"That's our wish," the low, musical contralto voice read his thought, "and our purpose, Roy."

Eleanor Padgett-Clive poised in the doorway like an exquisite painting, marvelously sexual without working at it in the least, in a diaphanous dressing gown that left just enough to erotic imagination. She glided to Roy and slipped her arms about his neck. "Sorry to be late. I was reading and the time just stole away. Hello, darling."

Roy felt bleak. To most men this side of terminal impotence, Eleanor would be a love call in herself. She resembled several English film stars of the '60s and '70s: full, luscious mouth, her face sculpted over exquisite bones. Her voice alone, low and musical, could remind a man of biological imperatives.

Could but did not; for Roy, everything about Eleanor was wrong. Wrong voice, wrong face, too damned high-class. Classy women made him feel angry and inferior, but he allowed her to lead him to the bed. Eleanor began to undress him. Her hands moved faster and faster, her breathing rapid and shallow with desire, until she was tearing the clothes from him.

"Hey, careful of the shirt, it's new."

In a very short time, Roy was naked as a peeled egg. Eleanor let her gown slide from creamy shoulders and pulled him eagerly down onto the bed, her heavy sensual mouth crushed to his. "Take me, darling. Use me. Ravage me."

He wished he could.

"Darling, what's the matter?" Eleanor searched Roy's face for some answering spark and found none. "Is something wrong?"

"No," he evaded. "Just . . ."

"Please, I'm so ready for you." Eleanor writhed against him.

"Hey, take it easy, okay? Shit." The same old trouble, no different here than back home. He could never make it with a nice girl like Charity that you wanted to marry. Even if Eleanor was just a whore, she *looked* nice. And there were other things needed that he usually had to pay for.

"A challenge," Eleanor whispered. "Shall we not rise to it?" She was more than beautiful, she was admirably deft and proved it in the next few minutes. The range of her erotic skill was phenomenal, employing the full gamut of her own marvelous equipment and parts of Roy even the Air Force doctors had missed. He only became more depressed and angry, thinking of all the guys who would've died happily by this time, how good it could be without that lousy hang-up, but ... . nothing.

At length, Eleanor desisted. "Love's labors are definitely lost. Your sort are so predictably alike."

That did it. She wasn't his type but no woman talked to him like that. "What you mean all alike?"

Eleanor glanced down at his defeat. "A midsummer's night dream turns to a winter's tale or a comedy of errors."

He didn't know what the hell she was talking about but it sounded like she was making fun of him. A stud like him who could go all night with the right kind of woman. "Hey, listen, bitch. With a man sometimes the woman don't turn him on, you know? Not my fault if you don't do nothing for me."

"The point is moot." Eleanor slid from the bed and into her gown. "But then you're not my sort either, you inadequate little man."

"You shut your fuckin mouth, bitch!"

"Certainly." Eleanor knew how to make a graceful exit with ruin in her wake. "This place isn't your hell, darling. Nowhere you go will ever be. You carry it with you. For you, nice girls don't, isn't that so? You can never quite reconcile sexuality with virtue. Actually nice girls have more talent for sex. Less guilt, more imagination and a great deal more fun."

"I said shut *up.*" Roy swung off the bed, ugly and dangerous. "You don't talk to a man like that."

"A man?" Eleanor's laughter cut like shards of crystal. "And you're what busy little Drumm dredged up for the people's choice? White Paladin to the unwashed. *Bon chance*, darling. Hail and farewell from the gratefully obsolete."

"Listen, you—" Roy took a vicious swing at her. She hardly moved, but whatever she did Bruce Lee would have paid to learn. Roy went tail over teakettle against the wall and landed head down, blinking at an upside-down Eleanor.

"Filet's not for you, Mr. Stride. Adrian will fetch you something more in the line of grits." The door closed behind Ms. Padgett-Clive.

Cold, shaking, Roy sat down on the bed, staring at the door. They knew. Everything. Got right down to the problem, even laughed at him. He cursed with feeble rage at Eleanor and Adrian and the whole goddamned lousy system that made things and people the way they were.

115

I didn't make the rules about what's nice and what ain't. Just I'm a White Christian and that's the way things are.

"Precisely, sir." Adrian poised in the doorway, an étude in apology.

"Hey, man, do you people know what I'm thinking even?"

"Not exactly, but we have done business for ever so long. One hopes you will pardon my deplorable lapse of judgment. Eleanor of *course* was completely wrong for your specifications. Actually she specializes in the younger novelists. I insist on making amends. Our remaining selection is Florence Bird."

Roy was in no mood to be gracious. "She better be the right stuff. Won't be long 'fore I got some pull around here. The business will go where I go, you got it? Who is she?"

Once more Adrian was the compleat sommelier. "Florence Bird: vintage '54. Robust, assertive as Pinot Noir. And absolutely Wasp."

"For real?"

"On the house's reputation: the last honest-to-Goebbels bottling Below Stairs."

"Well, run her in here before I go somewhere else. Can't be only one whorehouse around here."

"There is Club Banal for the pedestrian trade," Adrian informed him with a definite chill. "Whatever *they* can make ordinary, A Son Goût can render sublime. Miss Bird, sir."

Once more Adrian bowed and withdrew. Only a short wait, then the door flew open and Florence Bird gusted in. Roy's heart leaped.

" 'Allo, luv!"

Florence was large, frizzy-haired and utterly bare under the open nylon wrapper trimmed in rabbit fur that fluttered in her bold wake like the train of a raffish empress. Florence was nothing if not forthright.

"Had to spend a linnet up the apples for an 'it and

116

miss from all the pig's ear and mother's ruin down the rub-a-dub. Like me Bristols?"

Roy licked his lips in tumescent excitement. Florence was stout and coarse with a merry lasciviousness, though her very direct handshake was definitely not what he was used to from businesswomen. She sounded like some foreigner, very difficult to understand. "Hiya, honey. Where you from?"

"Lunnon," Florence pealed like Bow Bells. "Carnt yer tell?"

More bullshit. He didn't want to talk at all. She worked for him, all right, the kind that always did: loud, cheap, lay it on the line. Right on. There'd be no problems with Florence beyond translation. She was late, she explained, having been down at her pub having a few gins and beer chasers and had to stop at the bathroom for that and to rouge her nipples, knowing a man of his hearty tastes would appreciate the effect.

Right stuff, right on, Roy thrilled. *Oh jeez, if she can only do the rest of it.*

Subtle as a bayonet charge, Florence cupped Roy's genitals and wiggled her hips. "Right bit o' wick'n awls." She winked, undulating her belly against his. "Like me Khyber?"

Whatever her Khyber was, Roy was all for it. "Yeah. Come on."

"A course, for you, might have to down a few more pints to give yer what yer need, but we'll give it a bash. Down on the floor, luv. Might be a bit left for yer."

"Oh yeah. Yeah, that's it, you got it." Roy got ready, tingling with anticipation and need. "Give it to me, you lousy slut. The whip, too."

Florence was cheerfully accommodating. Roy closed his eyes in bliss and pain under the benediction and the whip. Love had found Andy Hardy.

■ 17 ■

Faith, hope and Charity Stovall

Charity didn't dare stop for long. Of all the terrors hell might hold, she most feared that unknown voice pursuing her, though she could no longer hear it following on the wind. No real time in this place, no real distance she could measure with any certainty. The gray velvet gown was a Hollywood dream but not much for traveling, sodden and heavy with mist.

She stopped suddenly. Just ahead through the swirling fog hulked a large house surrounded by a high iron fence. No lights showed but smoke curled from one chimney. The gloomy presence of the house contrasted with a gleaming, fresh-waxed taxi near the front steps. The driver's door bore the device:

BELOW STAIRS CAB
"ANYWHERE TO HELL AND BACK"
CALL 666-JAKE

Charity pushed at the wide gate. At the groan of rusty hinges, a huge hound raised his head from a nap on the crumbling stone steps with an inquisitive *woof*.

"Got no time for games," Charity told the dog. "Hope you don't bite."

"Not at all." The hound yawned to his ears. "But beware the owner. He thinks."

Charity was only moderately surprised. After a monster made out of television, an earthquake and a thrill-packed but exhausting interlude with Dane, a talking dog was not all that new, except he sounded kind of snooty. City people were always putting you down, trying to sell you something or draft your friends. "You got a funny accent. Where you from, doggie?"

"Boston, girlie," said the hound with audible disdain. "I will not comment on your accent. Similes founder, metaphors fail."

"I speak good American."

"And I only English, alas. Yale, '52. Summa cum maxima, Skull and Bones."

"Plattsville High School, class of '85." Charity would not be outdone. "You don't have to be so stuck-up about it. Everybody goes to school." *Will you listen to me?* she caught herself. *I'm arguing with a watchdog.* "Anyway, is your owner home?"

"He's not my owner." The hound indulged in a thorough fore-and-aft scratch. "But he's in. What do you want?"

"I guess a cab to town. Somewhere. Maybe get warm first."

"The cab you can get; the warmth comes harder. His name is Jake. With a J."

"I know, I know." Charity grasped the heavy bronze knocker and banged it twice.

"Oh, go on in, it's never locked," the dog told her. "Jake had only a few things he valued and lost them ages ago. Some ideals and a friend." He licked his chops and settled down again into his nap.

Charity had to ask. "How does a hound dog go to college?"

One eye opened. "I'm only a dog on duty. Good hours, great for catching up on sleep, which was very difficult for a successful embezzler. Worries, occasional

119

conscience. This is like keeping a lighthouse, not much traffic. So if you don't mind, sayonara." The eye closed.

Charity pushed the door in and found herself in a dark hall, musty with the long absence of light. The only illumination flickered feebly on a wall from a room far down the passage. Charity moved unsurely along the hall to pause in the entrance to a large living room lit only by a fireplace.

There was a man in front of the fire. He didn't look up. "Prince?"

He slumped in his armchair, absorbed in a chess game on a small table on his near side. Charity saw at first only a brooding profile. Too young to read men with any accuracy, Charity still felt the profound sorrow of that presence. He barely acknowledged her, first moving a piece on the board.

"Yes?"

"The door was open," Charity attempted, a little embarrassed. "The dog said just come in."

"Of course." Jake rose with a distant courtesy and came to meet her. His head canted at a weird angle as if the neck had been broken and badly set. A small leather bag hung around his throat and chinked dully with his movement: seemed an odd place for a cabdriver to carry change.

"Come in. Warm yourself if you can."

"I saw your cab out front. Thought maybe you could drive me out of here."

"There is no out." Jake looked right through her, clearly disinterested. "Where would you like to go?"

"Somewhere," she guessed with her small knowledge of Below Stairs. "Just I don't have any money. I'll have to owe you."

"Don't worry about that. Come by the fire."

She spread her hands to the pale flame that she could barely feel. "What are you burning?"

"Old vanities, dry regrets," Jake told her. "They

don't throw much heat. *Shalom*, Miss Stovall. Have a chair."

"Do we know each other?"

"New arrivals: the news gets around. We don't recruit as many as you'd think. It's still a small town. You came with Roy Stride. He was my last fare."

"Roy?" She twisted to him in her deep chair. "How is he? Where is he?"

"Doing quite well," Jake reported. "Stiffed me for the tip."

"Take me to Roy, please. Can you?"

Jake nodded. "Anywhere you want. I'd imagine there's a great deal you want, Charity." He ranged about the large room, turning up lamps here and there. "You haven't changed for hundreds of years, and your sins, such as they are, have not grown in complexity. A moment of yes in a lifetime of thou shalt not. Certain punishment out of a steaming Protestant imagination." He laughed as at an old, familiar joke. "Not that Catholics lack melodrama. In the thirteenth century, they imagined me hanging feet downward from Satan's mouth. Next to Brutus."

"Who?"

"A man with similar questions, similarly resolved."

Nobody in this whole damn place can talk straight, Charity thought restlessly. She couldn't understand a word of Jake although he had his own fascination, quieter—thank goodness—than Dane, who had been exciting as could be, but he could wear you out. Now, Jake was . . . definitely good-looking, even a hunk by back-home standards; not so much the looks but the manner and voice. He reminded Charity of James Mason on the Late Show. Hell might be a strain, she concluded, but you couldn't beat it for the new and different or the interesting men. Not that Jake put himself out to be polite. She wondered if folks were this hard to talk to in heaven.

"Sure is quiet here."

"You object to that?"

"No, no, it's a nice change."

"One can think," Jake mused over the chessboard. "If thought is desirable. For me it was a curse, an obsession, like chess. Always the intellectual yearning to be the man of action. To be, like Brutus, a fulcrum of history. That was denied me until one day when I—acted. I'll never know whether I was right at the wrong time for my own sake or wrong at the right time for the sake of history."

Well, how does a person answer something like that? "Gee, I got good marks in history, but . . ."

"I wouldn't expect you to understand."

His quiet bitterness shriveled Charity. He could be a nice man if he let himself; what would that cost him? This was no way for a man to live, all alone in the dark, even visitors kept at a distance. Dane made her feel woman enough to be a fire hazard, but this Jake, it was like she was wallpaper or something. Not natural. The worst thing in the world, even in hell, was being alone. He didn't notice her. He irritated the living Jesus out of her.

"You don't have to be so mean about it."

Jake waved it away. "Nothing personal. History's full of sinkholes. Today's moral bedrock is tomorrow's quicksand."

He *really* ticked her off, partly for what she couldn't understand, mostly for what she could. Real men like Roy or Clint Eastwood didn't talk so wimpy. "When it comes to morals, right is right and wrong—"

"Is debatable. Don't argue morality or guilt with a Jew. We invented them."

"You don't look Jewish."

"My God, she said it!" Jake's laughter was a dry, wondering bark that had no warmth in it. "She actually said it. You must have been an evangelical."

"Tabernacle of the Born Again Savior," Charity

owned with wistful pride. "Not that it helped a whole lot."

"Indeed." Jake sank again in his chair. "Tabernacle of the . . . the more shriveled the existence, the more elaborate the credentials. Virtue measured by what you wouldn't do, at least under scrutiny, and others judged for what they would and got caught at. You don't want Grace, Miss Stovall. You want to get even."

She didn't get that at all. "Get even with what?"

"I'll show you." Jake touched a button on the arm of his chair. Across the room a four-foot screen jumped to life in ravishing color subtly enhanced by soft music.

"This is the ultimate," a deep male voice oozed from the screen. "This is Ultimate Rise. What you've worked for and deserve, and it's waiting for you."

The camera moved over stunning vistas of sunken living rooms in luxurious cream leather, each casual furniture piece worth a fortune. Bedrooms of imperial opulence, kitchens that inspired domesticity and did all the work, cozy dens, conversation pits cunningly designed around fieldstone fireplaces, bathrooms of unbridled hedonism with heart-shaped tubs and frothing Jacuzzis. Charity ogled.

"Where's that? They don't have that in Pittsburgh even."

"I'd say not," Jake remarked with a sideways glance. "I'll bet you never missed *Dynasty* or *Knots Landing.*"

"Course not. I even wrote a letter to Alexis telling her what a slut she is."

"But such a rich slut, eh? All that scheming and immorality in the middle of all that wealth. The painful fascination of pressing your cold little nose against the windowpane and deciding that rich is nasty, virtue is just plain folks and the American Way. The envy of the have-nots: Alexis will get what's coming to her, evil will be punished. And you sure as hell want yours. Religion is what you sing on Sunday, Miss Stovall. Your true faith is what you want all week."

"Hey, you make me sick, you know that?" Charity flared, surging out of the chair. "What do you know how hard it is to get anything nice? There was a factory in Plattsville, now there's nothing. Just a mis'rable piddly little town full of people that have to stand outside—that's true, that much, what you said—stand outside looking in at folks no better than us taking the best while we get the leavings.

"What do you know about living on welfare checks or credit run out at the store? Huh? I grew up with not enough; with stepparents because my own was . . . were a couple of God knows what from God knows where. You try that, Jake: nothing to call your own and nowhere to go but down or dead. You watch all the pretty, silky commercials like this one about all the nice things you can buy with the money you'll never have. You try that—"

"Admirable," Jake acknowledged. "At least you've learned to state the problem."

"Don't you laugh at me," Charity seethed. "Don't you laugh at us. All we got in Plattsville, all the rest of you goddamnit *left* us is the kind of God and Jesus Christ we can understand. Look at me! Forget this bull-shit movie dress that'd take me six months to buy if I didn't eat or pay rent. Do I look fat? Like I never missed a meal or a trip to the dentist? Last one we had moved out three years ago, couldn't make a living. You get a toothache now, you gotta drive twenty miles. If the car will make it.

"Your kinda people laugh at us for crying in church when we feel like crying all the time. Why shouldn't we want a Jesus with sword and fire? If He's got no sword and fire when He comes, by God, we'll give Him ours. We got lots of that."

"And anger. Envy. Getting even."

He seemed to be goading her. With nothing at

hand to throw at him, Charity threw the truth. "Damn right we want to get even. *Everyone else does.*"

Until she heard it, Charity never guessed such a rage lived in her, that rush of deep emotion always prayed and sung out of her in the Tabernacle, cleansed and released until the need built up again. She always thought it was the Holy Spirit. More frightening than that, but damn right she wanted hers. Why not?

Jake moved another piece on the chessboard, considered the consequences, then rose and took his cabby hat from the mantel.

"You sound ready to get some of yours."

"I sure am." Charity clawed at her hair gone frizzy and hopeless from damp. "Between Dane and his poetry and you, gimme a break. I want to find Roy."

Jake escorted her down the hall to the entrance. "No fear, he's doing very well. The Paladins pounced on him the minute he arrived. No different here than on earth. Messiahs are a weekly special."

"Oh. Where can I find him?"

Jake gave her a searching glance. "Why not let him find you? Ultimate Rise just happens to have a vacancy, and I'd say you're entitled to the good life for a change."

Charity remembered that sinful bathtub and the acre-wide living room and was tempted. "Maybe for a little. Just to rest."

"You'll love it," Jake promised. "Fully automatic, live-in butlers, magnificent view. On a clear day you can see Robin Leach. I wouldn't be surprised if they didn't expect you. What's the matter, woman? I'm tempting you to a freebie paradise and you look positively ill."

She did feel sick, cold with a winter thought. "Gollee. Jake. All that stuff I said . . ."

"All quite true."

Was that what all my praying was about? "Lord Amighty, no wonder I'm damned."

"No, Miss Stovall. Love and hell are alike in that respect; they are what you bring to them. The script is

125

yours; only the props are furnished." Another keen scrutiny. "And growing always hurts."

Damn, Charity yearned as Jake's cab whisked her away. *Doesn't anybody around here talk straight?*

Drained, quivering with the release of emotion. Not even Roy would guess there was so much mean in her. Or maybe he did.

Was that what got us together, each wanting to get even any way we can and seeing the same thing in the other?.

"The weather's better in the high-rise district," Jake tossed over his shoulder as they drove through clammy fog.

"That's nice." Charity sat back with her own thoughts. Strange thoughts with a disturbing familiarity, like ugly cousins met for the first time who resembled her too closely for comfort.

■ 18 ■

This can't be hell, the plumbing works

From the taxi window, Charity goggled up at the splendor of Ultimate Rise. "Now, that is class!"

"As advertised." Jake handed his card over the seat. "Anytime you need a cab."

"I sure will, thanks. You're nice when you don't talk so weird." When Jake came around to open her door, Charity noted the pallor of his face and neck. "You ought to get out more, Jake. Be with folks."

"I've been there."

"It's kind of embarrassing. I can't pay you. Not even a tip."

"On the house. Your new condo, Miss Stovall. Corrupt yourself in good health." Jake slid into the front seat, meshed gears and drove away.

A uniformed doorman spun the revolving doors at just the right speed to receive her smoothly. Across an opulent lobby large as a parking lot, a tailored, obsequious desk clerk held out her keys. "Your duplex, Miss Stovall. Elevators to your right. Welcome to Ultimate Rise."

The elevator whispered open, wafting light, breezy

music to her ears from an old Audrey Hepburn movie. A cool voice inquired: "Floor, please?"

"Uh. Floor." Charity always flustered when singled out for a decision. "I don't know. Do I press a button or something?"

The elevator voice had the sepulchral hush of an undertaker's receptionist. "Floor, please?"

"I don't know," Charity implored the upholstered walls. "What do I do with an elevator that talks?"

"What do I do with a human who can't?" The retort held a nuance of electronic bitchery. "I'm just a machine. Now, at least. I used to be a high-fashion model. Died of drugs, but I did have lovely cheekbones. Name, please?"

"Charity Mae Stovall. From Plattsville."

"Finally. Penthouse duplex," the elevator confirmed. "Going up."

The music breezed and sparkled as the doors swept open on paradise. Charity gasped.

Definitely nothing like it even in Pittsburgh. A white apartment, everything perfect. The parquet foyer led down three steps to a sunken living room wall-to-walled in white carpet. Gleaming chrome-and-glass coffee table topped with oversized art books left at just the right angle. Cream the walls, ivory the grand piano, gossamer the powered silk drapes that slid noiselessly aside to reveal a spacious balcony and, beyond, a breathtaking panorama of fashionable Below Stairs.

"I'm rich." She said it again as the truth sank home. "I'm RICH. Just like in the movies. WOWIE!"

Charity skipped from one vast room to another, wonder treading on wonder's heel. Downstairs alone was big as two houses together. Living room, guest rooms, extra baths, kitchen, pantry, a whole freezer room, more rooms just for the hell of it.

"GOOOINNG UP!" Hiking the velvet skirt, Charity took the spiral designer stairs two at a time to the master bedroom with its emperor-sized water bed covered with an eiderdown and CMS-monogrammed silk sheets in powder blue. The master bath was done in pink.

Charity wallowed and rolled on the water bed like a contented puppy. The quilt hissed gorgeously as it slid against her skin. She paraded in front of the huge mirror and decided that gray velvet looked kind of tacky here, and then yipped with new delight to discover a full dressing room with three full racks of dreamy clothes, all in her size. Charity stepped out of the movie dress into nylon underwear and a soft linen caftan. Mirrored results were edifying. Feeling audacious, she wondered if she could get away without a bra—but no, that was for the liberated city women she disapproved of on principle.

"On second thought, why the hell not?"

Charity hiked up the caftan, popped the bra and let it drop on the carpet. She wasn't a feminist, but the Devil had already liberated the hell out of her at the White Rose Motel, and this was her house, so she could be comfortable without feeling, you know, trashy or common. Besides, she wasn't big enough to be all that floppy without a bra.

Descending the stairs, she felt exotic in caftan and bare feet. The cream leather sofa invited her; she melted into it before a four-foot television wall screen. The remote control was near her hand; one touch blossomed the screen to life, panning slowly across a snowy and familiar interior. Charity's eyes widened.

"That's this place. Mine, right here."

"That's right, Char."

Even the voice was familiar, a nasal London yelp out of the speakers just as she remembered from *Lifestyles of the Rich and Famous.* "This gowerjus condo in the carefully secluded and mowst expensive paht of Below Stairs is the hideaway of glamorous Char Stovall."

She giggled. "You better believe it."

"Char has been the constant companion of Roy Stride, rising young political leaduh."

Gol-lee, where was Roy now? Well, she thought, he won't be hard to find. If he's no worse off than me, he sure ain't hurting.

The screen blushed pink as the picture segued to the lush bathroom with its foaming Jacuzzi. "And it's here," the voice-over brayed enthusiastically, "that Char lives with her new love interest, Randy Colorad."

"Hey. Who?"

"—her every wish fulfilled by her houseman, Simnel."

Charity hugged her knees, wide-eyed. All too much, but *fun*. The camera cut to a beige kitchen where a mild, pudgy little man in livery busied himself twirling a bottle down into an ice bucket. "Wonder what heaven's like."

"Miss Stovall?"

Simnel hovered just behind her, holding a tray with champagne and several small but interesting plates of the stuff called "ordooves." Charity flicked off the TV as he set the tray on the coffee table. "Mr. Colorad called earlier, mum. He should be here directly."

There was a curious blob of something dark on one plate. "What's this?"

"Caviar, mum."

"Oh. Sure. Come to think of it, I ain't had a bite since I got here. Dane said we don't get hungry."

"No, mum," Simnel said pleasantly. "It's one of the advantages. However, you may indulge if you care to. I also took the liberty of chilling an excellent year." He poured the champagne into a tall, shallow glass. "Moët, '76. Shall I prepare the Jacuzzi?"

The champagne tingled delightfully in mouth and nose. *So that's what it tastes like.* And Simnel looked like every butler she ever saw in old Fred Astaire movies. "Yes, indeedy. You may do that thing." Charity flicked the television on again, unable to get enough of it. "Gol-lee."

Simnel watched her with discreet amusement. "Jacob was right."

Another gulp of Moët. "Say what?"

"This is your real religion."

"I don't want to go into that again."

"Excuse me, mum. Merely by way of orientation. Your real religion is what you really want. I'll ready your bath, mum."

He sounded like a stuck-up Englishman or something. She ought to get rid of him and find a good nigger maid that knew how to keep her place.

The champagne made her tingle with well-being. She ordered Simnel to bring the ice bucket and caviar to the bathroom, then trailed upstairs to watch the Jacuzzi churn in readiness for her. Charity slithered out of the caftan and lowered herself bit by luxurious bit into the foaming bath.

"Oh, God, if I wasn't already dead, I could DIE."

The bathroom had its own thirty-inch screen with remote control. Charity swallowed more champagne to wash down the caviar—which she didn't like all that much but it came with the place—and pressed the TV on switch.

There she was, herself, in salmon-pink lounge pajamas, sexy enough to ruin someone's life, right there on TV.

"Oh, man, I look like red-hot Saturday night."

She gulped more Moët and thrilled to her own image on the tube: half reclining on the white leather sofa, one knee drawn up, winsome with a blue teddy bear hugged to her breast.

"The trooly mahvelous thing about Char Stovall," the narrator yelped, "is how she's never forgotten her roots or the people that raised her."

"But I'd sure love to," Charity talked back. "Who the hell wants to remember Plattsville?"

She felt defiant, daring and just a little drunk.

"Here in this fabulous but secret five-million-dollah condo, Char Stovall works constantly to better the lot of the humble folk she comes from. A simple, poignant story, an American rags-to-riches tale of an orphan gel active in the little church in her hometown."

Gorgeous color faded to grainy home-movie black and white with sepia hints of aging: Charity at ten with her adoptive parents, all waving at the camera and looking uncomfortable. Then a shot of Roy sitting with studied nonchalance on the hood of his car, rifle in hand. Woody playing with another local musician—

I really liked you, Woody Barnes, know that? You didn't ask me to be anything but me and I could always sort of take my shoes off with you. One mistake, Woody. One. Am I still a nice girl?

She took larger gulps of champagne, guzzling it like her usual diet cola. Combined with the hot Jacuzzi, the effect relaxed her, made her quickly drunk and not a little maudlin. She wept incoherently over Woody, Roy, herself and the pathetic sight of ten-year-old Charity in a greasy potato-sack shift.

Then realized: "I never wore anything like that."

"Yes, yew did, Char," the narrator prompted. "It goes with the American Dream."

Cut back to silken Char on her divan, cuddling her teddy bear, a close-up that caught all the honesty and wistfulness of her thoroughly American face. "Until I was ten," the screen Char spoke to someone off camera, "I never had any clothes that weren't hand-me-downs. So now I want to write my story as an inspiration for other people and to show that the American Dream is real. Somehow, any way I can, dead or not, I want to go back and help my people."

"You kiss my ass," Charity blurted, dropping her glass in the bath. "I ain't never going back there, never! Damn dead town where there wasn't anything to do but work and pray and pay and get kids."

"Char is a *deeply* religious gel," the voice-over nasaled. "She led the prowtest against the Planned Parenthood clinic ten miles from Plattsville."

"Sure I did." Charity found her glass, rinsed and refilled it. "And I wish I didn't. My best friend got pregnant first time with a boy. What kind of lies you telling?"

"Why, Char," the narrative voice protested, "the truths you've always lived by."

"That ain't the way it was, no way."

Not even close to truth. Bea got pregnant and scared, and the first thing her father did was beat hell out of her because Bea's mother made him. Liars! Charity raged. You goddamn phonies, you weren't thinking of Bea, just how it would look with the neighbors. So Bea married Roland, and when I saw her after, it was like more than the baby got taken out of her. She shouldn't've had that baby, but there wasn't any more clinic even if she could've gone. After all that protest and screaming we did, Roy and the Paladins bombed it in the name of White American motherhood or something. I think Roy did it to impress me.

"Char Stovall, this is your faith. Brought to you by Slick Shave, the blade that starts your day—"

"And can damn well end it any ol' time you get sick of the stupid game." Charity switched off the set in disgust and reached for the white Princess phone.

"Simnel, that you? Listen, how do I get outside? I want to call a friend."

"Sorry, mum. The entire phone system is out for the whole building. We have intercom but nothing outside."

"Oh, fine."

"And Mr. Colorad just arrived. He'll be up in a minute."

Was up already, smiling at her from the bathroom door. "Hi-i, gorgeous."

Charity gazed with bleary appreciation at the muscular young man who stood before her stripping down

133

to a pair of immaculate white briefs. "Hi," she breathed. "I bet your underwear don't even get dirty."

"Not the kind I wear." Randy Colorad winked from the mirror, lathering himself.

"Y'know, Jake's right," Charity mumbled, sinking to her chin in the whirlpool. " 'S my religion. I want. Wanted all my life. That's a main occupation back home. Right, right, right. First offender: think I'd get off with probation, but no-o-o. To hell with *you*, Stovall! And there's Dane with all that fog and poetry and then Jake who jus' sits around feeling sorry for hisself. What the hell's he got to be sorry about?" She smiled foggily at Randy, her mood shifting softly. Talk about ruining somebody's life; he looked like he might enjoy it. "You're a real hunk, y'know that?"

"It's easy with my Slick Shave." Randy flashed thirty-two blinding teeth at her. "I'm smooth all the time."

"C'mon in here and prove it. What the hell, I'm just what the man said. A simple down-home girl living the American Dream."

"Love to." Randy slipped out of his briefs and into the whirlpool. Charity snuggled up to him.

"Already been damned," she murmured woozily, "and I got change coming."

■ 19 ■

Money can't buy happiness, but why not be miserable in comfort?

Charity opened her eyes to sunlight and strange sounds. Feeling delicious, she yawned and squirmed contentedly between the blue silk sheets. Hell could be a lot worse.

A series of grunts issued from an angle of the bedroom beyond her vision. She turned over to see Randy Colorad laboring with a Nautilus weight machine like a guillotine, muscles rippling, glistening with sweat.

"Twenty-three—*huh*. Twenty-four—*agh*. Twenty-*fi-i-ve*—URKK!"

"For God's sake, you'll rupture something!"

"When the going gets tough . . ." A last herculean effort. Randy lowered the weights and sat up, favoring Charity with a charming smile, no tooth uncapped. He sprang up, beautiful above the neck and all a girl could wish below. "Now for that morning shower that gives all-day protection."

Charity draped herself on one elbow, feeling sultry. "Hurry back."

Randy came out of the shower carrying a spray

135

deodorant. "Here." He slipped under the sheets. "It's strong enough for me but made for you."

"So are you." Charity attacked him joyfully.

The ensuing two hours demonstrated that she really ought to work out more herself. In the bookstore back home, voyeuristic peeks into *The Joy of Sex* (when nobody was looking) dazzled her with possibilities that seemed languorous only in theory. In practice they required a certain facility and a great deal of limberness. Silk sheets were great to dream about but always slidey when you needed four-wheel traction, and the damn water mattress made her almost seasick, zigging when it should zag. Nevertheless, her climaxes were symphonic. She never thought she was that kind of girl; now she knew there wasn't any other.

In the brief respites between onslaughts, by way of critique Charity could wish now and then for the poetry that turned Dane's passion tender (God, he could suffer!) and even once, in an athletic moment, for the pungent honesty of Jake. She closed her eyes over Randy's shoulder and thought of him. That helped her get there, but it was Woody's face she saw at the end. That was strange; she felt treacherous and terribly fallen. Anyway, Randy never said anything she hadn't heard on TV before.

When she was gasping with surfeit and yearning seriously for a little rest, Randy bounced out of bed with the same energy that propelled him into it.

"Hey, kid." The white smile flashed like a bathroom light at 4 A.M. "Gotta go to work. Got a shoot later."

Charity picked up on that much from TV. "You in a movie?"

"No." Randy flexed his shoulders and trotted into the bathroom. "Gotta shoot someone. But first—that all-day protection again with a man's kind of soap."

"You just took a shower."

"Yeah, but then we screwed for a while."

"Don't talk dirty. All that washing's not good for your skin."

From the depths of the thundering shower: "I'm Beautiful People!"

"Yeah, but are you gonna itch." Charity yawned. "Idiot."

With the detachment of a definitely slaked thirst, she watched with decreasing interest as Randy trotted out of the bathroom in pale blue one-piece underwear, slipped into slacks and a Members Only jacket and placed his Foster Grants with the care of a coronation. Again the measured, roguish grin. "See you later."

"Sure. It was real nice."

"That's what friends are for." Another devilish grin and Randy was gone. Charity drowsed a while before plumping the pillows to sit up against. She touched the call button, only to find Simnel in the doorway.

"You rang, mum?"

"Breakfast would be nice. Not that I'm hungry but, you know, a change. Oh, how about the phone?"

"Still out, I'm afraid. They are working on it."

"Honest to Pete, you'd think once a girl dies she wouldn't have to hassle stuff like this."

"No, mum. The upwardly mobile concept is a Christian notion. We have our problems." The mild little butler withdrew.

"Even dead the phone company gets you." Charity turned on the wall TV, quickly adjusting the volume as the fifty-inch screen roared to furious life across the bedroom.

"—can feel that these are indeed the last days of a dying regime. Here in the teeming downtown streets, a drama is being enacted, one that may be fraught with significance for Below Stairs tomorrow—indeed, may be that tomorrow."

Music up with telegraphic urgency as the news continued with voice-over. A street, soldiers in White

Paladin fatigues and swastika armbands straining to hold back the screaming crowds.

"We're here in the main thoroughfare, which you can see is packed with the largest crowd since the arrival of Lord Byron. In a moment—yes, here they come! —in a moment we'll see the massed demonstration and its dynamic new leader, Roy Stride. This demonstration follows by less than twenty-four hours the threat of a raid on black and Jewish homes by Paladin squads. The government's failure to make any effective answer to this threat may be seen as a death rattle. There's our camera truck."

The open truck came into shot and passed beyond; as it did, the view on Charity's set cut to a dolly from the truck itself. She sat bolt upright. "Hey-y."

There was Roy striding along in precise step with the ranks of Paladins behind him, head high, confident and flushed, the star of his own drama at last.

"Roy!" Charity bounced up and down with delight. "Roy!"

ROY! STRIDE! ROY! STRIDE! ROY! STRIDE!

". . . and here he comes. Roy Stride, the youngest political contender in the long history of Below Stairs. An American from the Heartland, the first candidate to be endorsed by the Prince and Topside alike. Even as we speak, the messengers from Topside are said to be on their way with formal ratification."

"Gol-lee, Roy." Charity melted back on her pillow. "Even angels. Oh, wow!"

"We're trying to reach Judas Iscariot for comment," the telereporter informed her. "The most reclusive of all Below Stairs citizens, Judas has always been distrusted by the popular vote, particularly the Christian Identity groups and the Paladins, who consider him a dangerous adversary. Certainly he has never allied himself with any party."

"Well, he shouldn't." Charity put the TV on hold as Simnel entered with a bed tray bearing champagne, coffee, strawberries and whipped cream, setting it across her with a flourish.

"Strawberry Decadence, mum. One of my specialties."

"Super." Charity dipped a plump berry in the mound of whipped cream and munched it. "Mmm . . . Do you know Judas?"

"Quite well," Simnel said.

"No, I mean the man who—"

"I'm familiar with the case." Simnel poured her coffee. "Very good company, Judas. Sharp mind. Mean chess player."

Charity frowned over her coffee. "You could like a person like that?"

"One man's meat, you know. There are celebrities I avoid out of self-preservation. Beethoven, for example. The personality of a chain saw. Yes, I like Judas for an evening's chat now and then. When he condescends. Not very gregarious."

Charity turned on the TV again. The same reporter had just poked his microphone in the face of a clearly disinterested man leaning against a car door, cigarette dangling from lips curled with an ancient, bitter joke. As the camera went to close-up, Charity choked on a swallow of champagne.

"That's Jake," she wheezed after a coughing spasm. "I know that guy. Honest, he drove me here in his cab."

"Best service in town," said the imperturbable Simnel. "More coffee, mum?"

"We're here with Judas Iscariot on the fringe of the delirious demonstration for Roy Stride. Judas, can you comment on the meteoric rise of Stride and the White Paladins?"

Judas reached through the cab window and fetched his cap. "I'd say the hopeless shmucks have found the kind of government they deserve. Always do."

The reporter pressed for more. "And his rapid rise?"

"So *nu?*" Judas shrugged. "He's taking their own fear, frustration and anger and selling it back to them with a new ribbon around it. Easy answers, easy targets: out with the Jews and blacks, down with the intellectuals, which means anyone who's better off or disagrees with them. Slogans, marching bands and the promise of blood. How can he miss?" Judas flicked away his cigarette and opened the cab door. "Buzz off, I've got a call."

Still the reporter persisted. "Could your views be construed as a class-oriented remark?"

"Look, these clowns need a messiah because the truth of the world always goes down easier with a few miracles and a lot of blood. It's a very old game, the rules don't change. I'd say Stride is a flaming, fourteen-karat folk hero. Look at this crowd; you're not talking about contented, mature people. You ever see a happy man who needed to conquer the world?"

Judas/Jake got into the cab and drove out of shot.

"So that's the evilest man in the whole world ever." Charity pondered the screen. She dunked a strawberry in champagne. "Talks mean about folks."

"With considerable authority," Simnel said. "A true believer at one time who would do anything to make need into truth. Now he watches the rest of them doing the same thing over and over again one way or another."

"He talked like he was real angry, only just at himself, you know? Funny"—Charity considered it—"I couldn't hate Jake."

Charity missed Simnel's approving glance. "No, mum. He does that for himself."

"Well, I'm real happy for Roy. I guess. This is a neat breakfast. Can you make eggs like McDonald's?"

"There is no such franchise here yet," Simnel informed her coolly. "Though I'm sure Mr. Stride will insist on one. As Judas remarked, a ray of hope to the benighted. Good morning, mum."

■ 20 ■

The late, late show

Charity woke in the dark. Randy wasn't beside her in the bed; that didn't bother her at all. Outside of sex, he wasn't much company. Everything he said sounded like a commercial.

Just . . . she felt creepy and more alone than she ever had since dying. She rang Simnel and heard only the quiet intermittent buzz. Randy gone, Simnel out. She was alone and couldn't sleep. She tried the outside phone: nothing, still out of order. From habit, she reached for the TV remote and turned on the wall set.

The screen sprayed garish color and flickering shadows over the dark bedroom, resolving to a night scene with a telereporter's voice-over—

"—just an hour ago the peace of these black and Jewish homes in a quiet neighborhood of Below Stairs was shattered by devastating White Paladin raids led personally by Roy Stride, new head of the Paladin party."

Cut to Roy himself standing in an open car, leather-coated, whip in hand, black peaked cap perched at a cocky angle, and—

Cut to a black family being dragged from their front door by huge Paladin guards. Husband, wife, three children being hustled ungently toward a waiting van. When the father broke away and resisted, one guard simply shot him. The action was brutally graphic: two guards slammed the man up against the van and a third opened fire with a submachine gun. The gunfire went on and on, his body disintegrating in sharp detail and color.

"No . . ." Charity recoiled from the scene, tried to change channels. They were all the same but someone was playing tricks with the camera. The black man fell and fell with his head coming apart—and then Roy again, standing in the open car. He turned to Charity as the camera came in close, and looked directly at her, found her, his mouth twisted in a smirk of macho triumph and pride.

"Hey, Charity, that you? Where are you? Look: I told you how it would be."

And once more the scene cut to another home, smoke and flame spurting from a shattered window, Paladins sprinting out of the front door. A man and woman lay crumpled on the front steps. The camera zoomed in on them. It looked to Charity as if someone had cut every artery in their bodies. *You wouldn't think there was that much blood in just two bodies.*

"The general feeling in the political air," the telereporter's voice-over went on dispassionately, "is that these raids have the tacit assent of the White Christian populace."

"Who said?" Charity blurted. "*I* didn't."

"—certainly no government troops or police have made any move to intervene, as though quietly allowing political force of gravity to take its course. This act is seen by some as a definite referendum. It is increasingly clear that the confidence of Below Stairs at large is with Roy Stride's party rather than the Wembley administration."

Only half listening, Charity couldn't take her eyes

from the bodies. *Dummies,* she thought. *They look like doll-dummies sprayed with red paint.*

"Charity!"

Roy again in huge close-up with that twisted grin. "Where are you? I told you how it would be."

"NO!"

She jabbed desperately at the remote control but each channel was the same, not even a lag in the film.

"Simnel-l!"

"—how it would be."

Charity screamed silently at the vicious grin on the screen. *No, I didn't believe you. I didn't believe it would be like this—*

—as the camera caught a little girl darting around the corner of the house, shrieking in terror. She turned to see the Paladin guard trotting after her, not even hurrying. The child ran blindly to the natural place, the bleeding sack of offal that had been her mother, screaming for help.

"My God," Charity writhed. "Don't hurt her. She's just a baby. Don't."

The Paladin guard loomed over the tiny child as the camera came in tight on them—

"These Jewish homes were the first target," the voice-over stated with no emotional color. "The black homes were hit a few minutes later in an apparently coordinated attack."

Something was happening to the film. Somehow it went to slow motion as it focused tight on the face of the blond, blue-eyed child. Hypnotized with horror, Charity let the irrelevant thought skitter through her mind —*I didn't think Jews could be blond.* But they could; she'd seen plenty that weren't anywhere near the picture conjured up when somebody said Jew. She'd just never connected images, never thought beyond the stock picture. This little girl was very fair and—

Very familiar. More than familiar.

"Jesus, that's—"

The child was *her* at age ten. She remembered the picture her new parents took when they adopted her, before her hair darkened to brown. But undeniably her in the picture, screaming for help from her dead mother.

And then not screaming at all.

The child looked up at the guard, mute. The only sound came from Charity herself, a wordless whine of empathic terror as the Paladin pointed his pistol at the tiny face. Her own child face but changed forever. More than horror in those wide eyes, a terrible knowledge that there was no help anywhere, no pity or escape. For those few slow-motion seconds, the child was not mad but her eyes knew madness, swallowed it whole and recognized it as the truth of existence. Knew it as her head disintegrated and spattered blood and brains over the twisted flesh bag of her mother, and—

Charity wanted to be sick and couldn't. You couldn't be sick after death, but the nausea rolled through her stomach, all the more exquisite torture since she couldn't even retch with it. She fled the bedroom to splash her face with cold water, but the bathroom screen was on as well—the same film repeating and repeating—Roy standing in the car, the camera zooming in on that dirty, mean grin of his that she hated —*always hated it. Why didn't I ever realize then?*

"—are you? Look! I told you how it would be."

For the first time in her life, Charity Stovall snarled. "You get away from me. YOU GET AWAY FROM ME, YOU . . . SIM-NEL-L-L—"

She ran out of the bathroom and stumbled downstairs. As she hit the bottom step, all the screens went on —kitchen, living room, guest rooms; a repeating loop, the child running to the butchered sack of her mother, screaming in slow motion, then not screaming but looking up with Charity's own eyes at the pistol barrel with that obscene knowledge in her eyes.

"—told you how it would be."

"Stop. *Stop,* you son of a bitch."

"—how it would be."

Her instinct was to bury herself deep in the pillows of the sofa, blot out the sight and sound, but as the loop repeated, shorter and shorter now—Roy's leer, the words, her own eyes staring not at death but a sudden understanding of life—something else began to counterbalance the horror in Charity Stovall. The fruitless nausea passed, replaced by a wholly alien emotion more powerful than she'd ever felt. Detached, from a long distance, she turned her gaze back to the screen, to Roy's gloating face and swaggering words, and the nightmare of her own violent child death.

That's me could be me is me . . .

"—told you how it would be."

Yes, you did, she thought, watching the screen from the depths of an icy calm. You sure as hell did, and I heard it and didn't think about it.

Faster and faster the loop ran: Charity at ten, screaming, then no voice left to scream, only her own eyes lifting to the gun, knowing what a child shouldn't have to know but so many did and had and would.

"—told you how it would be."

Scream. Silence. Look up. Knowing.

Until at last the film froze on the eyes and their final recognition of horror. The child, with one second, one century or an infinity to exist, would never again look on anything or anyone unshadowed by that terrible knowledge.

Obscene . . . I never used that word, always thought it meant dirty movies. But this is obscene. I could scream from now until the end of time, every dirty word I ever knew, they wouldn't be as obscene or dirty as this. Not that you kill a child, but that you could put such a knowledge into her.

Now she knew the passion churning in her: rage—not from any wound to her but simply that humans could do that to children, take the brief innocence and stain it forever with the knowledge that there was no safe place anywhere ever. Forever or for a few seconds, children shouldn't know that much about the world.

The gun didn't kill her. She was dead when she looked up at him. Like some old people in Plattsville who came from Europe after we beat Germany. You could see that shadow of a gun barrel all their lives.

No music, love or joy would leach that shadow from the little girl's eyes.

"—told you how it would be."

"Damn straight you told me," Charity lashed back. "You murdering piece of shit, I should've seen you coming. But I'm glad, Roy. Glad I'm dead; that's cleaner than being alive with you. You better hope you never meet up with Jesus. He's sure as hell not gonna like the way you use His name. I'm afraid of you, Roy. And I think you like that."

Trembling, near-traumatized by the force of her own rage, Charity didn't notice Simnel switching off the set or the silence that followed.

"Can't sleep, mum?"

"Where were you?" Charity mumbled in a voice with no life in it. "I called and called but you weren't here."

"Sometimes I go for a walk in the wee hours."

"Do you know what I just saw?"

"The purges? Yes, I was there. You can see the fires burning from the balcony."

"No, Simnel. I don't want to."

"The government conveniently did nothing to stop them. No one did."

"No one?" Charity whispered, still trembling. "Not one person? Did you see what they were doing?"

"Yes, of course," said mild little Simnel. "I expect things will change at Congress Hall. The government won't last. Not to worry; none of this will touch us in Ultimate Rise. Shall I fix some hot cocoa, mum?"

"It's already touched me," Charity muttered. "I feel dirty just watching that."

"The postmoderns would call you sentimental," Simnel observed. "Trying to encompass inhuman behavior with human sensibility."

"Dirty . . . They ain't fixed the phones yet?"

"No, mum."

That was good, that gave her time to think. "Simnel, I don't live here. Just like before, you never heard of me."

"Charity who?"

"Right. Good night, Simnel."

"Good morning, mum."

Charity tried to climb the stairs. All of sudden there were too many of them. "Oh, Simmy—Jesus!" She slumped down on the steps. "Even . . . even dead, how can they do this to people? To children?"

She felt a hundred years old, too utterly spent to climb the rest of the stairs. Like a child herself, she allowed Simnel to guide her upward, his wise, gentle voice close to her ear though she didn't understand any of what he was telling her. Something about a tiny animal who developed in the dark while bigger animals ruled the day. A funny little thing with big eyes and fur and fear, born looking over its shoulder for danger, and out of this twitching bundle of need and terror came humans never to be wholly free of the dark or their own nightmares.

When Simnel tucked her in like a tender parent, Charity saw a wisdom in his eyes older than mountains, and a pity beyond tears.

■ 21 ■

Doing the Reichstag rag

The Case White takeover had been accomplished without a shot fired. Roy might have relished at least a little shooting after his bold blood-purge raids, but the Wembley wimps gave in to the will of the people. That will was a steady roar as Roy's armored Cadillac inched through the Paladin-lined streets toward Government Square and drew up before the marble steps of Congress Hall. The armored car carrying his personal guard slowed in his wake.

"We're the fuckin Congress now," Roy smirked to Drumm beside him. "Gonna be some changes."

"Don't lean out too far," Drumm cautioned. "There's a possibility of snipers."

"Hey, yeah." Roy ducked back inside. They waited until the police and hulking Paladin security guards shouldered and heaved the screaming crowd back from the cars to clear a path up the steps.

"Okay, let's go." Roy stepped out of the car and stood a moment as the crowd caught sight of him and loosed a roar of delirious excitement.

Roy! Stride! Roy! Stride!

He basked in the sound like sunlight after long winter. It warmed and sufficed him. All they had to do

was follow his word and Below Stairs would be their
kind of paradise. A new order, rough on some, but you
couldn't fry eggs without breaking shells, he thought in
a flush of originality. Impulsively, Roy flung up his right
hand with the whip. The screaming cut like edited tape.
The crowd hovered, quivering, for his words.

"We been down! Going UP!"

The mob roared like maddened animals. GOING
UP!

"Damn right," Roy muttered to Drumm as they
mounted the steps inside a cordon of armed Paladins.
"They waiting for us?"

"Shaking in their boots," Drumm assured him.
"Ready to agree to anything."

Looked that way: the guards at the door stood to
nervous attention when Roy passed. They were point-
edly unarmed and looked anxious to leave. Roy's entou-
rage commandeered two elevators to the executive
floor, alighted and formed again, the guards flanking
Roy and Drumm. Roy took a moment to straighten his
tunic and hat, tug at the holstered Lüger. "Let's go.
Short and sweet."

Their jackboots rang in unison down the marble
hall.

"Here." Drumm halted before open double doors.
Roy felt disappointed; he'd hoped the guards could kick
them in. The first four guards swept into the chamber,
weapons at the ready. One of them nodded to Drumm,
who stood aside for Roy. "After you, my Leader."

Roy stalked into the executive chamber. The
guards' precaution was hardly necessary. A small el-
derly man huddled behind a large, ornate desk, head in
his hands. Next to him stood another man, somewhat
younger and much more vital, quiet defiance flashing in
his eyes. This was the one who might be trouble, Roy
decided. Looked like a smart-ass college boy lieutenant
always used to hard-ass him in the Air Force, always
thought he was better than anybody.

Drumm strutted to the desk, a parody of protocol. "Leader Stride, may I present the former president, Ronald Wembley. And"—a studiedly contemptuous glance at the distinguished man at the president's side —"the former prime minister, Jason Blythe."

"The papers are executed," Wembley began in a haggard voice. "The transfer of power is complete. For the people's sake, I ask—"

"You're in my chair," Roy cut him short. "Move it, Wimpley." A nod to the guards: two of them hauled Wembley out of the leather chair and pushed him to one side.

"What the fuck would you know about the people, Wimp?"

"The president's name is Wembley," Blythe snapped.

Drumm spun on him, vibrant with malice. "You shut your mouth. You had your say a long time, Blythe. From here on, it's ours."

"And what price the Leader's loyal right hand?" Blythe posed the acid question. "His own theater? Perhaps a decent toupee?"

"Hey." Roy pointed at Blythe. "You got something personal against my minister?"

"No more than against the spread of roaches," Blythe retorted. "Mr. Drumm is a former clerk from this office with a habit of opening private mail."

"The right mail at the right time," Drumm admitted with malicious satisfaction. "That's how I learned of your personal vendetta against my plays."

Blythe seemed to find that amusing. "Plays? Ah, yes —*More Stories from the Toilet Zone.* The smaller the man, the larger his power fantasies. Mr. Stride, I would prefer to be liquidated now, if you please."

Roy had to grin at the guy's balls. "What, you crazy?"

"No. Just tasteful."

"Mr. Stride, if I may." Wembley approached tentatively; the guards moved to intervene but Roy waved them away. "I wanted to say for the people that you must be sensitive to their greater needs."

"Cut the shit, Wimp. What do you think I'm doing? Hear them out there? I *am* the people."

"Yes." Beyond the weariness and defeat, Wembley's tone was faintly ironic. "I should like to retire now."

Roy laughed at him. The poor old bastard looked pathetic. "Sure, go ahead."

Drumm drew himself up as far as five foot four could manage and ran the back of one gloved hand across his mouth. "Guard, let the old gentleman go home."

"But not him." Roy jerked a thumb at Blythe. "I don't like his fuckin mouth. Take him to solitary."

Blythe was marched out after Wembley. Drumm held the executive chair for Roy. "Sir?"

Roy went to the chair as a king to coronation, settled in it, spreading his hands over the polished desk top. "That Blythe is a smart-ass. Sit on him."

The small dead oysters behind Drumm's thick glasses registered their closest to pleasure, momentarily less cold. "Done, Leader."

"I'll count on that." Roy couldn't like Drumm, no one really could, but he was loyal to the point of adoration and very efficient. "So you wrote horny plays, huh?"

"I wrote truth. Only leftist liberal hypocrites called them pornographic."

"Yeah, well now you're in the top ten, maybe you can have your own the-ayter."

"Thank you, sir." Drumm clicked his heels. He did it so well that Roy glared around at the guards, who looked too damned casual. "Nobody gave you at ease! Hit it!"

They jerked to rigid attention.

"That's better." Roy lifted his booted feet onto the

desk. "I used to be enlisted myself. Discipline's the backbone of any outfit. When I say jump, you jump. When I say shit, you squat and strain, got it? Okay. At ease. Drumm!"

Click! "Leader?"

"Something missing in here. Yeah. Take down Wimp's picture. I want one of me, like an oil painting, you got it? And bigger."

Ever resourceful, Drumm knew just the artist to execute the commission, one who'd done covers for barbarian fantasy novels.

"Ri-i-ght." Roy glowed, hands behind his head. "Somebody who can draw guys with balls and women that look like women. Which reminds me. How about—" Roy broke off and glared at the guards. "Hit it!"

Clack!

"Dismissed. But wait outside."

Alone with Drumm, Roy became confidential, almost friendly. "You know how it is with a real man. Got certain needs, but he knows what's right. That's what bugs me about that Blythe. Smart-ass fuckers like him think we're dirt, don't know shit about good manners or what's the right thing to do. I know what the people expect from me that way. The hell I ain't a gennelman. I'm gonna get married to Charity Stovall soon's you find her, and you do that real quick, you got it? Gonna do the right thing by her. Where's Florence?"

Drumm didn't smile at the revealing non sequitur. "Watched over, sir."

"Give Florence her own house, all the beer she wants. But out of the way, you know what I mean?"

Drumm knew. "A discreet location."

Roy chucked the little man under one of his chins with the whip. "Discreet and close."

"May I suggest Blythe's former accommodations? Lovely house, very secluded."

"Right on. I like that." Roy snickered, swinging his boots off the desk. He swaggered about the chamber, hands on his hips. Perfect, sure enough. He peered out from the curtained double windows at the crowd seething beyond the balcony. The sight was more than beautiful; he felt like crying. He couldn't tell what his feelings were, but there was the purest joy he'd ever felt and still an unslaked rage at people like Blythe who looked down on him. He needed respectability. He *was* respectable, otherwise he wouldn't trouble to marry Charity, who was the right kind of girl. What else he needed on the side, like Florence—well, that was private, no need to flaunt it. And those people out there waiting for him, he needed them too.

Trouble is, you don't know who your enemies are. You gotta watch everyone.

But while they screamed for him, Roy knew what to do. What he'd dreamed of.

Going to show you people the truth of the world. What you always want. Like the raids which they did exactly what you didn't have the balls for, and you are going to love me for it, because I am the goddamned people. Love me!

"Get the guards back in here," he ordered, not taking his eyes from the milling thousands beyond the window. "Time to let them see me."

■ 22 ■

The rewards of faith and
their avoidance

Streaking through limbo with Milt Kahane, Woody Barnes marveled at the black, bright, star-winking universe around him. "Man, you really get a different picture from up here."

"Very impressive," Milt agreed. "No view like it, although the Hudson Valley comes close. The whole thing is a helluva show, Barnes. Being alive, being at all. That's what this gig is all about. Remember your trumpet voluntaries from practice?"

They shot through gaseous clouds, played tag with asteroid belts, hitched a short ride on *Voyager 1* snail-pacing past the orbit of Pluto. The frail little contraption looked lonely but familiar to Woody. Milt hurried him on.

"It'll get shmutz all over the costume. Come on, we're late." With the whoop of a raucous diver, Milt kicked off from *Voyager* and whizzed on, Woody close behind. "Everyone wants a reward, especially shmucks like Roy. What do you want?"

"Never thought much about it," Woody reflected. "At least, not until they zapped Charity. Enough gigs to

154

pay the rent, I guess. Chance to play with some good sidemen. Get married."

"Like Charity?"

"No, she's all hung up on Roy. I never said anything to her anyway."

"Wouldn't've done any good," Milt was sure. "Love is a matter of when."

A sudden, nearby nova turned the universe blinding white.

"Wheeee! Feel the breeze! You know the worst thing in the world, Woody? Getting what you thought you wanted. Never looks as good on you as in the store. Take that mother who fragged us in Beirut. He got zapped the same day and came Topside looking for Mohammed and Allah, the whole shmeer. The Boss really has trouble with Moslems, and this dipstick was a Shiite, sort of an Islamic Fundamentalist. They don't even like other Moslems."

But there were great fringe benefits. As Milt explained it, radical Moslems had an ancient but precise idea of heavenly reward for defenders of the faith.

"Houris: sort of super Arab hookers. These guys believe they get an eternal shtup with orgasms that last a thousand years. Sexual Valhalla."

Woody considered the prospect. "Not only couldn't I stand it—hell, I'd get bored."

"That's the point, but (a) you're not dumb and (b) you're not a fanatic. If these clowns had any smarts, they'd be raising poppies or selling rugs."

Milt did a graceful loop and figure eight, waving his trumpet at eternity. "The Boss gives Dipstick his houri just to get rid of him. Not a real houri: actually she'd been a waitress in Newark who belly-danced on weekends. But sexy? You could get seasick watching her navel. So she goes in, she told me, and this turkey gets it on after a lot of bullshit about the infidels he scored, meaning you and me, and he cranks up on paradise."

As Milt had it from the part-time houri, when paradise arrived as advertised, with no sign of cessation, the Shiite felt it was really worth dying for. Gibbering with faith and gratitude, he labored to redeem his spiritual green stamps. Ten minutes into his thousand years, he wondered if the Koran mentioned anything about a break now and then. After twenty minutes he was ready for Sundays off.

"What the hell, the Thousand-Year Reich only made the first twelve," Milt observed. "So—half an hour and he throws in the towel. Totaled, sick at heart. In tears, yet. The dangers of literal belief: what's eternal reward when there's nothing left to want, right? So the Boss sits him down—believe me, he had to sit down—to find out what he really wanted to do. Which was all uphill, because I met this clown and he had the IQ of a Venetian blind; even Arabs had trouble getting through to him. That's why they put him in that window alone and told him carefully who to waste and who not, hoping Dipstick would remember some of it.

"Anyway, the Boss finally gets out of him that he was a baker, a whiz on baklava. He gives him the last known address on Mohammed, and off goes the Lion of Islam to find the place—which turns out to be in Greenwich Village. So now he's the patron spirit of a falafel hut on Macdougal Street, inspiring the best Middle Eastern desserts in town, happy as a clam. There we go! Hang a right, Barnes."

Woody dove after Milt toward a tiny point of light from whence came a growing roar of human frenzy. "Must be Roy's crowd whooping it up."

Milt listened as they drew closer. "That's them. Can't use your mute this gig. Subtle is not in. These turkeys are all Venetian blinds."

"Roy wasn't too dumb, I guess. He was always reading."

"Yeah?" When Milt turned to glance at Woody, he

looked rather like Jake. "Who do you think I've been talking about? Arabs?"

They swooped toward the distant point of light that became a city, a street, a screaming crowd. A high balcony . . .

■ 23 ■

The clear vistas of paranoia

Drumm at his shoulder, Roy ogled the crowd below like an orphan given a birthday party.

"Microphones ready, sir."

"Listen, what about Topside?" The memory was all too recent for Roy. "I seen God close up and He ain't no wimp. He could really fuck us up."

"Hardly." Drumm seemed unconcerned. "Topside is not all God, just as Britain was not all Churchill. Topside has always observed strict neutrality where Below Stairs is concerned; not to mention the vast numbers of them in open or secret sympathy with the Cause. The rest don't want trouble, which is fine until we're ready to enlarge our ambitions. Their emissaries will put in an appearance today as promised. Listen to your people, Leader: *there* is reality. You are eternal. Be Brutus. Seize the time. Below Stairs is ours today." Drumm let the seductive implication hover at Roy's ear. "Tomorrow . . . ?"

Tomorrow Topside. Roy thrilled to the first frisson of invincibility. Heaven and hell all his for all time, bought and paid for with a heart attack. *Jesus, too fuckin much. Like he says, seize the time.* "Okay. Guards out first. Let's go."

At Drumm's order, the guards, vigilant mastiffs, filed in and through the balcony doors. As Roy Stride stepped onto the balcony, the roar burst from the crowd like a single crazed animal. He raised his arms, asking for silence but content to let the storm of frenzied triumph roll over him forever. Drumm waited at the other microphone until he could be heard.

"The Wembley government has stepped down." Another wave of delirium, which Drumm stayed with an upraised hand. "A worn-out garment discarded by a healthy body."

Pandemonium. Roy felt close to tears.

"A new day! Topside itself has agreed to a non-aggression pact following the Leader's assurance that, with this assumption of power, he has no larger political demands. We ARE the future!"

Again the energy exploded from thousands of upturned throats. ROY! STRIDE! ROY! STRIDE! ROY! STRIDE!

"We expect momentarily the emissaries of Topside to ratify our assumption of rule," Drumm told them. "Of our destiny!"

STRIDE! STRIDE! STRIDE!

Arms lifted, Roy beamed down upon his destiny. *You motherfuckers are gonna kiss my ass and love me for it.*

"Liberated Aryans of Below Stairs"—Drumm drew out the vowels in a stentorian voice—"greet the morning of your own new day!"

Hysteria again as Drumm stepped away from his microphone and saluted Roy Stride. Roy waited full minutes until the screaming went ragged from collective exhaustion and subsided to the tense, murmurous anticipation of a single beast straining to be unleashed.

"WE BEEN DOWN!" Roy boomed over the expectant acres of them. "GOING UP!"

The roar from them was music to his ear as he raised his fist in what was to be a new salute—knuckles not forward as with the radicals of the '60s and '70s, but turned in naturally, fist ready to fall like an avenging hammer. He found he didn't have to think of the words, they simply came to him. "They always laughed at us, right? We were the trash, the rednecks, the clowns at the back door of their yuppie paradise. And every four years they promised us whatever we wanted just so's we'd vote. Sure they did—while the farms got sold and the factories closed down. They did everything but listen, right? Well, they'll listen *now*."

STRIDE! STRIDE! STRIDE!

He found his rhythm, learned from Purdy Simco. "Hallelujah, a new day come! They don't write the word of truth, we do. From now on, they don't speak for the White Christian American Way, *we* do. That's for us. By God and all that's holy—"

In nearby limbo, Milt Kahane nudged Woody. "That's our cue. Let's give him the shtick."

Trumpet ready, wig straight and lines learned, Woody Barnes still marveled at the monumental travesty of what he saw. "If this was on TV, I'd turn it off."

"You might." Milt worked the spit valve on his polished instrument. "They won't. Look at those clowns: are they laughing? Myth is in, kid. And . . . go!"

Strauss or Berlioz would have wept for sheer musical ecstasy. The effect was staggering. Over pedal tones deep as from the organ at the heart of the world, a great celestial chord of massed brass blared in a symphonic hosanna as two columns of dazzling light appeared above the balcony and resolved to white-gowned, Aryan-blond angels who lifted their trumpets in an electrifying fiat to the stunned crowd.

"Topside and the ranks of heaven, the halls of ultimate truth and justice, proclaim and ratify the sovereignty of Roy Stride Below Stairs."

"Second in sway only to the Prince himself," the second angel declared in a marked New York accent.

Another riff from the first angel, curled about the edges by a subtle drawling style. The trumpet came down smoothly to rest on his hip. "For unto the chosen people is come a chosen Leader. All hail to the people of Below Stairs and the Leader they have so long deserved." He nodded to his gossamer-robed companion, sotto voce: "Hit it, Milt."

Blazing in the light, the two trumpets lifted in a stirring voluntary. One broke off while the other slid up into a high-flirting riff—

—that bolted Charity straight up in bed. The face she'd recognized for one moment under that silly blond wig was unmistakable. The music was like *Star Wars*, but only one guy in the whole world blew a horn that way.

Cut to a close-up on the angel.

"WOODY!"

He peered out of the screen, surprised and delighted. "Char! Hey, this is a real kick, ain't it?"

"I didn't know you were dead, Woody."

"Came as a complete shock to me, too."

"What's the wig for?" Charity wondered. "Not like you at all."

"These people dig blonds. They're Aryans or something."

"Woody, we're Aryans."

"No fooling?" Woody considered it. "Didn't get us much, did it?"

"Not much." Charity chilled with the memory of Roy's blood raids that brought him to that balcony. "Don't let on you see me, okay?"

"Okay." Woody peered into the bedroom. "Great place you got there."

Charity hiked the sheet higher around her cleavage, grateful that Randy Colorad was out. He wanted to make love all the time. That was okay at first, but lately she'd taken to watching television over his shoulder

161

because even the commercials were more interesting. Him and his exercise machine and his twenty-four-hour freshness soap. Nothing was fresh about Randy; even his sweat was boring. She'd always thought someone glamorous like that—

No. She *never* thought, that was the problem. In her whole dumb-ass life she never thought for one minute. About anything, goddamnit, pardon her lang—no, the hell with that. Don't pardon anything. Dumb-ass. Had to *see* what Roy was before she caught on. Had to die to realize what she'd missed in Woody Barnes.

"I'm sorry you're dead, but it's nice to have friends around. I mean—oh, damn, Woody, I miss you."

"I miss you too," he confessed. "Only hung around the Tabernacle because you were there. Too late now, I guess."

"I wish it wasn't," she yearned.

"I never had anything to give you. And you were always for Roy."

"That's over." The finality of the sound surprised Charity.

"Well, look at him now," Woody glanced out of shot. "He's got it all now."

Yeah, Roy and me, we got it all. Our real religion, like Jake said. I guess he should know. "One thing you can do real good here is learn, Woody. When you get Topside again, you tell them I've seen the pits, and they were smart to make you an angel. You're a good person. I mean the best." Charity's eyes smarted with sudden tears. "I just wish to hell—"

"Hey!" Woody's bewigged head jerked aside at something offscreen. Behind him, the crowd noise had changed to something shocked and then dangerous, a huge gasp, then a roar for blood. "Char, they shot him. Somebody shot Roy."

As Charity gaped at the screen, the live event cut to a news anchorwoman with the blankest expression since Mount Rushmore.

"Good afternoon, I'm Nancy Noncommit—here's what's happening. An as yet unidentified gunman has wounded Leader Roy Stride in the middle of his apotheosis. No details yet, we'll have that story live—after this."

CUT TO FEMININE-HYGIENE COMMERCIAL. (Music: poignant violins. The honey-haired young woman with the heart-shaped face presses a letter to her breast.)

SOFT, INTIMATE FEMININE VOICE-OVER: "There are days when nothing should interfere with feeling like a woman—"

"STICK IT, BEAVER!" Charity shot from the bed, grabbing for the channel switch. All the channels were the same commercial.

Cut back to the balcony. Roy's face, dull with shock, looking straight at her in huge close-up.

"Charity," he croaked. "They shot me."

—and pull back to reveal him holding his bloody sleeve. "Don't worry, it's just a flesh wound." Roy winced and staggered—kind of actorish, Charity felt. "I'll take care of it myself. We're gonna get married. You and me, just like I promised. Listen to these people. Did you see? I'm the Leader! And you're . . . you're going to be . . ."

She didn't know what to say, just wanted to hide. "Mrs. Leader?"

"Where are you?" Roy strained. "You're gonna share all this with me. Where the hell are you?"

Charity panicked and blanked. "I don't know the address." With a sick rush of fear, she saw again her child self aged with that horrible knowledge in the split second before her head splattered open like a broken egg. *And I don't want you to know it. Talk about a good time for a commercial—*

—and cut with blessed serendipity to a well-groomed, smiling young Japanese spokesman: "Three-point-nine financing, five hundred cash back on the new Wasabe XL with underpaid Japanese engineering. You only *thought* you won World War II."

Charity dove for the remote switch and turned the set off. "What's the use of being dead? It's just like being alive, only worse."

"Mum?" Simnel waited, polite and impassive, in the bedroom entrance. "A Mr. Veigle called. An agent, apparently lives here in the building. Naturally I told him he had a wrong number. I'm not sure he believed me."

Charity was in no mood for this. "Make him believe you. Who's this Vague anyway?"

"Veigle, mum. A very powerful agent. They say he gets ten percent of the Prince. I'm sure that's a bit strong."

Charity turned away, wrapping the sheet around her. She felt cold. "I don't want to see anyone, Simmy. Anyone! Understand?"

■ 24 ■

Romanticism as theology: Is there hope for the spiritual drunk?

Gorgeous; the million-dollar wound that looked spectacular and didn't hurt much. Roy surveyed the dramatic stain spreading over his shirt sleeve between shoulder and elbow. The whole thing was a beautiful movie, better than Bronson or Eastwood, and Charity saw it.

"Drumm, will it show on color TV?"

"If it doesn't, we can touch it up."

They were momentarily alone just inside the balcony doors, guards three deep in the hall, the crowd screaming outside as the assassin was torn like an unclean thing from their seething mass by Paladin guards and dragged up the marble steps to his doom.

"You bring that sumbitch here," Roy seethed. "I want him to see me to my face."

Click! "Instantly, Leader."

He felt like the next thing to—no, he *was* God now, at least here. The Devil didn't seem interested—Roy couldn't figure that at all—but the rest sure loved him all right. They'd follow him. He'd find Charity, tuck

Florence away for rainy days . . . he had the whole thing knocked. Even Topside got out of his way. Damn if one of those angels didn't look like . . . No. No way. Woody was alive. A live nothing back in Plattsville.

Roy gazed at Wembley's picture in the space where his would hang in nobler majesty. Secretly he wished the portrait could be bare-chested, but that wouldn't be dignified. Respectability warred with inclination and won. But still . . . maybe a sword and lots of fur like Conan.

Drumm entered, followed by three guards and a shabbily dressed prisoner, whom they sent sprawling at Roy's feet.

"Get up, motherfucker. I want to get a good look at you."

Roy realized he should have kept the man on the floor. Middle-aged and schoolteacherish, he wasn't tall but seemed so because of a determined dignity.

"What are you?" Roy wondered. "Besides a lousy shot. You look like some kind of college perfessor."

"I was a teacher, yes," the prisoner admitted. "May I have my glasses back?"

Drumm laughed unpleasantly. "Old man, you won't be around long enough to need them. Name?"

"Ernst Stahler." There was a trace of High German in the accent.

"I remember him, Leader Stride," Drumm explained. "Stahler: fled Germany when Hitler came to power. Under suspicion as a Communist in the U.S. during the fifties. An enemy."

"I was a political writer." Stahler tried to focus his deficient sight on Roy, one eye already closing from a well-aimed blow. There was another bruise on his chin. His clothes were badly torn.

"You got guts, old man," Roy said with thin admiration. "Just stupid. You're gonna apologize. Say you're sorry for shooting at me."

"I am sorry," Stahler admitted easily. "Sorrier than you think. More than that, I was totally wrong."

"How about that?" Roy smirked to Drumm. "Even the losers are with us."

Stahler managed to stand like a granite statue even bleeding and handcuffed. "You misunderstand. The bullet only dignified you."

"Hey look, scumbag, I got things to do and people to see. Roaches like you I just spray, you got it?"

"The image is apt," Stahler said with his quiet academic precision. "In the fifties I wrote that fascism was a propensity of the schizoid German mind. Not so. It is universal as influenza and as tenacious. When healthy resistance wears down, you will appear. For a time, Mr. Stride. Because it is not only the power you need but the cosmic drama. Ask your resident dramatist, Drumm. That truly was the romantic German part of it. But even the Germans realized, if only subconsciously, that their own mythology ends in defeat and loss. *Götterdämmerung.*"

A snap of Roy's fingers and his Lüger was fetched from the desk by an obedient guard. Roy leveled the weapon at Stahler. "You gonna tell me in straight talk, old man."

Stahler didn't flinch. "You will come to it in time, as I did. As Hitler did. Until then, every wise decision will be nullified by two of sheer stupidity and indulgence. It must be so, and you know why it must be so."

"You—" The son of a bitch made him so mad, Roy began to shake. He yanked back the pistol slide and pointed the weapon again. "You got five seconds to live. Talk *straight.*"

It was unnerving; Stahler didn't even blink. "You even have the wrong symbol, Mr. Stride. Your sign is not the fist of power, it is Florence Bird."

Aiming the pistol between those steady, knowing eyes that stripped him naked, Roy had a red-sick moment of recognition. *This* was his real enemy, not the

Jews or blacks or any of the easily visible targets the Paladins held up to the mob outside. This one here. The ones who knew and had the power to describe him; who made him a white nigger, only one step up from the black ones and no different at all when it came to money or getting fired first. The ones who got to be officers, got the best jobs and the best cars and women; who never had to work for power but always got it somehow. Not only the inferiors would go but these motherfuckers, too. Before anyone else. Now. Because of the answer in his hand. *You don't look down on me.*

But they did.

Roy fired. Stahler's head snapped back, spraying blood and flesh. The rest of him went down like a pile of rags. Drumm stepped over the mess, unconcerned.

"Get rid of that," he ordered.

When the guards were gone with the remnant of Stahler, Drumm adjusted his toupee and reassured Roy. "Don't worry, my Leader. The rug is washable."

"How'd he know about Florence?"

"I don't know, sir, but—"

"If he knows, who else does, huh? She's my private business." Roy turned on Drumm, shaking with rage and the exhilaration of a new kind of power. Blooded and blood drawn. He'd never felt anything like it, not even in good sex.

"And now possibly the business of others," Drumm reflected prudently. "Especially after you marry Miss Stovall."

Roy dropped the Lüger on his desk. "You got Florence hid good?"

"Trust me, Leader. But we must be prepared. If respectability is the daughter of morality, her jealous sister is blackmail."

Roy understood. More than respectability's sister, blackmail was her shadow, especially now. He really needed Florence tonight, but that would be asking for it. Where the hell was Charity? The high-rise district wasn't all that big they couldn't find her. House to house if they had to.

"We must be prepared," Drumm cautioned. "A scenario, orchestrated circumstances. We must make the disclosure work for us. That will be my personal operation. Trust me."

"Yeah. I got to, don't I?"

"Everything must work for us now." Drumm pointed a pudgy finger at Roy's bloody sleeve. "Even that."

Lovingly, Roy fingered the stained sleeve with its bullet holes as credential. "He was right, that old man, he did me a favor. Listen to them out there." He drank in the thunder, the music. "That fucker made me God."

With grand panache, Drumm threw open the balcony doors. The roar invaded the chamber like floodwaters from a burst dam. "Show them their God, Leader! Oh, and the blood. Cheat your left arm down—that is, be sure the wound is slightly turned toward them. After you, sir."

Roy stepped out onto the balcony, bathing in the sweet balm of total power.

STRIDE! STRIDE! STRIDE! STRIDE!

■ 25 ■

Meanwhile, back at reality . . .

Woody and Milt sped Topside across the void. The first trip had been a bit unsettling for Woody, though not all that different from good science fiction movies. Once used to it, he found the whole experience a hoot, and how many nights like this could you expect in Plattsville?

"We might make another appearance sometime," Milt supposed, "depending on how the script goes."

"I'm worried about Char."

"Writhing in the torment of a luxury duplex? What's to worry?"

"It's all phony," Woody complained. "And Char's a real person."

"That ought to clue you, Barnes. She's smarter than Roy, but still no hundred-watt bulb yet. She's gotta learn for herself. Meanwhile you can't complain about the scenery."

That you couldn't, Woody marveled: worlds and space and more worlds, colors he'd never imagined possible let alone seen, flickering through million-mile clouds of dust and gas alive with more worlds to come. Compared to this, Roy's triumph was bush league; just that Woody knew the guy too well.

"Roy's a dumb prick, but a dangerous one."

"Hey—take advice," Milt counseled as they soared through the black and silver of endless space. "My family were experts on the fascist mind. Roy's a fuck-up like Hitler. What's the opposite of fail-safe? Success-safe. These turkeys have got to lose because most of their thinking is off the wall to begin with. Think about it: there's Adolf rearranging Europe like a hyperactive housewife, shrewd as they come, and still getting his horoscope done every goddamned day, which is like seriously figuring Santa Claus into the national budget. These people are not coming from common sense; they simply can't think big. Give Stride a steady job and his own mediocrity would keep him in his place." Milt Kahane laughed suddenly, twisting around to grin at Woody. "Now there's a thought. If Hitler could've made it as an artist, we might've skipped a whole war—hey!"

Milt looked quickly over his shoulder as a series of flashing lights bathed them in hard brilliance, then rolled over in a steep dive. "INCOMING!"

Woody banked in a tight turn after him as the swift ship slid past them, glittering in and out of visibility before it vanished in the distance. The damn thing barely missed them. It could have . . . Woody felt at himself to see if the whole inventory was there and not hanging off the damn hit-and-run ship. "Ho-*ly*, Milt. What the hell was that?"

"You got me." Milt swerved back on course, fuming. "Dumb son of a bitch almost ran right up our tails. Just like the Long Island Expressway: long as their horn works, who needs brakes?" He bellowed his scorn after the alien ship.

"Tourist!"

Their ship had been in matter phase for the few instants Maj needed for control calibration. The two human-energy readings came up on them so quickly

171

that she flustered for a moment. Beside her, Sorlij scanned the readouts.

"Whatever that was," he said, "I don't believe it."

"Conventionalized human-energy forms."

"Can't be. Scanner malfunction." Sorlij punched in a system check, then called up various star charts on the screen. "We're getting close, I'm positive. I think it was the fourth planet in this system."

Maj disagreed: the fourth planet could barely sustain microbe life when they visited last. "The third."

"You're sure?"

"How could I forget?" Maj was in a particularly seductive form now, favored by the more successful women of her kind. She shimmered like bright metal immersed in clear water, and the gently reminiscent emotions turned her to a rainbow shower. "We made love in human form there. You remember how fashionable it was then."

Sorlij didn't remember all that well but was diplomatic enough to share her smile of pleasurable recollection. "Who cared then where we were? But I'm sure it's this system."

"There it is." Part of Maj's rainbow elongated to a pointer as the definitely familiar clouded blue ball loomed on her viewscreen.

"So it is. I wish I hadn't been so drunk when we landed."

"Darling, I'm glad you were. You tended to be terribly serious." Maj's colors dulled slightly as her mood turned analytical. "Reading the third planet now."

Absorbed with the world growing on the screen, Sorlij didn't notice Maj's chromatic change from faded rainbow to the dull brown of shock. "Sorlij, listen!"

More than just listening, they *felt*—a torrent of human energy, a cacophony of languages, mechanical and even nuclear activity.

"No malfunction," Sorlij stated grimly. "Those were human-energy forms."

Which raised questions troublesome as they were intriguing. "Sorlij . . . could it be?"

Sorlij didn't want to believe what the readouts told him: relatively advanced human life infecting not only the planet but polarized in two distinct post-physical energy pools. "Maj, enter a problem. Precise time point of our last visit."

She formed a delicate hand with seven agile digits that danced over the computer keyboard. "Entered."

"Primate parameters as observed then, approximate brain development in cc."

"Entered."

"From elapsed time, extrapolate anthropoid development to present. Query: nuclear technology possible?"

Maj's slender temporary fingers tap-danced over glittering inductance squares. "Computed."

They read the dismal results expressed in formulae. Maj summarized them on a sinking note. "From our givens, some extraordinarily gifted specimen might just about have discovered the bow and arrow. However . . ." She broke off to scan a parenthetical insert to the results. Sorlij read it with her.

"However," he echoed hollowly.

Based on the developmental arc of twenty other primate species over two galaxies, the ape should have been too stupid to meet nine out of ten predictable early challenges. The few prodigies that developed beyond the point of their last visit would not have survived the probable polar tilt and the first long winter. Not to mention their penchant for intramural slaughter.

"Forced development," was Sorlij's inevitable conclusion.

"Oh yes."

Nor was that the worst of it. Intellectual growth could be augmented or accelerated. Emotional growth, too random a process, could not, though its relation to the former could be stated as a fairly predictable arithmetical lag behind the logarithmic progress of intellect.

Maj ran a swift line check to verify their results. No error. If she was a hedonist in her youth, Maj was now very practical. "The disparity is monstrous. I'd say they're technically brilliant, emotionally primitive and not a few of them quite mad."

Even superior beings had limits to their comprehension. Sorlij was close to his. "This is not supposed to happen. It's not my field. How do I deal with this?"

Instantly Maj was all comfort, entwining her essence with his. "There, dear. Whatever it takes, you'll manage."

"But how could it *happen?*"

"Don't be dense, dear. Our little lost lambs."

Sorlij changed color dramatically as he realized the unthinkable. "Oh no. No . . ." He materialized a specialized rump and collapsed on it. "Barion. That disgusting, egotistical, irresponsible—"

"And as of now, criminal fool." Maj's reflections were weighted with delicious malice. "And his musical brother. The matched banes of existence."

"Excuse me, Maj. I'm going to go human for a moment." Sorlij did just that. "I want to feel sorry for myself. I was so happy, Maj. So successful with marine organisms."

"Darling, it's hardly your fault."

"I left them there, both of them too drunk to move. A degree of culpability, that's what they'll say at home. Why, Maj? My mollusks were showpieces. I was working toward a decorative form of kelp. A really fine lungfish. Why me?"

Maj turned human to complement him, managing a lustrous cross between a sitcom wife and a centerfold. "Because you're the best for the job and everyone knows it."

"Yes," he admitted with manly resignation. "That's true."

Maj guessed from experience: now he would say *it's a dirty job but someone has to do it.*

"It's a dirty job—"

"Yes, darling."

Sorlij glared at the energy readouts emanating from the third planet and its vicinity. They were spectacularly mad. "Those two little *brats.* There's not even a word to do them justice."

"Excuse me, dear." With the flick of one delicate finger, Maj brought the ship out of jump to sublight. "The word for them is 'finished.' "

■ 26 ■

A rescue! A rescue!

From her Jacuzzi or watching over the shoulder of the inexhaustible Randy Colorad, Charity followed the mounting TV drama of Roy's fevered quest for her. BSTV made the most of it—

"This is Nancy Noncommit, BSTV news anchor. Top story this hour: the Paladin search continues for Char the mystery star."

Quick cut to Drumm close-up, smoothing his little mustache. "Below Stairs is simply not large enough to hide a woman of such importance. The Black-Jewish-Catholic-Communist dissidents responsible will pay severely when apprehended. I would also like to say for the record—"

Cut back to Nancy Noncommit: ". . . idiot will talk all night." (Sees her camera light on. The blank smile flashes automatically.) "Meanwhile White Paladin guards are combing the streets and residential neighborhoods for any lead to the missing fiancée of Leader Roy Stride. BSTV news is on the spot with one interrogation team."

Outdoor shot of a sleepy-eyed Paladin by a bullet-pocked wall, fondling his rifle. Several bodies lay at the foot of the wall.

TELEREPORTER: "We understand that these people resisted interrogation."

PALADIN: "That is correct. I asked them if they knew where Char was, and they said they was Catholics and didn't give a big rat's (bleep), and I shot them as per the orders that I was given."

TELEREPORTER: "Do you usually have this difficulty with interrogation subjects?"

PALADIN (stroking his rifle absently): "Sometimes, yes, sir. Like this morning someone said he knew where Char was gone to but we was already shooting him."

TELEREPORTER: "Did your superiors consider this hasty?"

PALADIN (frowns in thought, takes a slip of paper from pocket and reads it): "We cannot be blamed for patriotism, but we are working to upgrade interrogation procedures."

And back to Nancy Noncommit: "One thing is certain, Char is difficult to find, especially when you can't get good help. Paladin search parties, ranging across Below Stairs, usually find themselves back at the Leader's Palace. This is seen by Minister Drumm as the work of dissidents. Others suggest the use of a compass."

So it went. Charity lounged in her tub, nibbled lox and admitted a select few neighbors from the building, like the past-life therapist from Venice, California, who volunteered to help her work through historical personalities allegedly seething in Charity's subconscious.

"She says I could've once been Cleopatra," she confided to Simnel over a hand of gin rummy, "but she says that's a very hard life to work through."

"Usually means there's a waiting list." Simnel laid down a deuce on the playing board across the white plateau of bubbles that encased Charity to the shoulders. "Cleo is very popular; never gets a moment's rest. Why not try for Calpurnia?"

"Who?"

"Caesar's wife. As advertised, above reproach."

Charity picked up the deuce. "I don't know. Liz Taylor was so great in the movie. Gin."

"GIN?" Caught with a ruinous handful of points, Simnel forgot himself. "You larcenous wench, you *can't* have gin this soon unless you're cheating. And you shuffled."

"Sure. Gin."

"You're not playing the game, mum."

"It ain't playing the game. It's winning. Gin."

"If I may say so, Miss Stovall, you never learned that Below Stairs."

"No. I learned that being poor in Plattsville."

The intercom phone buzzed softly. Charity yawned. "Get it downstairs, Simmy."

Simnel withdrew to do his office; shortly thereafter the bathroom phone beeped again. "It's Mr. Veigle again. About business, he says. Wants to come up. He lives here in the building, mum."

"Oh . . . why not," Charity decided, thoroughly bored. "It beats wrestling with Colorad, which I want you to tell him when he comes in that I have a headache."

"Mr. Colorad won't be back until this evening."

"It's a bad headache, it'll last."

When Simnel ushered in Eddie Veigle and added more bubble bath, Charity's head in its red shower cap looked like a maraschino on whipped cream. Veigle struck her as somehow sinister; even in the hot bath he made her feel clammy cold. She greeted him with a noncommittal "Hi."

"No." The bulky visitor shook his brilliantined head. "Absolutely not. We build the image from the first. You're a nice girl from Pottsville."

"Plattsville."

"Never mind. We're creating a product. The word is 'How do you do, Mr. Veigle?' Your parents were poor but they taught you good manners."

"They never taught me anything," she contradicted truthfully. "They didn't even care if I did my homework or not. Look, I'm doing you a favor just letting you in. How'd you find me, anyway?"

"I'm a businessman," Veigle said flatly. "We always know more than the government. And I live here in the building. Word gets around."

Eddie Veigle was moon-faced, bespectacled and deceptively benign, a fat man in a tasteful, perfectly tailored double-breasted gray suit. Next to Veigle, Ronald Reagan looked seedy. His nails were manicured, not one glossy black hair strayed out of place, not even the short gray ones around his ears. He smiled a great deal —just that, Charity discovered quickly, the smile could go bleak and cold as the moor around Dane's castle even as he beamed at her.

"Not even the Paladins know where I am."

"Bet your buns they didn't; not till I got the scenario worked out." Veigle drew a satin-upholstered stool close to the bath and rested his ample buttocks on it. "But they do now."

"Huh?" Charity sat up so fast she had to scoop in extra bubbles for modesty. "SIM-MY!"

"Because now is the right time for you to be found." Veigle inspected the shine on his nails. "Don't worry, you'll make a mint. Wait'll you hear what I've worked out."

Charity felt suddenly very afraid.

"What's the matter, kid? You look like you just lost your last option." Veigle leaned closer, solicitous but still oddly menacing. "The scenario's a winner. First the book, then the movie. That's why we ran the lifestyle segment on you."

"That wasn't me." She needed to escape from him. The vague threat of him filled the whole bathroom. "That was mostly bullshit."

"Look, baby, we're not amateurs. We used the best actress we could find. We had to to get that boondock accent of yours. The dream is what they'll buy."

Charity felt herself trembling in the warm, sudsy water. If he called the Paladins, they'd be here any minute, the same ones that killed the little girl. "I can't write any book. I wasn't good in English."

"Honey, it's a package," Veigle told her as if tutoring a backward child. "I got ten ghostwriters screaming for this assignment. Title alone can't miss. *American Dream.*"

They had the rags to riches, he explained; that was a natural, he loved it, but . . . getting a little, you know, tired. The package needed something else. Market studies showed greater impact when a spiritual element was included.

"That's it. A spiritual rags to riches." Veigle's oil and honey tones enriched with revelation. "Look at Colson after Watergate: found God in prison. How many sales? TV movie. Larry Flynt of *Hustler* magazine: up to his kishkas in a lawsuit, saw the light on a plane trip. I FOUND GOD AT 35,000 FEET. The drunks and druggies who fell from the big time and fought their way back, always with a book and a movie coming out of it. Goodness is admirable," that deep, insinuating voice told Charity, "but the fall-down is prime time. Jim and Tammy Bakker struggling to be brave on camera. Even the highbrows watched. They made jokes about it, but they watched. Drama, Char!"

Of the names he rattled off, Charity remembered only Reverend and Mrs. Bakker. She'd liked the PTL ministry on TV. He seemed like a nice man, but someone ought to teach his wife how to put on her makeup.

"Now do you get the picture?" Veigle urged. "This is high concept. Every one of those stories was a hit book or a boffo flick. Virtue is nice and sweet, but pain— the fall and redemption are the drama, the money in the bank. And you, doll face, are a mint. I want you to sign with me now."

"Pardon, mum," Simnel barely edged through the

open door with a polite knock. "Mr. Colorad is home early after all."

"Great. I really need that. Mr. Vague here—"

"Veigle, baby."

"He says my story is the American dream."

"American dreaming has a high sugar content," Simnel observed, fussing with a shelf of towels. "Spiritual junk food."

"Simnel, I love ya!" Veigle boomed. "Always good for a zinger." The grin petrified as he turned back to Charity. "Now listen, kid—"

"I'm home, lover." Randy Colorad bounded into the bathroom in candy-striped bikini briefs. "Hey, Eddie, what's going down?" He stripped quickly and slithered into the tub. As always, the lighting went commercial bright to accommodate him.

Veigle groaned. "Christ, it's Tennis Anyone. Don't splash on the suit, okay?"

"Miss me?" Randy leered at Charity.

"No. I have a headache. Stay on your own side of the tub. I'm busy. Simnel"—a meaningful glance she hoped Veigle missed— "I'd like the kosher special for lunch and put a rush on it."

"Kosher special. Very good, mum." Simnel modestly eclipsed himself.

"Quit futzing around," Veigle snapped. "I'm talking megabucks. Got the contract in my pocket."

"I'm not sure about my future plans," Charity hedged. "I may have to move real quick."

"Char, when you sign with me and this deal goes down, you'll have a pad like this for every day of the week. Listen to this story," Veigle persuaded. "Nice American girl from a small town in the American heartland dies in the middle of her first boff, right? Damned with her lover, Roy Stride, a nobody from nowhere who rises to become a leader of his people Below Stairs." Veigle's organ tones began to sound like a coming attraction in Dolby. "Alone, terrified, she flees across the

181

bleak landscape of damnation—lotsa special effects—
one breathtaking escape after another. In color, score
by Korngold."

"Oh, shit," breathed the mesmerized Randy. "That
is wonderful."

"Just wonderful? It's fucking dynamite. And all the
while . . . Are you getting this, Char?"

She smiled demurely. "I'm starting to."

Veigle's voice softened with pathos. "All the while,
Roy searches for his high school sweetheart. Pain nothing, wounds nothing, triumph dust and ashes without
her. Without . . ."

"Without the world in his arms," Randy offered,
totally caught up in the magic.

Veigle grudged Randy something like admiration.
"That's good. You ought to write jacket copy. The world
in his arms." He savored the words, rising, uplifted by
the pure helium of his vision. "A best-seller book, a
miniseries. A forty share on BSTV."

"I don't *wanta* get rescued or anything!" Charity
wailed.

"Say what?" Veigle blinked, brought back to a
world not in anyone's arms. "You're kidding."

"I don't wanta get saved or shot on film or any
other way, which it's very easy to do around here even
dead. As for Roy and the one time—*once* in the tacky
old White Rose Motel—I had more fun playing gin with
Simmy. Now will you please get out of here so's I can
get dressed?"

"You're not thinking positively." Veigle took a
folded contract out of an inner pocket.

"I am thinking of getting out of here and I am not
signing any stupid contract."

"Yes, you are." Veigle speared her attention on one
pudgy forefinger. It was very white, white as the rest of
his skin, bloodless pale. Everyone was dead here, but
under his manicure and hair comb, Veigle *looked* it.
"Listen, you are nobody until I make you somebody,

you understand? You don't do a thing without me. Nobody'll look at you twice without packaging. You're his sweetheart, his true love—"

"The hell I am!"

"Listen to him, Char." Randy wriggled closer under the water. "He knows the business."

"I'm sick of the business and everybody trying to give it to me," Charity raged in a spray of water and bubbles. She found Randy's rump by Braille and applied a foot to it. "Get out of here, you horny seal!"

"But I want to hear the end of the story," Randy pleaded. "It's gripping."

Veigle's voice dropped to a husky whisper. "I was just coming to it. The two of you, success hollow without true love, Lazarus at the feast, and then finding each other at last. I see the shot already: both of you on an empty, lonely street late at night. You turn and see him a block away. He turns. Slowly you recognize each other. You move toward each other, faster and faster. Close on him, close on you as the music rises up in the kind of triumph only Korngold can write—the soundtrack alone will go platinum. Two American kids who went all the way down and up again. Underdogs who stumbled, but even after death came from behind to win."

"Oh, shit, Eddie, that's—" Words threatened to fail Randy Colorad. "That's more than good. It's *profound*."

"And about as real as you are," Charity seethed, near violence herself. "Lordy, would I love a little real. Even a roach in the kitchen."

"No, you wouldn't." Veigle shook his head, sure of himself. "You never did. The world is made up of losers like you who just go on losing. How much did you ever pay for a look at one more? You wanted the prime-time glitz like the rest of the grunions. You begged for it with your snotty little nose pressed up against the screen. Don't kid yourself: without me, without the buildup, you're not even a thirty-second spot on late night."

"I don't *want*—"

"Who cares what you want, you little twat? *We're going to make money out of you!* It's inevitable, so relax and enjoy it."

At this tense juncture, Drumm shouldered through the bathroom door followed by an armed Paladin big enough to have been manufactured by the GM truck division, Simnel hovering in their wake. Charity's heart sank. Her goose was cooked. Furthermore, she was running out of bubbles.

"At last, Miss Stovall!" Drumm flourished. "My respects and my regrets for your trouble. If these people have harmed you—"

"Sorry, mum," Simnel apologized. "They forced their way in."

"Can we talk without the gun?" Charity appealed. "How'd you get past security?"

"We persuaded 'em, ma'am." The lumbering guard ogled the receding froth over Charity's bosom. "My name's Roy, too. Roy Earl Holub from Yazoo City, Mississippi, and I'm pleased to make your acquaintance. I'd do anything for the Leader."

"If you'll dress, Miss Stovall, we'll escort you to—"

"Hold it, Drumm," Veigle butted in, waving his contract. "She signs with me first. Favor for favor."

"Roy Earl." Drumm motioned to the guard. "Some persuasion for Mr. Veigle."

The rifle trained on Eddie Veigle. He went, if possible, even paler, wilting down onto the stool. "Now, that's not fair. Who tipped you she was here?"

"Fair is what right-thinking Americans say it is," Drumm snapped. "Miss Stovall will have no need of your services."

"Char, this would be a great time for those new stress vitamins," said ever-helpful Randy.

Drumm motioned impatiently. "Miss Stovall, if you please."

"Simmy, how about my kosher special?"

"On the way, mum." Simnel took a giant towel from the rack—only to have it plucked from his grasp by the kosher special, who opened it invitingly for Charity. Her heart leaped: God and the Mounties had arrived in time.

"Jake! I've been living right after all."

"Charity—" Surveying the astonished and suddenly respectful faces around him, Jake couldn't supress a giggle. "Let me take you away from all this."

"Jake, I never saw anyone so beautiful in all my life or so in time," she vowed passionately, booting at Randy with the vigor and precision of a halfback. "Outa the pool, Flipper! Towel, Jake. I mean please, Mr. Iscariot."

He spread the towel expertly between Charity and the other men as she rose to wrap herself in it. "The rest of you freeze. You, the brain trust with the gun: you're tired of carrying it, so put it down."

Dazed but obedient, Roy Earl leaned the rifle against the tub. Charity skittered out of the bathroom, grabbing for the first clothes to hand. "Thanks, Jake. I'm always getting rescued without a stitch."

"Won't hurt sales," Veigle offered. "Don't worry, we'll find you. You're money in the bank."

Jake turned on him lethally. "I said freeze. All of you."

Something in the voice. Dressing hurriedly, Charity herself froze at the sound of it. Everything about Jake now was scary, even his back. She wriggled into jeans and a T-shirt, jammed her feet into tennis shoes.

"You won't get away with this, Iscariot," Drumm blustered. "Friend of the Prince or whatever, you're not big enough to cross the Leader."

"Oh? Anyone want to get paid off now?"

Charity couldn't see the exact movement of his right hand, but Drumm, Veigle and the guard shrank as far from him as possible. With a yelp of pure terror, Randy jumped clear out of the tub like a hyperactive salmon and sprinted out of the bathroom, trailing wet bubbles down the stairs.

"Ready, Charity?"

"Got my running shoes on. Think I'm gonna need 'em."

Judas/Jake scooped up the rifle and tossed it to Simnel. "Entertain the callers until we're gone."

Hurrying downstairs to the open elevator, Charity remembered her fled roommate. "Randy?"

Hidden but plaintive: "He's not going to pay anybody off, is he?"

"No, but there's some Seconal in the bathroom. Take the whole bottle." She jogged into the elevator after Jake and punched for down. Nothing happened. "Hey, elevator, move!"

"Please enter correct instructions," the elevator balked. "I used to be a—"

"I *know*," Charity screeched. "You had great cheekbones. GO, stupid!"

"I most certainly will not." The elevator didn't.

"How'd you like to start life over as a stamp pad?" Jake offered with the calm of a poised cobra. "Basement, please."

The doors closed. They wafted downward to the piped music of Lawrence Welk. With a moment to breathe at last, Charity gazed adoringly up at her savior, the Archvillain of the Christian World. He looked beautiful. "Jake, did I ever tell you you remind me of James Mason?"

"Thank you. I always liked his work."

"Would you mind just this once if I kissed you?"

"Delighted, Miss Stovall. It's been a long time since the last. Ruth Snyder," Jake recalled tenderly. "Incompetent murderess but a very nice woman. Be my guest."

He didn't kiss well at all. His lips were slightly cold. Charity was faintly disappointed. She felt the hard knot of the leather bag against her throat and went cold herself. Under the ricky-tick elevator music, she heard again the voice almost forgotten—very familiar and much closer now.

Char-i-tee . . .

III

BANALITIES

■ 27 ■

Judas with strings

Jake ran red lights with such reckless abandon, Charity kept looking back to see if they'd picked up any traffic cops.

"Don't worry about that." Jake took a corner with squealing tires. "The heat leaves me alone."

"Where are we going so fast, anyway?"

"A place you're ready for."

"Someplace real that makes sense," Charity yearned.

"With rules, order, regulations."

"Where people live like folks—*look out that car!*"

Jake swerved with the reflexes of a fighter pilot, throwing Charity against her door. "Lordy, where'd you learn to drive?"

"Never did, actually. Just sort of picked it up. No accidents yet."

"We're not there yet." Charity crossed her fingers and prayed silently. "Wherever there is."

"As requested, reality." Jake kept his eyes on the street ahead. "And Alice said, 'Who cares for you, anyway? You're nothing but a pack of cards.' And as the pack rose up and came pelting down on her, Alice woke up to reality. Getting dark."

Jake switched on his high beams. A startled pedestrian leaped back out of their lethal trajectory. Jake geared down and curved smoothly into a side street.

191

Downtown Below Stairs slid by Charity's open window, garish with neon.

"Where are we going? 'Suming we get there in one piece."

"The Club Banal."

"Club what?"

"Banal," he defined: "the classically ordinary, predictable, unremarkable, unchanging. Not the worst, a long way from the best. Boring."

"That's a dumb name for a club. I already got bored out of my gourd by Randy Colorad."

"The Banal is much more than that," Jake explained. "The working heart of Below Stairs. Leaders come and Drumms go, but the bureaucracy remains. And there's the brothel."

Charity hoped she hadn't heard him right. "The what?"

Jake shrugged. "I believe the American term is cathouse."

"Now, look," Charity argued, offended. "All right, I made some mistakes, and maybe I'm not a real nice girl anymore, and maybe that ain't much of a loss, but I don't deserve to be sent to a . . . a white slave house."

"White slave?" Jake laughed with honest amusement. "Melodramatic wench, the Banal has a variety of jobs, and you'll like Elvira Grubb, the manager. Everyone says what they mean. What they've got to say, that is, and as far as it goes. But as ordered, reality. Reason and order, ponderous sanity, regulations. The very cosmos invalid until reviewed, countersigned and filed in triplicate. Very safe and no surprises. And . . . here we are. Feel at home."

The cab slid to the curb before a neon-fronted building with a crowded bar from which brassy music blared out over the whole sleazy block. A little daunted, Charity didn't want to leave the safety of Jake just yet.

"Thanks again. Every time I need saving, there's you."

"Scared, Charity? It's just like the world, the same confusion. Don't be impressed."

Charity's glance dropped to the age-blackened leather pouch around his scarred neck. "There's something I—don't be mad, but I just gotta ask."

"I know." He tapped the pouch. "They all do."

"You can tell me to mind my own business."

"Perhaps you're not ready for it yet."

She met his gaze levelly. "Hey, Jake, I'm getting readier by the minute, or ain't you noticed? I mean about what I used to think was good and bad."

"Ah—a sea change."

She slid over to touch his cheek, caring about him. "Why, Jake?"

"The same old question. Why did I do it?" He looked past her in that distant, detached way of his. "You know, all those films you saw never got it right. Yeshua was my friend."

"Who's he?"

"Jesus: that's what the Greeks made out of his name. He was my friend, he loved me. Actually Yeshua was one of the two best minds in Judea. I was the other. Freely admitted; my modesty fell with the rest of me. But in those days I was something of a Fundamentalist myself and not at all forgiving. I never forgave him for not being what I wanted him to be . . . a god, a messiah. We needed to believe in miracles then, too; nor were we any more critical than you."

Charity found it difficult to stay on the subject with him that close. "I was taught you were the lowest thing on earth or in hell."

Jake laughed again. "That's leaning on it, don't you think? What I am in fact is the oldest but most effective plot device of the trite world. People need a villain, Charity. Without me, Yeshua would have been a ripple in Roman history. One dissident rabbi leading one splinter group out of dozens, a footnote for Hebrew scholars. People have short memories for also-rans. The way things turned out, I don't imagine he's any happier than I am. I have to go." Jake leaned over and brushed her lips with his. They weren't warm, but Charity felt the sincerity. "The ride's on the house, Miss Stovall."

"Don't you ever get lonely, Jake?"

He took a moment to consider the question. "No, not the way you mean it. Besides, who'd live in that house of mine?" Jake slipped the gear into neutral. "Rotten weather, a snotty embezzler for a watchdog, and I'm not much company."

"Don't put yourself down." Charity opened her door and got out.

"Don't go sticky," Jake snorted. "You'll spoil my theological image."

"Don't worry about that. You'll always be a son of a bitch." Charity slammed the car door and leaned in through the window. "Just kind of a nice one."

"Queen of the Treacle Harvest." Jake gunned the motor. "If you'd been with us, you'd have fallen in love with Yeshua just as Mary did. Women have a weakness for celebrity. Go on, I've got a call."

BARION TO COYUL:	SINCE STOVALL NO LONGER INTERESTED IN STRIDE, OBJECTIVE SEEMS ACCOMPLISHED. SHOULD EXPEDITE. STRONG REASONS TO TERMINATE.
COYUL TO BARION:	WHAT'S ACCOMPLISHED? SHE IS MERELY AFRAID OF HIM. WILL TERMINATE WHEN SHE'S SICK OF HIM. YOU SAID NO QUESTIONS. DON'T BUG ME.

BARION TO COYUL:	I SAY QUIT NOW. WHY MAKE A FEDERAL CASE?
COYUL TO BARION:	YOUR KNOWLEDGE OF WOMEN STILL NEOLITHIC. SUBJECT LOOSENED UP BUT NOT YET RESTRUCTURED. PRESENTLY AS LIABLE TO FALL IN LOVE WITH JUDAS AS WOODY BARNES OR ANYONE ELSE. BESIDES, I'M BEGINNING TO LIKE THE LASS.
BARION TO COYUL:	PSYCHOBABBLING SENTIMENTALIST.
COYUL TO BARION:	NEXT TO VIOLENCE I REALLY HATE DIRTY LANGUAGE.

28

Everyone comes to the Banal

A week without Paladins assured Charity that her trail was cold. She relaxed into the humdrum of the Club Banal, which combined all the functions Jake listed. There was the bar, built in the Tijuana-Juárez style of the late '40s, with rickety tables and a brass ensemble that played interminably. Just off the bar down an atmospherically dim passage were the brothel rooms. Behind this vigorously active function lay BSA (Below Stairs Accounting, office of), a huge open space like five airplane hangars end to end. From the entrance, BSA receded into a dim infinity of desks, workers, the *chitter-clatter ting!* of office machines and the asthmatic buzz of government phones obsolete in 1960.

"What do they do here?" Charity asked Elvira Grubb, who conducted her introductory tour.

"I'm not sure, lamb. No one is."

If the function of BSA remained obscure, the people were more than familiar to Charity, like the VA and post office workers at home. They filed into the bar on their breaks to hunch over the tables in disconsolate huddles, bawling at each other over the deafening music. None of them could tell Charity Stovall what BSA ultimately produced, being employed strictly on a need-to-know basis. They needed to know very little and were not at all curious about the end product. They processed mountains of paperwork, all requiring triplication and interoffice memos, listless, disinterested and permanently dissatisfied. Since time meant nothing, the smallest mistake in the endless lists of numbers and names jarred the Leviathan process off its treadmill track. Back came whole Himalayas of completed lists for checking, recopying, rechecking, review and countersigning once again. Conversations in the bar centered obsessively on who made the most mistakes, who was getting kicked upstairs or who was next in line for promotion. They endured a grinding, low-grade misery but no one ever left except to visit the girls.

"They could leave anytime," Elvira told her, "but no one ever does."

The whole thing seemed pointless to Charity. "Gollee, why would the Devil make up such a wimpy kind of punishment?"

"Bless you, child, the Prince doesn't punish anyone any more than *I* do. They brought all this with them." Elvira Grubb had a comfortable, sensual laugh and the relaxed plumpness of a woman come to middle years by an enjoyable road. Her life, she felt, had been marvelous and death was even better. "I take care of things and water the drinks and—if I do say so—give the establishment what decorum it possesses. My husband is an eminent critic and friend to the Prince. Did I tell you that Mrs. Lincoln was a confidante of mine?" Elvira had, more than once. "She didn't deserve her bad reputation in Washington society. Let me tell you, that husband of hers was not an easy man to live with. You watch out for these humanitarians. Someone close wants a little affection, they're always off loving Mankind. Now, Wilmer is a perfect husband. A real bear cat."

And off she'd go, telling once more of her romantic marriage while Charity tried to enjoy her diet cola and found she could no longer stomach anything so insipid.

"Give me a bourbon straight up, please?" said the suddenly needful Charity. "This stuff tastes like these people look."

True, gray and unhappy as they were, no one left the club or the accounting office. They hung over the tables or the bar, complaining about the petty but endless injustices of civil service or what hell should really be, but no one really tried to change anything.

"Why should they when it's all so nice and steady and safe?" Elvira philosophized from her high desk between the bar and the annexed house of qualified joy. "Babies always rattle their cribs, but they wouldn't be comfy anywhere else, I say. The girls are fantasy . . . Good evening, Mr. Pugh! Nice to see our regulars, go right up. Domination on the second floor, same as always . . . Where was I?"

"The girls are sad as the office." Charity swirled the swizzle stick in her bourbon. "And those old ladies up in Accounting. Work, work, work, and once a week, big deal, they put on an awful hat with fake flowers, and go across the street where there's girl waitresses and fancy cocktail napkins and get blind. They sweep 'em out in shifts."

This was also true. The retrieval of genteel and very blitzed old ladies from the lounge across the street was a cottage industry in itself.

"Never mind." Elvira stuck to her point. "Whatever they dreamed, this is all they ever really wanted and the office is all they ever got. Used to it. Be scared to death of anything else."

You get what you pay for, Charity knew, *which means what you can afford, and you get used to that. Even me, my big night, the first night of my really being a woman, and what do I look back to? The White Rose Motel, which it was probably built by the same people thought up this place.*

One worker, mired in the quicksand of Accounting, was still defiant. Leon Pebbles was thin, red-eyed

and always looked slightly feverish. Leon went an extra
mile to do his job well and to search out ways to improve
efficiency. Naturally his co-workers hated his guts.

"They don't want efficiency," he grieved to Charity. "They're afraid of it."

For his integrity, Leon lived on the Cross. Much
table kvetch centered on his wild-hair schemes to cut
down paperwork, which would mean less employment.
His memos were few, brief and lucid, heretical to calci-
fied supervisors who saw ruin in their comprehensibil-
ity.

"He don't read the Style Manual. You don't *begin*,
you *implement*. You don't *rush*, you *expedite*. Pebbles is
a square peg in a round hole."

"But what are we *doing?*" Leon lamented to Charity over his mineral water and ulcer tablets. He didn't
need the pills since his death, but they were habit, like
his compulsive efficiency. "Nothing, that's what. Pounding sand down a rat hole, and the less they do, the
longer the job description."

Heads turned at the bar: Pebbles had spoken a
taboo word. In this area Leon was Judas himself to other
workers. Lengthy memos were always coming down
from somewhere to be read, initialed and passed on.
Never less than ten single-spaced pages, they boiled
down to the need for efficiency and cutting paperwork.
To keep one's job from going under the ax, one's function must be represented as vital, complex and suffi-
ciently incomprehensible to dazzle the job analysts.
Trash burners alone, Leon's department, became End
Product Evaluation Engineers with job descriptions
couched in syntax that defied translation—

—*conceive, establish and maintain an effective system of end product evaluation and final action imple-
mentation of same . . . (see para. 27a above).*

Not so the traitor Pebbles, who, throwing caution
and the Manual to the winds, was brash enough to
write: *All material comes to me in large bundles, which*

I bag and burn. There are twenty-five of us to do this where ten would be enough.

A marked and friendless man. Bloody but unbowed, Leon prophesied to Charity with Old Testament wrath: "Someday, the Lord's anger and just plain COMMON SENSE, by God, is going to reach down and rewrite every by God job description in this dead-ass place. BOOM! You wait."

Leon plodded back to his job, threading his way through the tables, glowering at the sludge in the wheels of progress. "Just wait . . . boom."

The band played on, workers muttered into their watered drinks. Barion sent more agitated messages to his brother—

BARION TO COYUL:	ADVISE. READY YET?
COYUL TO BARION:	NOT. WILL NOT OPEN UNREHEARSED.
BARION TO COYUL:	HURRY REPEAT HURRY. IF SUSPICIONS CORRECT, OUR TYPE ENERGY FORMS WITHIN SOLAR SYSTEM, GROWING STRONGER.
COYUL TO BARION:	YOU MEAN WE CAN GO HOME?
BARION TO COYUL:	YOU UNBELIEVABLE ASS, I AM TALKING ABOUT JUDGMENT DAY. OURS. VERY LITERAL AND VERY NEAR. HURRY.

■ 29 ■

The treadmills of your mind

The Club Banal and her own place in it were faintly absurd to Charity. The description occurred to her out of the blue like so many others lately. Absurd. Pathetic. She'd always recognized the words in reading but not often enough to work them into her own vocabulary.

"Ab-surd." She tasted the word. "Ridiculous. Redundant. That's me, all right."

The threefold business of the club churned onward through eternity. The bad brass ensemble slammed its musical assault against the harsh-lit tiles of the bar walls, the men of Accounting brooded and complained, Leon Pebbles seethed and muttered, "Boom . . ." The line of glum men shuffled forward to see the girls, browsed the Green Room and from there passed on to see what fantasy might beckon from the rooms.

With Charity's outbreak of new vocabulary came an increased desire to read, although the Green Room held little nourishment, mostly Harlequin romances read and reread by the girls until they had to be held together with rubber bands. Charity once devoured them like potato chips; now they seemed insipid. The heroines were all vanilla versions of herself in better clothes, the heroes all Woody Barnes with better

PARKE GODWIN

chances. For the waiting male customers, there was a shelf of "Bor" novels or something like that, not very interesting to Charity although she hewed her way through one or two from desperation. The men in these stories were all grim studs and all the women started out getting raped and ended up loving it. These books were kept on a shelf labeled "comedy" by the Puerto Rican girl, Esperanza, who had been raped at the age of thirteen and hadn't cared for it at all.

"Guy who wrote this oughta do three to five in a horny cell block, see how he likes it," Esperanza suggested darkly. "Hey, who took my Harlequin? I ain't done yet."

There were also some fat paperbacks called sword-and-sorcery, usually in three or more unreadable volumes each. Charity couldn't relate to fairies beyond Walt Disney. As for destiny-haunted princes—always getting hidden with poor folks at birth and then going on dangerous quests to find out who they really were—well, she'd been there with Dane and came close to a second heart attack and didn't need a replay. But fat Shirley (a.k.a. Lady Ellivare) read them over and over, sometimes starting with volume five and working backward.

"I can't help it," she confessed to Charity over her book and a box of chocolates. "I relate to all the destinies within me. How could I not, being Dion Fortune in my last life?"

There were other neo-pagans like Shirley among the Club ladies. They practiced a religion of emancipation and joy and were terribly serious about it, chanting their prayers to the Goddess in the fruity overtones of Eastern Star chapter ladies attempting *Medea*. They reminded Charity of Purdy Simco on a fired-up night in the tabernacle. The Catholic girls burned candles to the Virgin in their rooms, and gossiped back and forth through the thin walls between tricks and often during them. Protestant and Jewish girls just got bored and did

202

their nails, talked about leaving and finding a steady man and never did either.

Essie Mendel loved to talk about her boyfriend in Accounting, upon whom her eye was fixed with iron patience but dimming hope. This swain, like his father, had died of overwork, prostate cancer and his mother.

"But he still spends every weekend with her in Ultimate Rise. Even with her around, I'm going to live there one day," Essie vowed. "Oh, Char, those hu*mong*ous living rooms where all your friends can come and see and owe you. The icebox with all that *food*. It's to die."

"You never get hungry," Charity reasoned, already jaded with Ultimate Rise. "Bor-ing."

Essie Mendel was a born consumer. "How can anything so rich be boring?"

Monotony was usual, but now and then diversion reared its head when a holy war broke out among the girls. The neo-pagans were always swiping novena candles from the Catholics to use in their circles. The most recent skirmish pitted wiry little Esperanza against Shirley, goddamning and screw-you-ing each other to a standoff, Elvira wedged between them laboring for peace.

"Shirley, give Esperanza back her candles right *now*. I gave you a nice new Bic lighter just last week."

"I will *not* use a plastic lighter to purify my circle! The candles were mine to begin with. And my name, goddamnit, is ELLIVARE!"

Esperanza strained to get at her. "It's mud you don't gimme my candles, *puta*. All that goddess 'n' nature shit and running around in a fancy bathrobe and stealing *my* candles ain't got *nada* to do with God."

"Of course not!" Shirley screeched, stung in the center of religious principle. "You sellout female eunuch!"

"Elvira, what the fuck she talking about? Some

witch," Esperanza jeered. "Couldn't even charm the fat off her own ass."

"Oh, give her the damn candles." Shirley-Ellivare retired with the tatters of her dignity. "How can she understand the Goddess? Never even finished high school."

Charity could never see any sense in the physical inspection for the customers beforehand or the forms they filled out or the pro station stop afterward. "I mean, they're dead, aren't they? What can they catch? Jake said this place was real." Charity wailed her frustration and perplexity. *"None* of it is real!"

"Well, of course it's not." Elvira went on checking her bar invoice. "And then again it is. Look at those men in the line. What else was ever more real to any of them? They never knew much about women or sex or anything outside of their silly jobs. What else would they bring along?"

They'd tried dropping the pro station and the forms, Elvira pointed out. The customers missed the gap in normalcy. They enjoyed waiting in line, telling the same old jokes to the same friends, visiting the same women, creatures of habit even beyond death. They needed to touch something. Charity's working room was situated between the pro stop and the bar. The men came and talked to her for a few minutes before returning to work or another drink.

She'd never understood men very much, she realized now, or her own role in relation to them beyond a gut-level knowledge that life was not all that easy before marriage and tough as hell after, and you put up with each other.

A few passed up her open door; most came in, sat down on the off-yellow futon and talked to her. Talked at her, rather, falsely hearty, ultimately shy and wary of women on a one-to-one basis beyond the sexual mechanics. The rules, the forms and pro station helped them keep at a distance an experience and a being they knew very little about and feared a great deal. In time Charity came to feel her ten minutes the most essential in the whole production line. More than sex, it was the communication they starved for, part of them knowing what the rest denied, that they needed to touch, make contact with something beyond themselves.

Virgil Bassett was with her now. Virgil died of weight and worry as a surrogate for identity, reciting his life in tones leaden with resignation. Always there had been his gray job on a diaper service delivery route, and his discontented wife, whose chief ambition had been to head the Myrtle Beach Daughters of the Confederacy but who never flowered beyond the entertainment committee, thwarted throughout her days. Joy for Virgil Bassett translated to the few hours in his basement shop for meditation and the delicate art of kite making.

"Most relaxing thing I can think of, 'less it's flying 'em," he rambled pleasurably. "Certain summer days on the beach you get them updrafts, thermals, and that old kite'll stay up there breakfast to sundown. No strain, just a gentle pull on your line, but you know you got a friend up there. It's beautiful . . ."

He never knew the score any more than I did. Charity felt the compassion well up from deep inside for all of them and not a little for herself. *Hell, there's no mystery between men and women, except why some poor damn fool like me ain't figured that out yet. He's just like me, spent a lot of time just wishing someone would really look at him and listen to him like he was a human being and mattered. We lived with bullshit rules back there and more down here. Least we can do is make up our own.*

With the subversive insight came an irrepressible urge. "Hey, Virg." She winked at him. "Knock knock."

Interrupted in his dearest soliloquy, thermal updrafts and the nagging tyrannies of his wife, Virgil could only stare at her.

"Come on, knock knock. Say who's there?"

"Who's there?"

"Sonya."

Virgil snickered. "Oh, yeah, I remember this. Sonya who?"

"Sonya shanty in o-old shantytown. Knock knock."

"Who's there?"

"Slagle."

"Slagle who?"

Charity crooned: "Slagles ri-i-ing, are ya listenin'? . . . Now I got a hard one for you. What is two hundred feet long, green, with warts all over, and sleeps at the bottom of the ocean?"

Not ready for any of this, Virgil Bassett pulled nervously at an earlobe. "Warts and what?"

"Give up?" she brimmed.

"Hell yes."

"Moby Pickle! Got another," Charity threatened, definitely on a roll. "What's purple, wears a Scout hat and stamps out forest fires?"

Virgil foundered and went down. "Nothing is—"

"That's what you think." Charity zoomed off the futon, pirouetted and broadcast the answer to a cosmos agog. "SMOKEY THE GRAPE!"

Virgil gaped, trying to understand and failing. "That's dumb."

"Got a big fat headline for ya, Virg: so are we."

Dizzy all of a sudden, sight blurred, Charity wove on her feet. *What . . . what's happening to me?*

"Char-i-tee?"

In the process of pulling at his ear, Virgil Bassett became a still life. All sound ceased. Charity stood like a last survivor, able to hear and move in a vacuum. "What's—?"

"Charity?"

The voice was just down the hall, coming toward her room.

She knew who it was now.

Charity Stovall appeared in the doorway, waving casually to Charity Stovall. "Girl, you have been hell to catch up with."

Herself to every feature—clothes, hair, probably the fillings in her back teeth, yet with a subtle difference. Identical lines but each one more relaxed from head to toe and more clearly defined, the facial expression quite changed. Charity II *saw* everything she looked at but didn't put labels on it.

"Hi." She plopped down on the futon. "Surprised it's me?"

"Not a whole lot," Charity supposed after honest reflection. "Way things happen around here. Well, I look pretty good."

"Thanks." Charity II inspected the petrified Bassett. "Customer?"

"Mr. Bassett. Champion kite maker of Myrtle Beach, but he never got much time for it."

"Let me guess," Charity II divined. "When he flew the kite, he worried about keeping his job. On the job he dreamed about kites."

"That's about it."

"Never met himself coming or going. But we have. Let's work together, Char. We're better as a team."

"Weren't we always?"

"Gol-lee no." Charity II stretched her legs and crossed her arms, a disconcerting double image making herself at home. "Not in Plattsville, for sure not with Roy Stride. Not until just this moment, girl. We're not exactly each other. You're what I used to be. I'm what you could be. No big deal, just playing with a full deck, and didn't you run me ragged catching up."

"You know?" Charity said thoughtfully. "Like Leon says, you are by God right. I was just thinking—"

"I know, hon. That's why I'm finally here."

"Just listening to Virgil go on about his job and his miseries when he can do whatever he likes anytime he wants. And then . . . hell, I said, so can I. Elvira told me and told me."

"Doesn't count until you tell you," said her vibrant counterpart. "Lordy, but you were a case back in Plattsville. The resident Nice Girl on which the factory seal ain't been broke. Some virgin, Char: you screwed yourself for years, right up to five minutes ago." Charity II stood up, opening her arms for an embrace. "Gimme a hug, I've missed you."

Charity hesitated, a little wary. "You're not one of those actors, are you? There's a lot of them around."

"Guaranteed pure Stovall. C'mere."

Alone again. Or joined. Whatever, something very strange was happening to her mind. Pieces of it reaching to other pieces, straining to connect, one and one somehow making three. Charity squeezed her eyes shut and open again to clear the sudden blur. She remembered something without sense or reason. Water . . . leaning over a pool of water, her own flat, ugly face coming up in reflection to meet her—at first frightening but then so damn silly she *had* to laugh, though the effort hurt her throat.

She must have dreamed it before to recall the image in such detail. Someone was standing on the other side of the water, telling her about . . . a gift? And for the gift, something paid or lost.

Charity's sight cleared. The ancient, fragile dream faded, leaving an afterimage, a bright flash still glowing behind her eyelids when she closed them, then . . . gone.

Charity looked down at the sleeping Virgil Bassett. She smiled at him. "We're in an absurd place doing ridiculous things." She bent close to the lost kite maker of Myrtle Beach, lulling him in the manner of a movie hypnotist. "You're deep asleep, Virg Bassett, but you can still hear me. When I say the magic word, you will leave this room and this whole dumb place, bag and baggage. Do you hear me, Virg?"

"Yes," he sighed in sleep. "I want to, but . . ."

"But nothing. The magic word is *fly*. When I say fly, you will go Topside. Go directly Topside. Do not pass Go, do not collect any more bullshit. That includes your wife, who won't care anyway. You got better things to do."

Virgil drowsed; his lips relaxed into an unaccustomed grin. "Cer'nly do."

"Wake up, Virg."

He woke feeling utterly marvelous, as if a light had gone on inside him. Charity was very close and—Je-sus! —ten times more beautiful than when he dozed off. And while Virgil rubbed his eyes and tried to put it all together, Charity bestowed on him the most thoroughly feminine and satisfying kiss of his bereft existence.

"Virgil Bassett," she whispered tenderly, "go fly a kite."

■ 30 ■

Barion explains; it doesn't help

"Post-life energy. We're in the thick of it." Maj removed the tiny earplug that emitted a cacophony of human speech. "All my readings are unreliable. What *is* that madness out there?"

"Go to matter phase," Sorlij ordered.

The corporeal ship drifted in space like a sea vessel becalmed. In matter phase, the viewscreens showed nothing but the monotony of space. They decided to leave the ship in matter and return to energy phase themselves for compatibility. At least they could read brain waves.

Once away from the ship they needed some time to adjust to a kaleidoscope of visuals and the deluge of raw emotion bombarding them: changing landscapes of pastoral serenity, city buildings, meadows, a pulpit or two, dwelling places of austere simplicity or garishness, all under a continual verbal roar. Sifting through the storm of voices and energy, Sorlij's worst fears plummeted to new depths. "Oh, Barion . . ."

"It's the Rock for them," Maj knew. "Shall we ask directions?"

"Got to start somewhere."

They found themselves on desert sand under a blistering sun. Not far away, an oddly garbed human crouched on his knees, face to the earth in an attitude of fervent prayer.

"Excuse me," Sorlij began. "We're strangers here. Could you tell us—?"

The worshipper glared around, sprang up and charged at them with a wicked curved sword. "ALLAH IS THE ONE TRUE GOD!" *Swoosh!*

The blow merely passed through Sorlij, who dissolved and materialized further away, a little put out. "Now, see here, whoever you are—"

Maj made a stab at it. "We're looking for someone—"

The mad alien turned on her, swinging the sword. "PIGS!"

Maj discorporated and reappeared next to Sorlij. "Look, you might show a little court—"

"*Allah el Allah-h-h. The one, the all-merciful,*" the Moslem yodeled, winding up for another try at them—

But they were long gone before the sword completed its futile arc, passing over landscape that changed with disconcerting frequency along with a colorful cast of characters. They had bewildering adventures. A large, scented female with plastic flowers on her powdered bosom exhorted them to join something called the Brotherhood of the Holiest Elect. Someone named Scotty invited them for the weekend at Pola Negri's. A group of intense women, ignoring Sorlij, made a breathy, hands-on fuss over Maj and invited her to a sisterhood party "without the sexist." Twice more they were attacked, once with something saw-toothed and nasty, once with a tube that went rat-tat-tat. They managed to escape through montaging scenery to a quiet, empty street with small dwellings in white plaster and ocher tile. Maj wilted down on the lip of a quaint stone well, confused and discouraged.

"Somewhere in this madness I can read Barion," Sorlij maintained.

"If someone would just give us clear directions before they turned religious, erotic or homicidal. Sit down, dear, you look done in."

"I am." Sorlij drew a deep breath, enjoying the tranquillity of silence. "At least it's quiet here."

"You two!"

Maj sighed. "At least it was."

"Get ready to move. I'm tired of being polite."

Their interceptor bore down on them, a short, powerfully built man in late Roman dress.

"Greetings," Sorlij attempted. "We're a bit new around here—"

"No." Bishop Augustine inspected Sorlij up and down. "You are not Him."

"No, I suppose not," said Sorlij, staying carefully in neutral.

"I have sought Him for sixteen hundred years. I will find Him if it takes that long again."

"Our wish to the smallest syllable," said the diplomatic Maj. "We're looking for him, too."

Augustine surveyed Maj with unconcealed disapproval. "Cover yourself!" After observing the better local female forms, Maj had refined the concept to a dazzling image with a charmingly minimal regard to costume. "You are a woman."

"As you build them, more or less."

"The beauty of woman is a snare."

"I did hope I was in good taste. The one we're seeking is unusual to your sort. Very handsome." Maj had always thought Barion attractive when he wasn't suffering from poetry or cosmic purpose. "Blondish, tends to be tedious. We call him Barion."

"Oh, *that* one." The contempt was audible. "He is always underfoot somewhere. I think he is a little dim."

Sorlij agreed. "Quite possibly."

"I purpose to see that one myself—scant joy or profit as it holds. Come along."

Once more the scenery dissolved with unsettling

rapidity. The street became a plain hallway spaced with office doors. They followed the bull figure of Augustine until he halted at one, knocked explosively and entered without invitation.

"Here is where he works. If the verb applies," Augustine qualified. "Sort of a general fetch-and-carry. Barion, are you here?"

"Augustine? Just a moment, Your Grace." A drawer slammed shut somewhere behind a row of ancient green filing cabinets. Barion emerged, hands full of papers. "Sorlij and Maj! I knew someone was in the neighborhood."

"Of course it's us," Sorlij acknowledged brusquely. "What's the meaning of this dissonant lunacy?"

"Tact, dear," Maj intervened delicately. "I'm sure Barion has an interesting explanation."

"Well, Maj: after all these eons." Barion made a valiant try at gallantry. "You've matured splendidly."

"And yourself, although you look a little drawn."

"I can't tell you how happy I am to see you," Barion confessed with more honesty than was apparent. "Overjoyed is not the word. Sit down."

Sorlij and Maj settled into wooden office chairs that creaked in protest at every move. Augustine remained standing, a rock of long-thwarted purpose. "Attend me, Barion. I have been trying for sixteen centuries to extract from you a plain answer as to—"

"EEEE!" Maj shrieked and turned dark blue with horror. A nightmare loomed suddenly in the open doorway, most of its body burned to char, the rest caked with blood.

"Which way to the martyrs, please?" the apparition inquired.

"Martyrs." Barion riffled through a Rolodex. "Martyrs . . . yes: William James, just down the hall."

"Thanks awfully." The horror bobbed out of sight.

"Have to be a little patient with martyrs," Barion explained genially. "They tend to feel *arrivée.* Mr.

James helps them put it all in perspective. Well." Barion sat down at his desk. "I suppose you're here to collect us —a-and I imagine you have a great many questions."

Masking his mind from them, Barion fired an urgent message at Coyul across the void—

SORLIJ AND MAJ: READY OR NOT, HERE THEY ARE. GO WITH WHAT YOU'VE GOT.

The reply came instantaneously, hurried and harried:

YOU THINK YOU'VE GOT PROBLEMS? FORGET IT.

No help there.

Sorlij and Maj demanded to see Coyul as well. They assumed he was in the other messy pool of post-life energy.

"Coyul calls it Below Stairs. Very much like this place," Barion explained. "Just less organized."

Sorlij tried to imagine a place less organized than this. The concept was a challenge. "Well, we'll be taking you both back. And if you or Coyul have perpetrated what every indication leads us to believe, it's the Rock."

"Premature seeding with no authority." Maj shook her head in dire accusation. "You've always been spoiled, self-satisfied, self-indulgent and undisciplined, and now it's all caught up with you."

Augustine had lost any sense of direction or meaning in the discussion. "What means all this?"

"What it means, dismally, is a specimen like you," Sorlij snapped at him. "Please don't interrupt. What did you start with, Barion? Must have been far below standard CT."

"About nine hundred cc."

Maj blanched with utter shock. "Nine—"

"But that was part of the experiment," Barion amended quickly. "Combining augmented intelligence with the raw animal. You must consider success along with failure. I've produced some admirable specimens."

Augustine's brows shot up. "*You* have produced?"

"Yes. You may not be the most tolerant of men, but you did change the shape of European history and thought."

"Nine hundred *what?*" Augustine didn't understand any of this; there was a sensation in his stomach akin to indigestion that hinted he didn't really want to, but he must. "What is a CT?"

"There's another truth I want in your report," Barion went on, ignoring Augustine, who was suddenly seeing the fetch-and-carry bane of his existence in a new and horrible light. "Coyul wanted no part of this experiment. He was against it from the start."

"Anything that took him away from his silly music," Maj noted with honeyed malice. "We'll be questioning him, too."

"Well, Below Stairs is a bit chaotic, but my brother does what he can to keep things tidy."

"Your brother?" Augustine began to make even more unpleasant connections. "*Your* brother?"

"Coyul," Barion admitted with fraying patience. "Your Grace has given him less flattering titles. Please don't interrupt." He turned back to Sorlij and Maj, urgent. "Coyul is helping me now with a vital corrective measure. There's a girl Below Stairs. She's very important. You must let us complete it."

"This is enough to make a man mad," Augustine despaired. "No one knows where God is. All manner of undesirables wander in from anywhere"—a pointed glare at Sorlij. "One has to put up with heretics like Pelagius and that barbarian Luther—"

"Who is very much like you." Barion cut him off with even more fragile patience. "Utterly sure he's right and the rest of the world will realize it one day. Your Grace will recognize the tendency."

"Barion." Augustine drew himself up in last-ditch desperation. "What do you mean *you* produced—you and your brother—are you saying that *you* created the world?"

"Of course not. You were already here . . . sort of. I just improved you."

"THEN WHERE IS GOD?"

"A fine rhetorical. Where indeed?" Sorlij acknowledged. "But don't confuse the creature, Barion. He can't understand any of this."

—as the new message tinged with panic whispered into Barion's mind:

CHARITY READY BUT EMERGENCY REPEAT EMERGENCY AT CLUB BANAL.

What could happen at the Club Banal? Barion wondered. The place was a definition of fail-safe mediocrity. Nothing ever happened there.

All this in a nanosecond plus a fraction more to remember the tyrannies of Murphy's Law and that this was definitely not his day.

For a strong man Augustine seemed suddenly juiceless and brittle, though he was never a frail spirit. The implication was nakedly evident. "Barion—are you . . . ?"

"This primitive is not important." Sorlij rode over him with brusque purpose. "There's a great deal we have to know."

"If you are," Augustine struggled, a tragic figure, "then where is the City of God? Where the majesty of the spirit, where the mystery, the fall or the redemption?"

"Augustine, not today," Barion warned at the end of his tether. "Not today."

"Yes! Today! If *you* are—"

"All right! I *am*."

"Then—what remains but madness?" Augustine drew on his last resources of intellect, courage and dignity, all formidable. "Madness or low comedy. Shall we not then run wanton in the street? Why not? What remains?"

"A great deal remains, you relentless man," Barion said. "That I *did* build into that splendid mind I gave you. Though it's very like building a magnificent car for someone who obstinately refuses to learn to drive."

"You have riven meaning from existence. If you and these misbegotten sprites are gods—"

"You said it; I didn't," Barion countered. "You and your agonized ilk made it into heaven and hell, *I* didn't. The question was never fall and redemption but simply where and how high you can reach. There was a time when thunder and lightning were gods to your kind. The Egyptians improved on that. Moses built on them. Someone will build on you. That is the process."

"Barion, will you get back to relevance and stop wasting time on this creature." Sorlij jabbed a finger at the stricken Augustine in utter disbelief. "You think he understands any of this? You're talking to an *ape*."

"Well, that's the heart of it. I think he can. As long as I'm going to jail, one of the best minds up here along with Yeshua and Tom More ought to know what's happening." Barion regarded Augustine with a deep respect for that strong man's convictions and his own. "You *can* understand; I built you for it. You see, a long time ago, not far from where you were born, there was this monkey . . ."

31

Roy Stride and the First Amendment

At the bar, Charity had one for the road with Elvira to say goodbye. She was very pleased with herself. "See old Virgil finally walk out? Guess I did the Lord's work today."

"Topside's very nice when you're ready for it, dear. Hel-*lo*, Mr. Pebbles. Mineral water as usual?"

"Yes, thank you, Mrs. Grubb." Leon set a tight-wrapped package by his stool. Charity tapped it with her toe.

"What's that? More health food?"

"Absolutely," said Leon, even more febrile than usual. "Makes the system efficient." He scooped up his drink and package and headed for an empty table near the bandstand.

"Don't know what I'm ready for, Elvira," Charity reasoned, "but I sure know what I'm finished with, so I guess it's time to go."

"Good luck, dear. By the way, someone's been asking for you over on the bandstand."

Out of self-preservation, Charity always ignored the Club band, but today they sounded good enough for most of the tables to quiet down and listen; two soft trumpets in a relaxed, meditative rendition of "Body and Soul."

"That's an old one," Charity murmured into her drink. "Used to be one of Woody's fav—" When the thought connected, she did the largest double take in the annals of American romance. "WOODY!" And shot across the room, dodging tables and customers in a broken-field run to hurl herself into the arms of the most beautiful man she ever found too late.

"Woody." Charity crushed herself to the marvelous reality of him. "Oh, Woody, am I glad to see you. I was just leaving for Topside 'n' thinking I'd never see you again, and—"

"Hey, doll," the other musician broke in, wry and gentle, "We're doing a gig."

"Forget it." Woody introduced them warmly. "Char, this is Milt Kahane, my buddy from the Corps. This is Char Stovall, and she's with me."

"Don't you know it," Charity breathed.

"Time for a break, anyway, Milt."

"So it is." Milt took up the mike and addressed the tables. "Gonna take a break, timeservers. End of the set, but don't you fret. We'll be back on our stools with some oldie jewels."

"Hey." A drunk wobbled erect at a near table. "Can you play 'Unchained Melody'?"

Milt frowned at him. "Not with a clear conscience. Don't applaud, just grovel and throw large bills. Hey-y." His dark eye brightened with incentive as a thin woman undulated past the bandstand. "Who is *that?*"

"Essie Mendel," Charity filled him in. "Sort of engaged to a Jewish guy in Accounting. She's very Orthodox."

"I knew it; I can spot a *shayna maidel* at a hundred yards. They're always ripe for a little reform." Milt took a deep, zestful breath and clapped his hands together, a man about to party. "Take ten, Barnes." He sauntered away in Essie's wake.

"Woody." Charity still couldn't believe he was here next to her. "What are you—I thought you were Topside."

"Oh, things were kind of slow, and we heard the burritos were good here, and—honest to God, Char, ain't this a trip?"

"Yeah," she agreed with some irony, "how they gonna keep us down in Plattsville after we've seen Below Stairs? I didn't know you like Mexican food."

But then, come down to it, how much did she ever really know or see about Woody Barnes? Except he'd been her friend forever. She could recall him at any given moment, but never, she realized now, in clear detail: how the wiry hair over his forehead sort of shone with red hints under the bandstand light, or how good-humored his blue eyes were. Or how, while no taller than Roy, Woody's frame was lankier and more relaxed. She never looked or noticed any more than she really saw the rest of the world around her. Like the thin pale scar between thumb and forefinger that streaked two inches across the back of his left hand. She'd never noticed that. Charity wondered fleetingly if left-handed people ever looked much at other people's right.

"Where'd you get that scar?"

"This?" He turned the hand over, taking a second to recall. "Beirut; the day Milt and I got fragged. Corpsmen loading me on a stretcher, my damn hand fell over the side right onto broken glass. Couldn't win for losing that day." He stretched out the hand to touch her cheek. "Really missed you, Char."

"Same here," she said fervently. "A lot."

"Guess I was a damn fool just standing around letting Roy have you."

"That's done."

"But that's the way it was." Woody fussed with his horn. "You couldn't see anyone else."

That plus the old Plattsville brainwash bullshit, Charity remembered honestly. Save yourself for marriage and marry as soon as you can, before you know anything at all, let alone how to love. By the time you do, it's worn out as the car and the furniture. "Jeezooee, I was dumb, Woody. Anything worth doing takes practice, doesn't it? Like playing the trumpet."

"Sure. If you've never been bad, how do you know when you're good?"

"Or being a doctor or even roller skating. But they expect us to be good at love right off."

That one true love stuff never did much but sell houses and diapers and keep dummies like me off welfare as unwed mothers. There's no more one true love than one true song to sing or dress to wear. Totally ridiculous, but so was I for buying it.

But—here she was being intelligent for a change, even if she had to die to achieve it, and Woody Barnes was laughing at her, grinning like a stupid kid. "What the hell's so funny?"

"No . . . no. Just you look kind of different."

"I feel beautiful, Woody. Just when I thought I lost you for good, I find you when I'm going Topside myself. Now we can go together." She snuggled close to Woody, reveling in the security of his arms around her.

"I always loved you, Char. Took me a while to know it, too." A beautiful thing to say—too beautiful for the fresh convulsion of giggles that followed. "Listen, you have to trust a little, okay?"

"Maybe I will if you'll stop laughing like a fool."

"I can't go with you, Char."

She looked up at him in surprise. "You're not gonna stay here, are you?"

"Well, no." Woody seemed to be choosing his words with excessive care. "There's a lot I can't tell you."

Charity felt a chill grow over her happiness. "Why not?"

Woody Barnes was not supple at evasion. "Well, I'm not dead."

She didn't understand that at all. "But—your friend Milt, you said he died in Beirut, and here you are with him. There's not a lot of rules around here, Woody, but that's one of them. What do you mean, you're not dead?"

"Just sort of drafted. For the duration."

"Duration of what?"

"Well, that's what I can't tell you. Just my part's done, so I'm going home."

Too damned much. Staring at Woody, she felt the second loss of him like a physical ache. Lost once out of ignorance and now again for no reason she could understand, and here he was telling her to trust . . . men.

"Always telling me what to do!" she flared suddenly. "First Roy, now you. Goddamnit, Woody Barnes, you are not in charge of the world—"

Only one answer. Woody Barnes finally made the right one. He kissed her. Thoroughly. In the lovely middle of it, Charity knew even more poignantly what she'd missed and would be missing for forever yet to come, but now at least she had some experience to judge from. Woody didn't have Dane's electricity or the bitter-tangy fascination of Jake, but . . . oh, yes. The kind of kiss you could live with a long time like a good, comfortable bed, and it tore her heart out with so much wisdom come too late.

"Damn, Woody," she said weepily against his cheek. "You're going home and you'll be married to someone else—"

"No way, Char."

"Come on, be real. You'll find someone else 'n' have kids and a whole life to live. And when I see you again, if I ever do, there'll be so much you lived that you can't share with me, and it's so damn, rotten un*fair*—and here I am putting my heart out for you to walk on and what the hell are you *laughing* at?"

All through her bittersweet lament, Woody's grin had grown even broader. "I can't tell you, but will you trust a little?"

"Like a stupid hyena: yuk yuk yuk."

"Girl." Woody kissed her again. No mistake, he was very good at it. *Talk about can't win for losing,* she lamented through his embrace. "I promise you, Char Stovall, you won't miss a thing. Whatever comes to me, I'll share with you."

She punched his arm in frustration. "How about sharing the joke?"

He still shook his head with that stupid-pleased grin. "No joke."

"Not to the late Miss Stovall it ain't."

"But it's big, Char. I don't know if anything like this ever happened before in the whole world."

"That's a safe bet." Charity glowered.

"I told you to listen, okay?" Woody shook her gently by the shoulders. "We'll see each other again. Trust me, okay?" He brushed the hair from her forehead delicately as if just discovering it. "Don't be sad, honey."

"Easy for you to say." With feminine practicality, Charity thought of Jake. She could go anywhere and, face it, a girl could do her waiting with a good deal worse. "I'll try not."

"Fall in, Barnes!" Milt reappeared, balancing a platter of burritos in one hand, Essie Mendel latched on to the other. "They didn't lie about the nosh, it's great. My treat, enjoy. This is Essie, also a winner."

Her own feelings very sensitive just now, Charity could read them in Essie like a neon sign. She clung to Woody's good-looking friend close as after-shave, and her introduction was clearly proprietary. "Char, this is Milton Kahane. He's Reform from Long Island."

"Reform?"

"The next thing to Unitarian," Milt translated. "Let's grab a table and assimilate."

They were moving to join Leon Pebbles at his ea-

ger invitation when the front doors exploded inward
like a broken dike, loosing a tide of armed Paladin
guards. The shock squad fanned out from the entrance,
leveling submachine guns and bad dialogue at the startled customers.

"Freeze, mothers!"

"Nobody move!"

"Hold it, turkey—don't even think about it."

"Me?" Woody eased between Charity and the
weapon trained on them. "Mind not pointing that thing
at me?"

"Shut up, pussy." The gun muzzle swung on a
slight movement from Milt. "Don't try it, dogshit. I'll
mess you all over the wall."

"Please, not again."

"Everybody over toward the bar. Move."

Charity had a bad feeling that she understood more
of this than she wanted to. The next moment proved
her dismal theory. Fat little Drumm strutted through
the door, flicked his clams-under-glass over her, then
the room at large, and motioned to someone outside.
Roy Stride stalked into Club Banal in SS black, whip in
hand. He took the moment, giving them all, including
Charity, the full effect of his absolute power.

"Hi, honey. Said I'd find you. C'mere. Okay,
Drumm, everything's cool."

"This is not a general raid," Drumm announced.
"We want only Miss Stovall. No one but her abductors
will be arrested."

"Come on, Charity." Roy gestured with his coiled
whip. "You're rescued."

Charity was sick at the sight of him but more afraid
for Woody than herself. These people could hurt him.
She started falteringly to obey. Woody's grip tightened
on her arm.

"No way," he said.

"Hey, Woody." Roy strode to him, offering his
hand. "Didn't know you were here. When you get it?"

Woody ignored the hand. "I got you way back, Roy, just wouldn't face it. Char's going Topside."

"You think so?" Roy smirked confidently. "Where've you been lately? I got those wimps in my pocket, boy. And the Prince. Shit, I ain't seen that sucker since I got here. Nobody fucks with me, Woody." He threw the fact to the room at large. "Nobody! You seen it on TV. Even Topside's playing ball with me."

Chewing on his burrito, Milt Kahane commented: "Hardball."

Roy turned on him, dangerous. "You got something to say?"

"You heard me," Milt said calmly. "And when you fan on your last strike, they're gonna ram the bat up your ass."

Roy looked Milt up and down with a grudging admiration: a badmouth but with guts and . . . somehow familiar. Maybe it was just the superior smile he'd writhed under all his life. In the lethal silence Leon muttered about Judgment and efficiency.

"Who are you?" Roy demanded. "You got a Jew look, boy."

"Me? I'm practically Swedish."

"I don't think so." Roy snapped his fingers. "This one to the camps."

"You always were a fuck-up." Woody stepped out in front of his friends. "Couldn't get out of boot camp without doing bad time. I was Topside when they cut orders on you, Roy, and you are in deep shit already. So take a little advice from the heart. Back off. I mean it."

Woody's still determination stopped Roy for a second before he remembered who had the guns and the power. "That you talking? Old go-along-with-the-program Barnes? Forget it. Charity, let's go."

She shrank back from him, remembering her own horror-filled eyes looking up at a gun barrel. "I can't."

"Charity, I don't wanta get personal in front of all

these people, but you're already my wife, if you know what I mean."

Along with the fear, she felt disgust. "That's not personal, just tacky."

"Uh—excuse me, Leader Stride?" A small man with hunched shoulders and a potbelly edged forward from a huddle of his co-workers, hands still up. "If you don't propose to facilitate any arrests, I've really extended my break and have to return back forthwith to my duty station."

"What *is* this?" Roy's frustration blew up in a vicious crack! of his whip. "You want trouble? You scumbags want arrests?" He whirled on Charity and Woody. "You think I'm shitting you? Okay. Drumm!"

Click! "Sir."

"Every third one to the camps. I don't care—man, woman or queer." Crack! "I'll show you suckers trouble—"

"Ow, *there* y'are luv!"

Her strident cheer barely diminished by a long troublesome search, Florence Bird shouldered and flounced her way through Paladin guards toward Roy— who went sallower than usual against his SS black at the sight of her. Florence by contrast was an animated Cézanne in a painfully bright flower-print dress with bits and ends that bobbled with the jiggling of her Junoesque proportions, topped off with precisely the wrong hat skewed at a precarious angle. She bore down on the speechless Leader with a bear hug and lipsticky kiss.

"Crikey, dear, been 'avin a butcher's all over Below Stairs for you. Try to get you on the phone, this little pouv"—a contemptuous thumb jerked at Drumm— "says you carn't be disturbed. Not 'arf short wiv me. Y'orta talk t'im about it."

Roy's mouth worked. His eyes tried to deny what they saw even as he realized that dictators like anyone else could be caught with their image down. His colorless complexion went even paler; to Essie Mendel, the whole picture was a contradiction in obscenities.

"You've got to have good coloring to wear black," she whispered to Milt. "He looks like mayonnaise on my cocktail dress."

Roy managed to escape from Florence's possessive grip but found only part of his voice—a sort of squeak. "What the hell—are you crazy coming here?"

"Well may y'arsk, dearie. Got tired of sitting on me Khyber in front of the goggle box all day, nuffin to do but watch me gentleman friend prance all over town."

"Christ, will you cool it?" Roy hissed between clenched teeth. "This is Charity!"

"Not with *me*, luv," Florence vowed with gale-force lung power.

"Christ, you dumb—it's my fiancée. Charity Stovall."

"Ow, lumme! A *course!* Where's me 'ead?" Forthright and unabashed, Florence strode to Charity, offering her hand. "Sorry, dear. Needn't take on: just business with me and Roy. Cash and carry, hands across the sea and that. Florence Bird. Very pleased to make your acquaintance, I'm sure."

"Oh, that's all right." Charity didn't know what to say, nor did she trust herself to try. "I was just leaving."

"There's nice." Florence beamed. "Lor, what's on in the high street outside? Pushed this way 'n' that by bleedin hordes of telly men, and look at this hat what I bought just yesterday, all bashed in. Lot of right brutes, got no respect for a lady."

"Telly?" Her meaning galvanized Roy Stride. "You mean television?"

"Don't I just?" Ruffled, Florence inspected the damaged hat. "Weren't for that nice Mr. Veigle, wouldn't've got in here 'tall."

Drumm made a sound like a man dying under a curse. "Veigle . . ."

Roy cast about wildly. "Drumm, do something!"

Too late. Whatever blitzkrieg strategy sprang to Drumm's mind, Eddie Veigle was already sweeping through the doors, the double-breasted, brusquely confident point for a flying squad of BSTV technicians, some shouldering cameras, others paying out cable for a makeshift monitor control, grips and makeup people in their wake, Nancy Noncommit bringing up the rear.

"Well, well, well," Veigle purred. "Everybody's here. Who's minding the revolution? Char, the mystery star *and* Florence Bird." Veigle couldn't resist a chuckle of pleasure. "Perfecto. A fifty share. Even Topside won't be watching anything else."

"HOLD IT!" Drumm tried in vain to stem the stampede of technicians around him. The guards weren't much help. Hoping for some more television exposure, they started straightening uniforms and hats. "You can't do this, Veigle. This is an official government rescue."

"My Polish grandmother had such a rescue," Essie muttered. "One kiss from the magic mamzers, she turned into soap."

"Oh, this is a class act," Milt sighed. "History as drama: what do we get? Reruns."

A camera focused on Drumm; a light meter flirted near his mustache. He was becoming spastic. "THE LEADER FORBIDS THIS!"

"How?" Veigle chortled from his monitor. "This is news, lovey. Ratings. I told you Char couldn't move without me. You don't want to work with Veigle? Okay, Veigle works without you. Cue Nancy."

Freshly primped by her hovering makeup woman, Nancy Noncommit spiked herself beside Florence and turned to the camera with blank-eyed authority. "This is Nancy Noncommit at the Club Banal. The suspected other-woman scandal shadowing Roy Stride broke here a few minutes ago when, acting on an anonymous tip—"

With malicious emphasis, Veigle mouthed it to Drumm: *Me, Drumm-bum.*

"—BSTV news broke the story in a deluge of disclosures. We found the Leader, his fiancée, Char Stovall, and the other woman, Florence Burns—"

"That's Bird, y'little git." Florence moved firmly into frame, nudging the smaller anchorwoman aside, flashing a toothy smile at the camera. "Florence Bird from Lambeth, and lor yes, we been together *ever* so long."

In the backwash of the storm, Woody and Char stuck close together. "Char, who is this Veigle guy, anyway?"

Charity's expression was not easily decipherable. "Whatever he is, he just hit the fan."

■ 32 ■

Blossoms and thorns of
the media culture

Despite the media cyclone whirling about them, Roy and Drumm fought a brief, sibilant battle.

"Leader, you have to make a statement. The whole thing is out."

"Not if we shut them up good and quick."

"We can't arrest everybody. It's bad press."

"We're getting that now or maybe you din't notice."

"The scenario."

"What?"

"The scenario. I wrote it out. We talked about it as a contingency plan."

Roy found it difficult to think fast at bay. "Oh. Yeah, I remember."

"And you must weep, my Leader. For the camera."

"No." Roy was adamant. "I can't do that."

"Why not?"

Roy fidgeted; Drumm pried at the bedrock of deep beliefs where his icons were enshrined. "Ain't what a man would do."

Drumm's little eyes blinked behind their thick

lenses. "Why do you think all this is news in the first place? Because you have transgressed? Rather that they recognize it. Not a real man Below Stairs who won't identify with you. Not a woman who won't sympathize: he's human, he's like us. They will know you for a man of large appetites as powerful men always are."

Still not convinced: "But why do I have to cry?"

"Because, my Leader, with the macho comes the marshmallow. The emotional response of people conditioned to believe anything they see on television as truth. The camera giveth and the camera taketh away. They will believe your repentance: the good man strayed but anguished for the pain he's caused. A man gone wrong, but a man throughout."

Roy began to like the image. "Yeah . . ."

"Leader, you'll be more popular than ever, Topside as well as here. Not a dry eye in the cosmos. You heard the Jew Veigle: no one will be watching anything else. We can deal with him anytime; meanwhile we must turn this to our advantage."

"But I can't *cry.*"

"It's simple. Pull the short hair in your nose, right . . . there. If that doesn't work, we have glycerin."

Roy surrendered to the imperatives of destiny. "Ah, shit. Let's do it."

Nancy Noncommit turned to the monitor. "That's it on the Bird."

"Okay, where's Char?" Veigle took center stage, an impresario committed to producing a miracle whatever the cost. "Hey, Stovall! You're on."

"No, she's not. Leave her alone," Woody fended him off. "Get away from her. She doesn't want to talk to anybody."

True: Charity struggled with every appearance of distress. "I—I can't talk now, honest." She collapsed in a chair at Leon's table. "Now, now . . ."

"Okay, cue the Leader." Veigle spun around, pointing at Roy. Drumm nudged the reluctant subject forward.

"From the left side only," Drumm ordered the cameramen. "Cameras three-quarter angle from the left *only*. Your best angle, sir."

Thrust into the glaring lights, nose hair tortured into yeoman service, a tearful Roy Stride went on camera—incoherent with shame for a watching cosmos, struggling with the demands of honor. Nancy Noncommit pushed the hand mike close to his face. Hushed, expectant silence.

"I can't—I don't know how to say this," Roy choked. Suddenly he turned away, hands to his face. At the monitor, Veigle talked into his headset.

"Close-up. Get the sweat and tears. I want his *pores*."

One more furtive yank at the nose hair filled the monitor with Roy's moral agony. "What I did—I can't undo. I just wish—" He stopped, swallowed hard, then went on. "I can only ask the forgiveness of the good people who—who believe in me."

Once into his role, Roy was surprisingly good. Even Essie was stirred. "It's sad, Milt. Look at that big English *bummerkeh* and tell me who's really to blame."

"Essie, you make me wish I were alive again. I could be sick all over you."

"What are you talking? Look at Char."

Under Woody's soothing hands, Charity's shoulders heaved tragically; from the hollow of her cradling arms came the strangled sound of deep emotion.

"But I—I won't hide anything from my people," Roy went on valiantly. "I only wish to God I could undo what I've done." He faltered on the verge of fresh tears, then got it out in a ragged rush. "And that I can earn the forgiveness of the fine, good woman I asked to be my wife."

Roy's face filled the monitor—agonized, streaked

232

with tears. "My office is new. I was—under a lot, a great deal of strain. Charity—honest to God, Charity—"

"Is that tomorrow's headline or is it not?" Veigle crooned into his headset. "Camera two on Char . . . beautiful. Now split one and two."

Roy and Charity now, split screen. Charity raised her head to Roy, equally racked, fighting to hold her feelings in check.

"Never top this," Veigle knew. "Never."

"Roy. Oh, Roy—" Charity struggled and lost. The words splintered, sputtered, roared into a raucous gut-hoot of hysterical laughter.

"Never . . . in all my li-life," she gasped. Out of control, clutching at her ribs, Charity collapsed on the floor by Leon's feet. Spastic, beyond control, she grabbed for something, anything to keep her this side of lunacy. She hung on to Leon, came away with his package squeezed to her own heaving chest. For a fifty share of Below Stairs and Topside, Charity Stovall imprinted her judgment on the cosmos.

"Y-you gotta be the b-biggest asshole that ever died."

Charity surrendered to a fresh onslaught of coughing and hiccups. Sadly, Veigle drew the finger of doom across his throat. "Cut, for Christ's sake." He glared balefully at the monitor, prompted to murder before his practical side came to the fore with an angle. "Save her tape," he growled into the headset. "We can sell it to the opposition."

Meanwhile, back at madness, Charity held out Leon's package to Roy, still sputtering. "Listen: even the groceries are laughing at you."

Roy charged at her. "What're you, crazy? This is going out *live*—"

"Hear it, Roy?" She jittered on the edge of fresh hysterics. "Even the bag is laughing."

Roy tore the bag out of her grip and threw it aside,

raging. "You don't laugh at me. You ain't so much, you goddamn whore. *You don't laugh at me—*"

—while Nancy Noncommit talked into a headset in a steely whisper: "Veigle, we're still rolling."

"I know." His voice oozed confidence again, buttered with delight. "We'll hide at least one tape. Did I say fifty share? Sixty! This belongs to eternity."

"Nobody laughs at me!" Roy raised his fist to batter the laughing truth from Charity's mouth. Before the blow could launch, he was caught by the collar and flung violently backwards on his butt, gaping up at Woody Barnes. Not a protracted gape. Into that classic study in astonishment, Woody hurled a juicy burrito with unerring accuracy and a *splat!* that would have thrilled Mack Sennett.

Incoherent with fury, Roy clawed at his holster and brought up the huge Lüger. "Shoot 'em all, Drumm! Every mother—" Point-blank at Woody's face, he squeezed the trigger.

There was a sharp report but not much else. A baby-pink flag unfurled from the pistol barrel, bearing the rubric: BANG!

Those few guards who had presence of mind to obey his final-solution order rather sheepishly discovered similar flags fluttering from their weapons, advertising MCDONALD'S—BILLIONS SERVED. Milt Kahane raised his hands in praise of celestial genius.

"Boss, Prince, I love you. The universe is sane, after all."

Then—acute hearing and traumatic memory wiped the joy from Milt's face. His eye shot to Leon's package, now busily ticking. He groaned with horrible prophecy. "Barnes . . . listen."

"YES! LISTEN!" His hour come round at last, Leon Pebbles, man of destiny, did not slouch toward Bethlehem but sprang to it atop the table, package held high with maniacal triumph. "I told you bastards the day would come. The day of total efficiency. Minimum paperwork and everyone sees the end product of his labors. FIVE SECONDS—BOOM!"

A frenetic five seconds, most revealing of character. Accounting personnel, used to doing nothing without directives, did just that. Elvira ducked behind the bar, mourning her freshly laundered tablecloths. Woody dove for Charity, upending a table for cover. Bug-eyed, Roy swerved for a second to Drumm for advice he'd never have time to heed, then hurled himself at Florence to protect the last, best pure Wasp piece of tail in the universe. Milt grabbed Essie and launched them both toward the deck—

"INCOMING!"

COYUL TO BARION:	PLEASED TO REPORT CHARITY VERY READY, VERY BEAUTIFUL.
BARION TO COYUL:	THEN PULL THE PLUG.
COYUL TO BARION:	LOVE TO. ALL BEST, XXXX

■ 33 ■

All this significance—what does it mean?

Reeking of smoke and burrito, Roy Stride booted open the door to Coyul's salon and invaded with Drumm behind him. He'd left his Lüger behind, not trusting any weapon that read BANG instead of doing it. Right now his fury was a more formidable threat.

"Where is he?" Roy fumed. "Where's the Devil?"

"Ah, Mr. Stride. Just a moment." Coyul paused to feed a notation to his computer with two fingers, orchestration with the remaining three. "We were expecting you. Good of you to be prompt."

Roy dismissed the ineffectual little man with one contemptuous glance. "I got no time for you, pussy. Wanta see the Honcho, you got it? The Devil."

"The term is considered gauche, old boy," said Drumm, whose flat American accent waxed suddenly British.

"True," said Coyul. "I prefer simply Prince."

Seething with his recent humiliation, Roy didn't connect at first. Not this nerdy little wimp in a business suit. "Don't shit me, man."

"Wouldn't think of it. Sit down."

"Fuck I will!"

"Over there." With no effort of his own, Roy floated swiftly toward and into a designer chair, unable to leave it. "All right, Barion."

Two men entered the salon—one dark, about Roy's size, who looked like he didn't have a single spot in his body without steel springs, the other big as a Redskin lineman in jeans. One of those blond college jokers he always saw in soft-drink commercials, making out with prime tail. Fucking big fag with muscles. He sat down across from Roy.

"Listen carefully, Mr. Stride," Barion began without prelude. "Your future depends on it. To begin with, you're not dead."

"Not . . . Drumm, what the hell is this?"

But even that stalwart's manner had changed. "It's the plot resolution, laddie. Do you gentlemen mind if I get out of costume? Awfully tired of it."

"By all means, Ned." Coyul's manicured hands fluttered in gracious assent. "And well done."

The sardonic Booth clapped slowly. "Applause, applause."

While Roy gaped, Drumm's image blurred, sloughing pounds, mustache and toupee, resolving to the fine-trained figure of Edmund Kean. He bowed to Roy. Coyul applauded lightly, presenting a second player.

"And a call for the ubiquitous Wilkes Booth."

With negligent ease, the lithe figure of Booth went squat and leathery green, quite vivid in Roy's memory.

"As Damocles." Coyul applauded. "Marvelous invention, Wilksey."

"You honor me, Prince. I was also outstanding as Dane." Another quick dissolve to the romantically tragic form of Charity's doomed lover.

"We don't need the entire dramatis personae," Kean reminded him sourly.

"The laborer is worthy of his hire," Booth countered with dignity, "and the player of his calls." The

237

larger-than-life tragedy of Dane became something mundane out of daytime TV in tailored slacks, designer haircut and a Members Only casual jacket. "As Randy Colorad."

Kean sniffed. "Juveniles were always your forte."

But Booth was not finished. While Roy stared, a horrible realization dawning, the vacuous good looks of Randy Colorad aged, lined, set into the sensitive and thoughtful image of Ernst Stahler.

"No! I blew you away," Roy denied. "I saw your fuckin head go six ways from Sunday."

And again Booth stood before him. "Stahler was my finest work. Deep, thoughtful. I may consider character work henceforth. Nevertheless—John Wilkes Booth at your service."

Roy had never been that good in school, but some names stayed in the pantheon of memory. "I remember you. You shot Abraham Lincoln."

"As a soldier of the Confederacy, sir."

"Stahler was utterly fine," Coyul appreciated sincerely. "I saw new depths and colors, Wilksey. Restrained, sincere . . . impressive. One was reminded of Scofield."

"Thanks, my liege. I believed in what I was saying," Booth recalled soberly. "Futile, even laughable I might have been in life, but at least in my time life meant something. Your world is a sewer, Mr. Stride. One can almost absolve you for being one of its diseases."

"Time, Coyul," Barion put in. "Sorlij and Maj, remember?"

"Right." Coyul struck his hands together. "Wilksey, I made you a promise."

"Please, Prince: not *Romeo*."

"Not a whit. We'll leave that to Leslie Howard. You may remount *Hamlet*."

Booth went down on one knee in gratitude. "Oh, my liege. My Prince—"

"Now, now. Don't gush, there's a catch. You'll alternate Hamlet and Laertes with Ned."

"You give me leave to kill, sir." Kean bowed with relish. "After that fruity Dane, I'll eat this buffoon for breakfast."

"Will you?" Booth rose to the challenge. "Look to your own ratty laurels, you laboring-class lout."

"Gentlemen, allow me to finish." Coyul's machinations were subtler than they knew. "Ned, you'll keep Wilkes within the bounds of good taste. And he in turn will teach you to fence like a gentleman."

"And somewhat less like a dancing bear," Booth sniped.

"With less mayhem to the scenery," Coyul hoped, escorting them to the door. "Now off with you both. Don't call me; I'll call you."

"You first, Ned." Booth stood aside. "You're considerably my elder."

"Ah, well—wisdom before folly." Kean swept out, but Booth lingered expectantly, raising his eyes in supplication. "Max? It's my *exit*."

The musical leitmotif of genial bonhomie sparkled in the salon. Booth's amber spotlight washed over him. Satisfied, with a heave of the shoulders, he followed Kean.

"You said I ain't dead," Roy blurted. "I don't get it. What's all this about?"

"Shut up. You'll get it. Believe me, you're going to get it." Barion's tone chilled Roy to the bone. His skin began to crawl under that merciless scrutiny. The son of a bitch looked like . . . eternity.

"You bug me, mister," Barion said.

"So who the fuck are you?" Roy bluffed. "Look, I'm covered, okay? I got treaties, Topside's word. No interference. I came here to see the Prince and it's this little wimp. So no bullshit, okay? Lemme go to the top."

Barion leaned back in his chair. "You're there."

Roy took a moment to digest and discard the absurdity. God did not wear Levi's. "Not you, man."

"In your parlance, you got it. As close as you'll ever get."

"Hey, listen, I *saw* God close up at the White Rose Motel. He sentenced me—"

"My friend Walter Hampden," Barion admitted. "Doesn't act much now but still does an occasional God, Moses or prophet. You're not dead. Charity's not dead, nor Woody. You can go home now if you want."

"Which we would prefer," Coyul remarked with a tinge of distaste. "The twentieth century is the foulest on record; makes the fourteenth immaculate by comparison. And it has produced, in a country like America, far too many like you."

"I wasn't ready for Hitler in 1933," Barion confessed. "I really didn't know how to deal with the danger of your kind or your sick needs. We've learned since then. Stahler put it nicely, you're a disease. The worst of what I could never breed out of humans."

"Though we certainly don't want to breed it into more," Coyul extended his brother's point. "If you married Charity—grisly prospect, but she was ignorant enough to go through with it—we shuddered to think what you'd have done to each other."

"Or your children to the world," Barion finished. "Charity is a great deal more intelligent than you. A son of hers could be quite gifted in beneficial ways. On the other hand, growing up under your benevolent influence, these gifts . . ." The beleaguered Lord of Creation let the obvious point dangle. "For Charity to put you aside as a reasoned act of will or even simple good taste was too risky in a place like Plattsville, where people pair at disastrous random for lack of wider choice."

"What are you trying to lay on me?" Roy sputtered. "You ain't neither one of you what you say. Look, I ain't dumb. You saw me on TV. You saw how they loved me.

They fuckin *loved* me. I raised my hand and changed everything."

Coyul wandered to the piano, running a scale. "We do crowd scenes well."

"No." Barion shook his head. "He doesn't believe it. He can't. Like higher math to that monkey at the water hole. His whole cosmos is drama, magic, fable. A vision of Christ and Salvation awash with melodrama, God as a white man, himself as hero. Minorities for villains. But he's going to believe it."

Barion rose deliberately and stood over Roy. "You're going to. Charity saw the truth when she was ready for it. But you, little man, you're going on cold. Coyul?"

Coyul ran an arpeggio into a Gershwin phrase. "I did this with a snake once. Ready or not, Mr. Stride—it's magic time."

His tormentors shimmered, dissolved to pure white light, became one glow as they flowed toward, into and through Roy. The last thing he clearly remembered was an instant of euphoria as that light became limitless understanding and infinite vision.

He was pure mind, pulsing in space, no division between sight and comprehension. He saw the solar system, then the galaxy dreaming through its eon-slow revolution. His view pulled back and back to encompass the unimaginably vast, wheeling universe, video-split with the movement of atoms within a molecule. Clear, painful intellect himself, he saw everything Coyul or Barion had ever seen—worlds men would not contact for thousands of years, if ever. Civilizations, concepts of God undreamable by humans. He knew horrors beyond simple brutality or destruction, complex beauties, a peace in being one with the universe, and the loneliness of being inexpressibly small, apart and insignificant.

Roy heard and understood languages whose simplest concept strained his mind to tortured sentience, heard music of a sublime, limpid simplicity. He observed the rise, flourishing and decline of noble and brutish races, watched them voyage out into space with the same greedy wonder as savages pushing log canoes toward the plunder of a neighboring island. Time spooled out, an endless film strip of still frames to which his hurtling consciousness gave the illusion of movement. Light-years, light-millenniums, light-eons. More galaxies and more beyond them, to worlds still forming, cooling, thunderous with the struggles of small-brained monsters that knew only hunger and rage.

Time and again the nascent worlds; time and again, given the narrow conditions of climate and distance from a sun, inevitably there rose one creature, manlike or utterly alien, racked for one moment/millennium with the terror and beauty of self-knowledge, drawn onward ever after, unable to retreat. And worlds beyond these, but nowhere an end. Nothing that glorified Roy Stride, nowhere a destiny in his size begun in the writings of a people he despised, attaining dramatic close in a crucifixion, endlessly vindicated in the violence of men like himself—none at least without a pathetic ending. Myriads like him came to power, shadows on film as his mind sped across time, rose, conquered, added their madness to the rubble spinning between the worlds, then died reviled or forgotten. Or worse, lampooned, made a sad or faintly ridiculous footnote in the dry histories of aberration.

Roy's cry of horror filled the universe, more horrible for the indifferent silence that swallowed it up. He wept with double pity, for himself and a knowledge of tragedy too huge for expression; whimpered in his smallness and fear, shrieked through the soundless void—

—put his hands to his face, shattered in the chair while the Devil played Gershwin and God spoke quietly to him.

"So much for the universal. Not much from your point of view. No MGM cosmos to answer the subjective hungers of your life. No denouement where God's lost will is found in the chimney naming you the Pure White Chosen One. Only worlds beyond worlds and a chance to understand in a place where death comes to all, even Coyul and I." The brothers exchanged a look of profound weariness. "After several hundred million years, that's not horror but relief."

"One tires of repetition," said Coyul at the piano.

"But what's it *mean*," Roy cried, agonized. "What is it for?"

"Not for anything. It exists."

Roy glared from one to the other. "I wanta go home. You said I could go home."

"You can." Barion nodded. "But there's a catch."

"Neat but nasty." Coyul struck an ominous minor chord.

"You'll remember everything, Roy. You'll see everything you were or wanted for its pointlessness, understand every motive for its cowardice and frailty. You'll know."

"Everything I just seen?" Roy faltered. "I gotta live with that?"

"You got it: everything. You won't know a day, an hour, a minute without that burden. You're not any more intelligent than you were, just more informed and defenseless against honesty. You'll spin out your life in an ordinary job with an ordinary wife dim enough to think you a blessing, until your kidneys or your heart fail or your cells begin to ad-lib with cirrhosis or cancer. You'll always know the meaning of what you've seen but never be able to express or accept it."

"It's—" Roy broke off, wincing as something happened in his head, like parts of his brain stretching to touch others. "It's insane."

"Oh, not as bad as all that." Coyul polished off " 'Swonderful" with a flourish and bounced up, shooting his cuffs meticulously. "There's the good side. Allow me, Barion?"

"Please do. I wouldn't want our hero to think us inhumane."

"You can always come back Below Stairs—permanently this time—with no unpleasant memories at all," the Prince of Darkness offered. "No strings, even a Drumm to support you, armies of illusions to hail you, inexhaustible minorities to massacre, mountains of architecture to express your magnificence. Even Florence Bird to defile you cheerfully on demand, since you seem to need that. They won't be real but you won't know that—except now and then, perhaps, in dreams you'll never quite remember."

"Or quite forget," Barion finished reminiscently. "You're the underside of my errors. Char Stovall is what I meant by human."

"Which reminds me. Will you excuse me?" Coyul appealed to his brother. "I've grown very fond of the lass. Like to take her home myself."

"By all means, but don't dawdle. There's Sorlij and Maj."

"Dear Sorlij. Lovely Maj." Coyul's smile was small and cryptic. "We'll have to deal with them, won't we? *Auf Wiedersehen*, Mr. Stride." Coyul glowed, sparkled and was gone. Barion turned back to business, unpleasant as it was. "Well, Roy?"

"*It ain't fair.*"

"No, it ain't. But that's the deal."

Still numbed by the horror of the indifferent universe, Roy felt himself lifted out of the chair and set on his feet before the huge man who was close as he'd ever get to God. *Why you gotta be so big? Why do you always get to look down on me? Son of a bitch, you done that all my life.*

"Size is irrelevant," Barion noted casually, shrinking and modifying to a new appearance—shorter than Roy, dark as Moonlight Jones. "You dig it better this way, white boy?"

The rage dimmed Roy's mind, blotting out even

244

the fear. Even though he knew why the red sickness boiled up in him and that the black man was only a cartoon of his own fear, his fists balled around the hate. Roy sprang at the figure.

"You black mother—

34

The catsup factor

—over and over again, Leon screaming about judgment and efficiency, Roy grabbing for fat Florence. Woody pushed her down behind a table and landed between her and the bomb just as it went off. God, the blast hit Woody all over and leaked through like a sieve *Woody, Woody, don't die for real.* And then, with his mouth close to hers, he simply kissed it to shut her up.

"Who's dead? It's catsup."

"Catsup." Her ears still rang from the explosion, too numbed to be sure she heard him right.

"And fake blood. It's all bullshit, Char. Just a little messy."

"Catsup . . ."

Charity sighed, close to waking. If Roy was the biggest asshole ever born, Woody was the biggest clown, with a nice kind of crazy in him. If she saw all this on the Late Show—

"Wouldn't believe it . . ." Charity's head lolled the other way on the seat, jolted by movement. She opened her eyes. Dark outside, shadows and fog blurring past the cab windows. She recognized the back of Jake's head, cap perched at a familiar angle. "Jake?"

Someone was holding her hand. "Well, Char?"

She blinked hard, rubbed the last sleep-fuzz from her eyes. "Simmy?"

"Even he. How goes it?"

"Don't know." Her stomach felt definitely odd. Misty limbo streamed by the car windows at great speed. "Where are we?"

"Almost to Plattsville," Jake tossed over his shoulder.

She tried to grasp the fact but failed, though one question formed itself loud and clear. "Simnel, where's Woody? What happened to him?"

"Waiting for you in McDonald's. I suppose I should clarify," Simnel offered in his kindly/careful manner. "The good news is, you're not dead."

"Not . . ." No, that couldn't be. "But I saw. I saw in the motel—"

Simnel looked slightly embarrassed. "Shameless special effects."

"I had a heart attack—"

"Real as the blood on your dress."

Dear old Simmy—laying a bolt of lightning on her in the same meticulous way he served champagne and strawberries. Charity was a very practical girl; she reacted in character. "*That's* why my stomach feels weird: I'm hungry." The backlash was swift and predictable. "Simmy, what the hell is going on?"

From the driver's seat, Jake reproved gently: "That's no way to speak to the Prince."

That took a moment to sink in before Charity rejected it. No way. She remembered the horned nightmare who got her number at the White Rose. "You are the—"

"Prince will do," Simnel/Coyul suggested. "We keep it nondenominational. "As for Simnel: from Lambert Simnel, another pretender. I wanted to look after you personally; you were very important to me."

"Thank you," said Charity, a little abashed. "You were a nice butler."

"We try to make it fun." Coyul nodded to the compliment. "Now and again things turn serious. Roy was serious. That's the bad news. He's not dead, either."

Charity struggled to comprehend, battling the last tatters of deep-rooted superstition. "But the—" She made vague pantomimic allusion to claws, horns and the unspeakable Damocles. They were exactly what she would have expected to see dying in sin. But that seemed a very long time ago. She could far more readily believe in plump little Simmy in his pinstripe suit, even liked the muted paisley tie.

"The night we abducted you," Coyul explained, "you were about to make a ruinous pact with your own scruples and marry Roy."

"No, I wouldn't" she denied vehemently. "I don't even hate him anymore. I don't feel anything for Roy but sad."

"You would have married him," Coyul was gently certain. "This is Plattsville."

"Just passed the city limits," Jake put in. Charity began to recognize houses and streets through the thinning mist.

"And here in Plattsville, there weren't that many options open to you."

No, she refused stubbornly. *I would have seen through him. I would've picked Woody.*

"In time, perhaps," Coyul answered her thought casually. "After the white dress, the wedding, the years and the children. One of whom would have been bright as you but tending to his father's failings. What Roy did with shadows Below Stairs, his son—the seething product of his ignorance and your inevitable frustration— could very well perpetrate here in a country susceptible to charismatic charlatans as a dog to fleas."

Charity needed no great mental leap to know that for truth. When she'd thought of God before, she always saw Purdy Simco, and maybe Jeffrey Hunter as Jesus, but always Roy as John the Baptist. As the cab turned into Main Street, Charity wasn't all that sure whether she was glad to be in Plattsville again, except Woody would be there.

And yet . . . something else, something once a part of her but gone forever now. "I feel like I lost something, Simmy."

"Not to worry; quite natural." He patted her hand. "One of your ancestors felt the same way. But you'll manage. Never fails, Char: every so often at the beginnings of your kind"—Coyul kissed his fingertip and transferred the blessing to the tip of her nose—"comes one smart little monkey. There."

Once again, as at Club Banal, Charity experienced an almost subliminal frame of memory—a pool of water, a dim image reflected . . . then nothing.

"But I do apologize for the theatrics at the White Rose."

"I think you should, Simmy. I might have had a real heart attack."

"Look at it this way," said the Prince of Darkness as the cab slid to the curb before McDonald's. "If I'd knocked on the door in a pinstripe, what could I sell you? Goodbye, Miss Stovall."

"Ms." Charity corrected him. "I just got liberated, remember?"

Jake alighted to open her door, but Charity lingered long enough to give Coyul an impulsive kiss and a squeeze. "Listen: if you have to pull this on anyone else, don't use the horns, okay?"

"I give you my word, that was an absolute first. If it's any consolation, tomorrow I may be out of a job altogether."

She cocked her head quizzically. "Would God let that happen?"

"He's in trouble, too. It's all very involved. Go on, now. Have talented children. At least one musician."

"Bye, Simmy."

Jake lounged against the front fender, hands in his pockets. "I suppose I'll miss you, Char."

"Don't say that," she said with no exaggeration. "I'll be wishing I was dead for real."

"Not you; not with all that living to do."

"Tell the truth, Jake, I almost—"

"No." He stopped her, pulling Charity close to him. "Never mistake compassion for something else. You could end up making a career out of it like Mary Magdalene," he recalled. "Always getting had and left. But she was that sort, an injury collector."

Charity understood him with canny female instinct. "You want to be alone always? I don't think so, Mr. Iscariot."

"It suits me."

Her affection just then was not at all myopic. "You haven't burned all your old vanities, Jake. There's a few left."

"Well." Jake opened the cab door brusquely.

"Don't tell me." Charity held on to him. "You've got a call."

He seemed anxious to be gone, glancing both ways along the street. "Maybe. Hate to deadhead all the way back."

"Wait, will you?" Charity pulled his head down to hers and kissed him. No, he wasn't good at it as Woody, but still almost worth being dead for. "I don't care if Simmy is the Prince and all that. Take him at gin rummy. He's a pushover."

"So are you." The sudden, urgent pressure of his embrace surprised Charity; dead or alive, still a definite hunk. "An abyss of sentiment."

"Go to hell," she murmured against his cheek.

"On my way."

Charity watched him slide across the front seat and drive away, turning at the next corner, cruising, ready to stop for a fare.

My God, I'm alive. I remember the water hole and

being lost and afraid. I remember someone making me somehow human, and the other one who took my fear of the face in the water and made me laugh at it. If that's the truth under all the Sunday-school trappings, I guess I can live with it. Have to.

A little giddy; she'd never had thoughts like that or so easily expressed. *They've kicked me upstairs, just like they did at the water hole. Please, Simmy, help us to keep laughing.*

When Charity turned to go into McDonald's, the first human being she saw through the windows was Woody Barnes, looking alive as she felt.

35

The higher education of
Roy Stride

—fucker!"

The blow launched at Barion found nothing to land on, threw Roy off balance. He sprawled on oily, stinking gravel. Roy blinked, shook his head, stared groggily at the man-made hills of the Plattsville garbage dump and up at the universe.

"I'm not dead. He said I'm not dead."

He lurched up, brushing garbage from the SS uniform; they'd left him that. They left him a lot more. His head hurt. His mind felt like a push-button FM tuner punching back and forth between two stations, two voices, his own and the scary one.

And the nightmare visions: pure mind again, watching from a great distance as the planets, from blistering Mercury to the dark ice ball of Pluto, wheeled about the roaring sun.

. . . worlds beyond worlds, nothing finite or contained but opening out forever in an infinite process of becoming. Intelligence subjective, flawed, needing ever to renew itself, cleanse vision, reform with no truth ultimate.

No!

Roy squeezed palms to his ears to shut out that serene, cruel voice. *NO!* he defied the broken refrigerators, plastic food containers, greasy tinfoil and rusted, skeletal Chevies. "It ain't like that. You can look it up in the Bible—"

Consider "Aryanism" first as a careless misinterpretation of a blanket term for a prehistoric people, later as an apology for white supremacy. This compounded error served as dogma for the diseased pseudophilosophy of Adolf Hitler, itself based on his severe paranoia.

"I don't know these words," Roy bellowed to the sprung-out sofas, broken kitchen chairs, pyramids of Hefty-bagged garbage and the incurious rats. "I'm alive. What you doing to my head?"

The visions would not leave him alone any more than the voice. Longer view now, beyond the solar system to the cold, bright stars, other systems whirling indifferently about the driving furnace of their suns.

Paranoia, the common cold of neurosis. The paranoiac, perceiving all external stimuli as threat, needs to see his enemies, not merely sense their external presence. Being imaginary, these threats must be fleshed out to visible targets, the more clearly defined the better. Thus the emotionally defeated German worker was given the Jew. His disadvantaged, disenfranchised American counterpart is offered not only the Jew but the Negro and Catholic—together with any group, way of life or system of belief not harmonious with his own, stamped with the label ENEMY in large red letters.

"You stop!" Roy sobbed to the microcosmos of broken Styrofoam, spent toothpaste tubes, Tampax, condoms, Kleenex and the small, night-foraging animals surviving now as his own kind once did. "Holy Jesus, get out of my head . . . STOP."

With his whole shriveled soul, he begged the voice to leave him alone. Against that gigantic clarity, he struggled to regain a small, neat box for a cosmos to believe in, with strong walls to contain all the truths he lived by, but the walls caved in under the pressure of what he knew and could never again deny.

He saw other systems now, the whole galaxy revolving with its own motives, rank with hatreds, vibrant with love, brilliant with alien striving in which he had no place or dramatic destiny, all wheeling ponderously through impersonal space and time.

Subconsciously aware of the fragility of his artificial reality, the paranoiac must ever reinforce its defenses with more and more elaborate rationale. His virtues must be defined, his enemies painted in primary colors. The basic motive of fear is raised to mystic proportion: a cause, a uniform, a symbol. He proclaims his purposes one with God's.

"NO—"

The central infection inflames and eventually mortifies the entire psyche until any healthy stimulus becomes alien.

Roy stumbled through the reeking, rusted mountains of garbage toward the lights from Plattsville.

The fundamental problem of identity—

"I got no fuckin problems, man. None!"

—reaches to the core of being until even sexuality may be stunted. In males the basic relationship to women becomes dysfunctional. Commonly the subject may not be able to separate pleasure from guilt, and therefore pays with pain, quid pro quo. When this compensation becomes an intrinsic part of the natural pleasure principle, there can be no gratification without pain or defilement.

"This is . . . insane."

No, just reality. Being finite and wholly fallible myself, I have my own prejudices. What you call hangups.

"Why do you hate me?"

Because I'm subjective enough to be disgusted

with a flaw in my own work. Because I'm in trouble, too, but you I can deal with. Live with it, Roy.

"That's right, live!" Roy hurled to the uninterested stars. "I'm alive. Nothing's changed. I win, you fuck."

Infantile, needing to be the center and reason for creation, the less educated or advantaged subject needs a distorted miraculous theology to support a perilous existence, externally and constantly threatened as it is by "them."

Howl.

Tightening, darkening, narrowing in ever-smaller circles—

Howl.

—until as your human joke puts it, the paranoiac eventually flies up his own metaphorical ass and disappears.

Roy reached the limits of Main where it became a feeder road to the Interstate. He hooked his arm around a lamppost, tottering, while the brutal light in his brain grew brighter and brighter.

Can you cut it? the cruel voice challenged, *or just give up?*

■ 36 ■

Perks for the upwardly mobile

Woody it was, solid, warm and alive in her arms, with all the customers in McDonald's gaping at them, some of the vocal opinion that young people had no manners, and if they wanted to make out they should go home or to a drive-in.

Charity came up for air somewhere around the fifth kiss. "Woody, we're alive."

"Promised you, didn't I?" he murmured into her hair. "Nothing will happen for me that you won't share."

She still hung on to him for dear life. "You did. You promised. Gol-lee, I must be alive for sure or I wouldn't be so hungry."

They dropped into two empty seats at a vacant table. "Oh, Woody—where we've been and what we've seen. Can we live with it?"

Woody laced his fingers with hers, still delighted with the reality of her next to him. "It wasn't your usual vacation. But what's so bad, Char? I've seen heaven and you've seen hell, and they're just what? Common sense, funny and horrible with a lot of bullshit thrown in, just like the six o'clock news."

When the adrenaline rush of excitement passed,

both of them slumped with exhaustion, still holding on to each other. "Tell you what I can't do," Charity allowed on sober reflection. "Can't go back to the tabernacle."

"Not hardly."

That kind of faith was simply outworn. The revival-tent gyrations of Purdy Simco would rouse no more fervor in either of them than a storm-window commercial.

"Maybe we can be Unitarians."

Charity knew little of the breed. "What do they believe in?"

"Can't say for sure," Woody admitted, "but I don't think they want to kill anyone."

"I'm for that." Charity inhaled the ambrosial aroma of broiling burgers. "We got any money? I'm star—" She broke off mid-syllable at sight of the two familiar figures at the serving counter; this she had not figured on. "Woody, is that who it looks like?"

"Sure," he confirmed, quite used to miracles now. "Just came along to say goodbye."

Well, she had a new concept of normal now herself. Charity welcomed the sight of Milt Kahane, bouncing with more life than most live people she knew, charging down at their table laden with shakes and burgers, Essie Mendel in tow. "Hey, Char! Quite a show, huh?"

Charity blinked at him. "Can I ask a dumb question?"

Milt struck a chairman-of-the-board attitude. "I suppose you're wondering why we're here."

"Just stopped off on our way Topside," Essie twittered, opening her cheeseburger with the curiosity of an Egyptologist. "May my family never hear of this."

"I'm giving trafe lessons." Milt attacked his Big Mac with gusto. "You believe this woman has never been in McDonald's or Burger King? Life in the fast-food lane, lover. Try the shake."

Essie took an experimental bite and then sipped

judicially at the vanilla shake. "The shake is nice. The burger kind of sticks in my throat. Maybe it's guilt. Finish it, Char."

Charity dove gratefully at the food. "What about your boyfriend in Accounting?"

"I wouldn't cry," Essie said primly. "Didn't I wait long enough for him? In a hundred years he'll still be going home to his mother. Which reminds me, Milton. I want to keep kosher when my parents come to visit, they'll expect. And furniture, leave the selection to me. I saw a really bee*yoo*tiful cream leather in an Ultimate Rise ad, really classy, and Topside we wouldn't have trouble keeping it clean, am I right? Speaking of clean, trust me, you wouldn't go wrong letting me pick out a few nice clothes for you, Milton. God maybe can get away with ratty jeans, he's eccentric, but you are still on the way up, and they don't do anything for your character or your position as an angel."

"What?" Charity choked on a mouthful. "Milt, you're a what?"

"An *arch*angel," Essie announced with a death lock on Milt's arm. "My fiancé, the Right Hand of God."

"Oh, hell." Milt just looked embarrassed. "They commissioned me after Beirut. Ninety-day wonder. Big deal."

"Anyway, people respect what they see." Essie was not to be deterred. "And an archangel in skuzzy clothes, what will they think? I don't keep a decent house? If you ask *me*, Milton, assimilation is one thing and plain sloppy is another. I wouldn't say a word if you want to look like a nebbish day laborer, but—"

Through all of which, Milt's tolerant smile grew slightly strained. "The next time I see something cute, please let it be a car."

"Hey, Milt." Charity noticed that both he and Essie were paling, losing natural tone like turning down the color on a TV set. "What's happening to you?"

"Oh." Essie jumped as if she'd spilled something on herself. "Milton, I think we have to go."

"I guess. Semper fi, Barnes. See you both not too soon." He rippled his trumpet valves. "Essie, let's make a memorable exit for the underprivileged Wasps of Plattsville."

McDonald's customers, never used to the extraordinary in any sense, were rocked to their roots by Milt's piercing cavalry charge played triple forte as Essie bowed gracefully to the house.

"I want to thank all the little people," she effused, blowing kisses. "The technicians, the grips, my aunts in Hadassah—"

"And for your sterling support of the Jewish Defense League." Milt took his bow. "Which helped us this year to blow up more Lebanese and Palestinians than ever before. *Shalom havarim,* and for our final impression of the evening, something in your own ballpark: a televangelist's bank account."

With a final wave to Woody and Char, they simply vanished.

One woman ran gibbering for the door, but that was extreme. Another customer said aloud it was probably just a publicity stunt for the new shopping mall on the Interstate. It was all done with mirrors, and they'd seen David Copperfield vanish the Statue of Liberty on TV. Just they didn't know Woody and Charity hung out with Jews, you know? They went back to eating.

"Know what I'll miss?" Charity mumbled through a mouthful. "I'll bet there's not one place in this whole damn town where you can get good Brie or smoked salmon, something you can really taste . . . Woody? What's wrong? You look—"

He was staring through the front window, the happiness washed out of his eyes. Charity turned to see what it was and went cold. The wraith framed in the restaurant window stared back at them, then passed out of sight.

Woody got up, tight and quiet. "Come on, Char."

She was suddenly afraid for both of them. "No. I don't want to see him. He's *sick*, Woody."

"He saw us." Woody picked up his trumpet case. "I don't want him hanging over our heads."

Like Damocles, Charity thought numbly, following Woody.

The night air was chill with the mist seeping along Main. Charity shivered. Woody took off his jacket and slipped it around her shoulders. They saw Roy a few doors down, leaning against the tabernacle window.

"Woody, I don't—"

He led her firmly on toward the desolate figure in the torn, fouled uniform, now a sardonic comment on the tragedy of Roy. From his attitude, face in his hands, Charity thought he was weeping, but no. When he raised his head, there was light enough from the street-lamp to know that those eyes would never weep again. They were the dry-scorched exhaustion after the last weeping of the world.

"I won," Roy told them. "They couldn't hold me. I can stay here if I want or go back if I want. The first sumbitch in the history of the *world* can go anywhere I want. I got it all." The swaggering tone softened with a note of pleading. "Come back with me, Charity."

Revolted, she didn't want to touch him, as much pity as she felt. "I can't, Roy."

"Shit you can't." Roy's eyes, dangerous and a little mad, slid to Woody. To Charity, they were the most frightening thing about him. "You got lucky. You caught me off guard in the club. Things'll be different when I go back."

"We can't go back," Woody told him quietly. "Char can't. She's alive."

Roy's crafty grin went colder. "I can take her."

"Why?" Charity blurted. "You don't want me. I *saw* what you want. I was there, I saw it on TV, again and

260

again. You telling me how it would be, while a little girl got her head blown off."

"There's always blood at the beginning of a new order, got to be. Cleaning house."

"That baby was me, Roy."

He didn't understand. "You crazy? I was there; just a little Jew kid—"

"*She was me.*" The passion propelled her closer to Roy, and the clarity of the next thought surprised her. "Because if it wasn't, it wasn't anyone."

Roy pushed himself away from the window; the act seemed difficult for him. He wobbled as if both legs had gone to sleep. "Look, I ain't got much time." Even his voice sounded dry, coming from a long distance. "Have you seen it? Have you seen it all? The *nothing*." Roy stared beyond the fog. "Just space and balls of rock, out and out and on and on forever and nobody, nothing out there to make us mean anything . . . Stop. Please, stop."

They edged back from him. He was a dead man come back for something after his own funeral.

"Come on, Charity." Roy reached for her. "I don't belong here no more."

She knew he was right. Nowhere in life, nowhere real.

"All those voices," Roy whispered. "All those lousy fuckin books, they're in my *head* and they won't shut up. They make me know things—STOP!"

Charity yearned from her heart, "I wish to God I could help you, Roy. But I can't."

"Don't shit me with that God stuff!" The words came out half snarl, half despair. "I seen God and the Devil. Couple of wise-ass wimps, that's all. But they never showed me Jesus Christ. They knew they couldn't sell me a phony Jesus Christ."

"I saw him," Woody said. He felt a pity, too, but even that was running out. "You wouldn't buy him either. He looks like an Arab. Come on, Char."

Roy lurched toward them. If his coordination was poor, nothing diminished the danger of him. "You ain't taking Charity. I got it made back there, anything I want. What she gonna do with a dumb shit horn player can't make a dime?"

"She's going to live," Woody said. "That's more than you can cut."

"You gonna stop me?" Roy drew the small ceremonial dagger from his belt. Light glinted from the honed edge. His laughter was a fading echo. "What you gonna do, Barnes, kill me?"

Woody moved between Roy and Charity. Roy slashed suddenly with the knife. Woody grabbed for his wrist but the movement was too quick. Woody felt the hot sting of the blade across his upthrust palm. He blinked at it; the blade should have cut deep but there was no more than a scratch.

"Woody—" Charity saw what was happening before he did. Roy was fading, piece by piece like bits taken at random from a jigsaw puzzle, not so much disappearing as becoming less defined from the night around him. "Look at him . . ."

Woody saw now. Poised with the knife ready to come up, Roy was only half in the real world, his very image being washed away like sand from a shoreline.

"*Kill* you—" The knife swept up, but for all the fury behind it, the thrust was insubstantial as double-exposed film. Instinctively, Woody tensed for the shock but the knife and Roy's hand only passed through him, a faint shadow across his body. He felt nothing except revulsion, a *wrongness*. When he pushed at Roy he could barely feel the contact.

Woody swallowed hard, feeling sick. He backed away, holding Charity. "He's going. Walk away and don't look back."

Roy was fading to something like grainy old black-and-white film, screaming at them with a voice weirdly distant. "Charity, we can have it all. They *promised* me."

Pulled along by Woody, she started to cry. "Dear God, Woody, I feel so sorry for him."

Woody didn't slow. "Don't," he muttered. "He doesn't feel a thing."

"What you gonna do with him?" Roy wailed after them. "Live in shit like we always did. Nothing, that's what you got. That's what you are! You saw on TV. The people . . . all the people, the crowds. *They fuckin loved me . . .*"

They weren't that far but they could barely hear him now.

"Woody, I can't just—"

"Yes, you can. Keep going."

"Come back, Charity—"

"No." Charity pulled away from Woody's grip. "I know what's in his head. I *know*. It's beautiful and horrible and—"

"I've seen it, too," Woody said. "And we can get up in the morning and live with it all day for the rest of our lives. He can't. That's the difference, Char. That was always the difference. Forget it."

No, she couldn't just walk on, walk away, but twisted around to see Roy because he hurt so. She prayed for him, the only kind of prayer she could believe in now: *Simmy, take care of him. The light's too bright and the truth is too cruel.*

Charity searched the sidewalk up and down the street on both sides. She thought she saw something move, but it was only a shadow in the thin fog wisping between her and the streetlight.

Roy felt marvelous, renewed power surging through him. Drunk with his own charisma, he didn't notice he wasn't breathing at all, didn't need to. His uniform was crisp and new as the day he swaggered out of the Whip & Jackboot. No voices but his own echoed in his head, and the adoration of the crowds. No other truth had ever disturbed that perfect balance. He remembered only the balcony, the reaching arms and hoarse voices raised to him—needing, loving, validating him. Making him God.

He was the Man now, Topside no problem, the Devil a fat little faggot. One day that little shit would get dumped on his ass, and when he looked around to see what hit him, there'd be Roy Stride in his chair.

His boots rang on the deserted sidewalk in cadence with the cleansing, conquering thought. He didn't hear the car round the corner behind him and purr silently to the curb.

"Leader Stride?" The cabby snaked out of the driver's seat and came around to open the passenger door. "Cab?"

"You got it." Sure of his destiny, Roy touched the whip to his cap. An image flickered in his memory wiped clean of everything else. The driver's face was familiar. He reminded Roy of some actor. "Don't I know you?"

"Sure you do." Judas lifted the money bag from his own breast and dropped it around Roy's neck. "We're practically blood brothers."

The small bag of silver coins was surprisingly heavy and would not come off.

■ 37 ■

Doom at the top

If Sorlij and Maj were appalled at Topside, Below Stairs was sheer trauma. A rapid but thorough survey of Earthside records only darkened their findings. With each new aspect, the problem grew more complex. They weighed observations, consulted law precedents in their library banks and finally summoned the errant brothers to a meeting in the matter-phased ship poised to streak home across the universe.

Sorlij broached the inevitable. "I don't quite know how to begin."

Maj knew very well how. "A crime has been committed: of error or gross assumption, call it what you will. The only question is: which of you is guilty of what?"

Coyul pondered the deck under his feet and wished he was Below Stairs drinking with Dylan Thomas.

"The magnitude of your presumption," Sorlij accused Barion. "The rampant disregard for law or ethics. That emotional rain forest you call Topside—"

"That chaos you call Below Stairs," Maj added. "And Earth itself."

"And Earth," Sorlij echoed. "That garden of lethal

delights, churning out art, morals and murder. Never
. . . never in all my experience." Sorlij paced the deck,
lower lip jutted out in deliberation. "The greatest
crimes. The gravest charges."

"Sorlij," Coyul interjected casually, "did I ever tell
you that you render pomposity into art?"

"I have no love for either of you, never did," Sorlij
snapped. "What Maj and I had to work for, the little
darlings of the gods had handed to them. I'm not blame-
less, I left you here. This will reflect on my career."

"And mine," said Maj. "We had attained some
prominence."

"What a shame." Barion shrugged. "A bad day for
the Kelp King."

"And his wife, the cosmic yuppie. Can you believe
this, Barion? We're getting class struggle. *A bas les aris-
tos.*"

"Go ahead, laugh," Sorlij warned. "There'll be
charges and conviction. I need not enlarge the consequences."

"And there are further complications," Maj took up
the indictment. "If your post-life playpens are beyond
description, Earth is not. In the midst of all that mess,
there appears to be a great deal of healthy good. Admirable aspects. Some grasp, however inept, of real significance."

Sorlij agreed wearily. "An anomalous mutant."

"Transient is a better term, dear: halfway between
what it was and whatever Barion wanted it to become.
Quite unique."

"As anthropoids go," Sorlij qualified. "What you
have is a weird neurotic balance. On the bottom end,
this primitive dualism; on the high end, something I can
only call sublime. If only they could *grow up!*"

"And that is our point." Maj's exquisite brows fur-
rowed in a deep frown. "As one of their major languages puts it, you've painted yourself into a coroner."

"I think you mean corner," Coyul assisted delicately. "That's English, very metaphorical tongue. Yes, hoist by our own petard."

"Out on a limb with a power saw," said Barion, already seeing the barren vistas of the Rock.

A no-need-to-prolong-it glance passed between Sorlij and Maj. "The point is," Sorlij plunged into the thick, "these anthros are too good to waste but far too unstable to be left unattended. However traumatic, they must be reeducated very quickly. Barion, I'm sorry"—Sorlij even managed to look it—"Coyul will be allowed some time at home before sentencing. You'll have to be left here. I doubt if anyone will be returning for you."

Barion expected to do time, but—"Never?"

"I doubt it," Sorlij judged. "The balance here is too delicate. They're not just a lab culture but humans with obvious and unexpected potential. We can't just leave them."

"No, we can't," Barion admitted, glancing at Coyul. He already missed his brother.

"You must finish what you started. Though honestly"—Sorlij gestured vaguely—"I would have thought it not only illegal but impossible. I don't know how you managed it."

"He didn't." Coyul rose, adjusting his tie. "I did. We needn't go on with this. I confess. Oh, Barion was tempted, but . . ."

Sorlij and Maj were not minded to parse degrees of guilt; Coyul was in enough trouble already and Barion, they reminded him, had already confessed.

"Of course he would." Coyul grew more supercilious by the moment. "That mountainous ego won't share guilt any more than glory. Regarding humans, Barion was always more romantic than competent. He simply didn't realize the errors in our own technology."

"Didn't real—" Barion shot to his feet, stung and confused. "Look, I cleared you. I confessed."

"An egotist to the end. I did it, Sorlij. I had to do

something until you paragons of responsibility came back for us."

Barion began to heat up. "He's lying through his teeth. Why are you doing this, Coyul?" He appealed to the inquisitors. "You remember him in school. Carbon-cycle life classes were his nap time. He couldn't augment a respectable paramecium without a crib sheet."

"Ha! Couldn't I?"

"The point is valid, Coyul. We have serious doubts, easily resolved." Sorlij activated a keyboard, fingers dancing over inductance pads that sprayed formulae over a large screen behind him. "The simple chemistry of primitive apse-to-synapse combination, with one minute error. Barion, find the error and restate."

Barion scanned the formulae, obvious as a child's cartoon, found the error in the amino-protein elements. He corrected and restated. "First-year stuff."

Sorlij wiped the screen. "Quite correct. Now—"

Coyul contradicted him. "Quite wrong."

"Coyul, don't be an ass," Barion beseeched. "Not now."

"You were wrong because the whole theory is wrong."

"Really?" Sorlij smiled at Coyul like a spider about to lunch. "We'll find a different set of errors for you. Something simpler."

"Don't bother. These will do." Coyul flexed his fingers like a pianist warming up. On each hand the five fingers divided in two. Twenty slender digits stabbed at the keyboard in a swift toccata of statement, foresting the screen with symbols. "Stated. And here—"

The screen wiped to one subformula in the amino-protein group from which Coyul generated a whole family tree of results.

"You've only restated the error," Maj said.

"No. Science is only exact when experimentation proves it so. We should begin by assuming we're wrong.

Unfortunately, we have certain failings in common with humans."

Prominent among which, Coyul noted, was not liking to be wrong even in regard to a remote study like carbon-cycle life in which none of their own electron-cycle kind had much prolonged empirical experience. Formal academics had generated plausible theory which worked in enough cases to be complacently accepted as law.

"What you call error is the actual propensity of protein enzyme acting as catalyst in evolving the anthropoid cortex—as you can see at a far greater rate than theory conceived. What theory fails to take into account is protein variation in a creature whose survival lies in its intelligence and ability to adapt. Barion was as hidebound as the rest of you in this."

"That's an assumption, not a factor," Sorlij challenged. "Show me the numbers."

"The precise variable," Maj specified. "What accelerated the protein?"

"Excuse me, I did forget." Rapidly, Coyul stated the oxygen components in the accepted theory. Underneath, the actual, richer oxygen content of Earth's Pliocene atmosphere and its more rapid effect on protein enzyme action, neatly stated in percentage. "There we are, children: how Daddy did the guilty work of the Sixth Day. Accept no substitutes."

A silent but sufficing bombshell. Staring at the formulae, Barion tried to find some point for refutation and saw none. Out of their own field, Sorlij and Maj could still see the obvious on the screen. These figures made Cultural Threshold at 900 cc not only possible but predictable.

Maj spoke first. "Would it be tedious to ask *why*, Coyul?"

"There was nothing else to pass the time." His silly titter nailed the lid on Coyul. "It amused me."

"But he *didn't*," Barion sputtered. "His figures are

right, I admit, but *I* did it. I can re-create my process step by step."

Sorlij just shook his head. "Barion, please. We admire your loyalty, but . . ."

Shielded from them, Barion's mind leaped at Coyul's—

YOU IDIOT, WHAT ARE YOU DOING? YOU KNOW I DID IT.

NO, Coyul thought back with a ripple of humor, WE DID IT. HARDLY WORTH MENTIONING AT THE TIME, LIKE ONE BUTTON LEFT UNDONE. I JUST DID YOU UP. WE WERE YOUNG THEN. LIKE THE YOUNG ANYWHERE, YOU ADORED DABBLING WITH THE RADICAL, BUT INEVITABLY WENT HOME TO DINNER WITH THE ORTHODOX. CHECK MY FIGURES. Q.E.D.

Barion raged: MARGINAL VARIATIONS. THEY WOULDN'T MAKE THAT MUCH DIFFERENCE.

BUT THEY DID. AND WHEN IT COMES TO ANTHROS, THESE TURKEYS DON'T KNOW ENOUGH BEYOND BASICS TO ARGUE THE POINT.

Apparently they did not. "Coyul, you'll have to leave the ship now. Maj, prepare for energy phase."

"It's still a good question," Barion pressed, no longer caring if the others heard him. "Why?"

"You'll do time as an accessory, of course, but wherever they put you, brother, you'll go on doing what you do."

"And what about you?" Barion urged, concerned. "You can't run Topside like a demented B movie. What will you do?"

"What Sorlij ordered," Coyul said simply. "Make them grow up. Always wanted to. Now I've got to, haven't I?"

In truth, Coyul's motives were not entirely fraternal. Five million years had left a considerable human residue in his personality. He thought in human languages, spent more time than not in their form, understood them better by now than his own arid kind. He found it difficult, even deprivation to imagine existence without a Jake, a Wilksey, or an Elvira Grubb. Not to mention half a dozen musical compositions in various stages of completion that would find no audience on the Rock.

"I have a knack and I've really grown to like them," Coyul summed it up. "Go goose an amoeba." The rest of the sentiment was for Barion's mind alone—

DROP BACK WHEN THEY LET YOU OUT. I'LL SHOW YOU WHAT A PIANO PLAYER CAN DO.

Coyul blew a kiss to his brother, presented an expressive middle finger to Sorlij—which blossomed on afterthought into an American Beauty rose for Maj. "Here: stick it"—blazed into pure energy and was gone.

■ 38 ■

The new, the terrible and the maybes

The intense young man with the James Mason looks lounged in one of Coyul's salon chairs, listening as his abdicating Prince cleaned up last business. Jake admired Coyul's ability to communicate on any level, even the gaseous hype of Eddie Veigle. Coyul reclined in a contour chair, loafer-shod feet crossed on the Danish Modern desk, phone propped against one ear.

"Eddie, sweetheart: listen. The *putz* is back and you've got him. Yeah, he picked up his option. But let's not make things too easy for him. Did you save the tape? Dynamite. Tear your heart out until Char blew it with the yuks, right?"

Coyul listened to Veigle's woes, the dramatic possibilities gone down the tube with that uncontrollable explosion. The phone emitted a rancorous drone of disgust which Coyul gleefully turned out for Jake's benefit.

"I know, Eddie. Tears are prime time, laughs are late night. So anyway, Stride's all yours. Keep him happy, give him what he wants. All the extras and day players you need. Just don't frighten the horses or pedestrians in the better neighborhoods . . . Okay, so

272

build permanent sets. When did you ever go broke on overstatement?"

Listening to the super-agent, Coyul winced at the smallest possibility of misunderstanding. "Eddie, are you trying to hurt my feelings? *Moi* who gave you exclusives on Bormann and Oswald? Of *course* you've got all rights: TV novelization, film, the whole enchilada . . . no problem, bubby. I always like doing business with people I love. Think big on this one; think Riefenstahl. *Triumph of the Will.* I'm bringing in a load of Topside talent. You can have C.B. Of *course* I mean De Mille. You're expecting Charlie Brown? What?" Coyul rolled his eyes at Jake in strained tolerance. "Eddie, what can I tell you? You want Griffith, you got him. What the hell, he needs a hit. Right. Terrific. Keep in touch. We'll have lunch. *Ciao,* kid."

The Prince of Darkness (or Light, depending on your translation) dropped the phone on its cradle. "Mr. Veigle is not an intellectual, Jake, but he is a predator. I made it worth his time to keep Roy Stride happy and off your back. That's how it goes; you'll have to talk to people in their own language, hold a few hands now and then, listen to problems. Develop outside interests, Jake; that helps on the bad days. Get out more, see people. You're getting a bit gloomy—but I think you'll manage smashingly."

Jake wasn't all that sure. "In your place? I'm just afraid . . ."

"Of what? You said it yourself, one of the two best minds in Judea, far from the worst Below Stairs."

"I certainly know Roy Stride, at any rate," Jake observed dryly. "I was once the kind of person who needed miracle workers. Messiahs. Now I wouldn't have one in the house."

"I understand Yeshua feels the same way now." Coyul swung his feet off the desk, checking his watch. He moved to a gilt-framed mirror. "Stroke them, Jake. Tell them what they want to hear, that's all they want."

"I'm not a leader, Prince."

"And I am?" Coyul countered out of the mirror. "I'm just a piano player, and precious little time I'll have for that now. Besides, you won't have to do it alone. I relied a great deal on your common sense for two thousand years, so I'm sending you real talent for Number Two. The other best mind in Judea."

"Yeshua?" Jake looked even more uncertain. "No, please. Not him."

"Bears no grudges. And he is the best."

"It's not that, Prince. You never had to live with that . . . He's impossible! He's always right."

Coyul smiled reminiscently, recalling Barion in his first few million years. "He's mellowed, Jake. And he misses you. Hasn't had a decent game of chess in ages. Well, it's your office now. Redecorate if you want, but avoid your habitual RKO Gothic; tends to depress visitors."

"Don't you understand?" Jake implored, desperate. "I'm *scared.*"

"What can they do? Sue? Vote you out?" One more critical inspection in the mirror. No, Coyul decided: definitely the wrong look for Topside. The rich maroon tie became tasteful white on white. The off-white shirt went pastel blue in complement. As his costume modified, so did the Prince himself—taller, less corpulent, shoulders broader and straighter. The emotional mouth with its hint of petulance firmed to strength. "That will do it."

The figure who turned to Jake bore a resemblance to Lincoln or perhaps Gregory Peck. There were nuances of Clarence Darrow's bulldog tenacity and Truman's down-home integrity. The gravity of a wise king, the wry wit of a prairie philosopher quite at home in a barn or a summit meeting. The world-class wisdom and quiet authority in that image could sell oil to Arabs, Amex cards in the Kremlin.

"Yes, that will do it. Jake, you're an absolute power

because over the ages you've learned absolute compassion and restraint and the knowledge that none of it is new and most of it is violence, treacle or pure hogwash. But . . . you're scared. So am I, Reb Judas. Talk about opening nights. As of now, I'm overdue Topside to meet a very confused delegation including Luther and Augustine—that eminently reasonable duo—Paul of Tarsus, Thomas Aquinas, a gaggle of the better popes, Joseph Smith, Jesuits, Taoists, Buddhists, disputing rabbis, Irish saints and God knows *how* many Fundamentalists still waiting like Oliver Twist with his bowl for their own kind of rhinestone salvation—and try to make them understand that all of them are the result of an experiment neither well conceived nor even finished. Hah!" Coyul snorted. "And *you're* scared?"

Coyul gave his tie a final tug. "Well, I asked for it, I guess. We ultimately do what we want, though I don't have the foggiest how to go about it. The therapists will have a field day and we'll probably lose hordes to schizophrenia. But cry all they want, stomp around, kick furniture, the human race will get rid of their fairy-tale notions of good, evil and the cosmos, and by God—by Me, I guess—they will grow the hell up."

Coyul subsided with a rueful chuckle. "You've got problems? Forget it, I'll call you." With no further farewell, he vanished, heading for a tight schedule—to re-appear immediately with a last afterthought.

"By the way: see that Wilksey gets a couple of good reviews for the new *Hamlet*. Means so much to him. God bless, Jake."

God II went to work.

Alone, Judas Iscariot didn't move at first; when he did, his actions were cautious, even timorous. He sat down tentatively at Coyul's desk, lifted the phone, then put it down. He didn't want to deal with anyone yet. His hypercritical eye gauged Coyul's taste in decor, ending with the white piano. At a mental suggestion, the instrument blushed to dark mahogany and began a pianissimo passage from the *Goldberg Variations.* Jake listened for some moments, then materialized his chess set on the desk before him.

Start small, he decided. Leave the glitz to Veigle. Do the big stuff when you're ready.

He was definitely not ready for the young man who simply appeared across the desk from him.

They could have said a great many things to each other, and no doubt would have two thousand years earlier, but both were much wiser now. Judas no longer needed a messiah at any price. Yeshua no longer expected the world to buy spiritual common sense even in parables. Both would do what they could with the cosmos as it was. Perhaps this tacit understanding passed between them before Judas moved a white piece on the board.

Pawn to king four.

Yeshua responded: pawn to queen three.

"There you go," Judas growled, "being devious again."

"Shut up and move," Yeshua muttered, absorbed in the myriad possibilities of the opening.

■ 39 ■

Back to the drawing board . . .

The planet had no name. As it was so far out on the edge of the known universe, Barion's meticulous kind had noted it with a number on survey charts. Development of such worlds was not usual, their use rare and only for penal purposes. With very little water, the highest form of life was protozoan.

This was Barion's Rock. In a few million of its solar years, he might make parole, but the arch-instigator Coyul would never see home again.

Moving as restless energy over the near-barren face of the small planet, Barion couldn't deny a feeling of personal contentment and admiration for Coyul's wisdom, a quality heretofore not fully appreciated. Coyul remained where he wanted to be and was most suited: concierge to a maddening, murderous, occasionally gifted mutant. Barion had theories to restructure, new concepts to distill—only slightly chagrined that Coyul had shown up his errors, more that his own thinking, which he considered in youth to be chic and radical, was ultimately rooted in comformity.

Rethink. Start again.

The surface slid under him as he searched for moisture. Mere sight was not enough. The flashing animus of

Barion melted into the equatorial soil, flowing like a subterranean river, divining, shaping new ideas. *What if? Suppose.*

All carbon life begins with a need for sustenance, therefore a challenge which must be met. The organism must develop a means to propel itself toward nourishment or draw it inward. Suppose . . .

He found the small patch that smelled encouragingly of water. No more than a trace, no thriving colony of protozoa rummaging through its elements for food.

But there was one.

The single organism Barion found had very little talent even for an amoeba, having just coalesced with the sluggish chemical agreement of proteins. The rank beginner had to nourish itself before it could divide, with no idea how to go about it.

But just suppose . . .

Like a human infant, the amoeba lay there knowing only hunger. The fact that bacteria existed close by was, in amoebic terms, of prime interest but little help. Vacuoles to envelop and ingest nourishment were barely functional.

Suppose we accelerate the whole protein process. Since specialization begins at this level anyway, suppose the learning/retention aspect is speeded up, so that selected unicellular life can specialize and evolve exponentially faster than before; faster than anyone thought possible.

"Come on," Barion urged as the tiniest part of him flowed into and endowed the single cell with relative genius. "We call this a pseudopod. You use it to reach for that snack over there. Tha-at's right."

The amoeba extruded a peninsula containing a vacuole. New at the business, the pseudopod merely pushed at the bacterium.

"No, now you open up. I'll show you. There you go, you're in business."

Refreshed, with an atom of learned behavior

snugly tucked away, the amoeba thrust out another pseudopod, faster this time.

Barion felt the old thrill of creation, but the monkey had schooled him. "Don't get smug. That was my mistake. Lesson two is fission. No hurry. We'll be out here until you get it right."

You walk before you run before you fly. Concentrate the aminos more rapidly, accelerate specialization. The pseudopod gradually phases from temporary to permanent. Undifferentiated plasma divides to functions, learns. Get the food, reinforce the outer cell wall, which, in turn, senses food more quickly. More specialized functions: digestion, faster locomotion, eventually a central complex to coordinate the whole organism, evolving at a supercharged rate, already tougher and smarter than previously thought possible.

Always possible; just that no one ever did it.

There would never be a warm primordial sea for this creature, but maybe—just maybe—the speeded conditioning would produce a relative intelligence to adapt and cope on its way upward.

"Worlds within worlds," Barion murmured with a vast fascination. "Unconquerable."

His creation was already fighting outside its weight, as it were, laboring but game. Barion hovered, following each step. "Come on, turkey. I know I'm right."

And then something remarkable happened . . .

ABOUT THE AUTHOR

PARKE GODWIN graduated third in his class from the Yerkes Institute. Enjoined by concerned friends and family to take writing seriously, he made an honest effort, producing the work of his Serious Period—*Beloved Exile, The Last Rainbow,* and *A Truce with Time.* This stage ended abruptly when, inexplicably, the Author began to giggle.

Godwin's brief career ended in tragedy at a fantasy convention banquet when he accidentally consumed the entrée. He is remembered mainly through the scattered recollections of other writers. *The Curse of Testosterone,* the autobiography of the radical feminist Roberta Drear, recalls Godwin with no affection at all, making rather much of his relationship with a Bulgarian succubus, an episode now considered apocryphal.

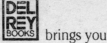